WESTERN   Reynolds, Clay,
Reynolds   1949-

        The vigil.

THE VIGIL

Clay Reynolds

Texas Tech University Press

The Vigil, a Sandhill Chronicle

Copyright © R. Clay Reynolds

The Vigil is reproduced from a 1988 First Southern Methodist University Press edition.

New preface by R. Clay Reynolds copyright © 2002 Texas Tech University Press.

The paper used in this book meets the minimum requirements of ANSI/NISO Z39.48-1992 (R1997). ∞

Cover design by Brandi Price; painting by Jacqueline McLean

Printed in the United States of America

Library of Congress Cataloging-in-Publication Data
Reynolds, Clay, 1949–
    p. cm. — (Sandhill chronicles)
    ISBN 0-89672-457-3 (pbk. : alk. paper)
    1. Mothers and daughters—Fiction. 2. Loss (Psychology)
—Fiction. 3. Runaway teenagers—Fiction. 4. Missing persons—
Fiction. 5. Waitresses—Fiction. 6. Sheriffs—Fiction. 7. Texas—
Fiction. I. Title.

PS3568.E8874 V54 2002
813'.54—dc21

                                  2001041471

  02 03 04 05 06 07 06 07 08 09 10 / 9 8 7 6 5 4 3 2 1

Texas Tech University Press
Box 41037
Lubbock, Texas 79409-1037 USA

1-800-832-4042

ttup@ttu.edu

http://www.ttup.ttu.edu

The Sandhill Chronicles are dedicated to Kenneth W. Davis, a gentle man, dedicated scholar, and lifetime student of the hearts of the souls of West Texas.

The Sandhill Chronicles: An Author's Apology

My small Texas hometown was fairly typical of hundreds of other small towns in Texas during the "boom years" following World War II, probably fairly typical of tens of thousands of small towns across America in those days of "I Like Ike" and television sitcoms' idyllic visions of family life and community spirit. In most ways, I was an ordinary small-town kid of the baby-boom generation. I wore dungarees, ugly striped tee-shirts, and a flattop held up with Butch Wax, and had a passionate longing for a V-8 engine and a girl who looked like Annette Funicello or, later, Ann-Margret. My father was a blue-collar working stiff, a combat veteran of World War II who came home after trouncing Hitler and his minions to settle down and grow prosperous. He settled down, but never did grow prosperous, not in the way he planned. He always wanted to raise horses, as his father and grandfather had done. He wound up working for the railroad until they farmed him out with bad eyes and a bad heart, at least some of which was probably the result of trouncing Hitler and his minions when he should have been home raising horses. My mother was a typical small-town girl who married a guy with a good job so she could have children and grandchildren and grow old and beam proudly whenever her progeny were paraded in public. She got most of that—the progeny, anyway—but my father died fairly young, and her children moved away to hold their parades in other places where no one knew her, or them. It probably is one of the great bewilderments of her life that her elder son, always somewhat of an oddity and outcast, became a writer.

It was her fault, though. She read all these books to me as a child and then encouraged me to spend afternoons visiting the

library instead of watching television. Mothers rarely understand the damage they do in the name of what's right until it's
manifested in oddities later on.

I think, though, that I began the process of writing about
where I was from and what I was doing early in my life long before I left home. Because I refused to play football (a heresy in
small-town Texas when you're as large a person as I am), I
made myself an oddity and an outcast from the start. I preferred music and books to other teenage pursuits that were, I
think, as boring to most of my friends as they seemed to me,
only most of them wouldn't admit it. Many of them just couldn't
quite think beyond our hometown and the surrounding county.
Neither could many of my teachers or any of my preachers. For
me, and for my friends, the world ended at the city-limit sign,
or later, at the county line. We knew there was something else
out there, but we were afraid of it. Only a few of us would ever
go there, and almost none of those who did would come back. I
think we knew that would happen, and I think, for most, that's
what the big fear really was.

I believed, though, that if there was pleasure in books—
and what I knew or could learn of music, art, and theater—in
my remote corner of Texas, there would be more of it elsewhere, "out there." So off I went, seeking beauty and truth and
the meaning of life in the big city—well, in San Antonio and
Austin at least, with an occasional sojourn to Houston or Dallas. Those cities were, after all, big enough and exotic enough
to intimidate any small-town boy who wandered agog in their
concrete environs and studied the temptations and blandish-
ments of their darker haunts.

In that precomputer, pre-color-television era, "out there"
was something of a challenge, and we suspected that it held
secrets. We weren't really ignorant, backward, or poorly informed. We had AM radio beamed all night at us from KOMA,
Oklahoma City, after all; through those static-filled airways,
we heard of far-off places such as Kansas City and Omaha, Chicago and St. Louis. We marveled over the wonders of a "hemi
under glass" and "double overhead cams" as they were de-
tailed in the rapid-fire commercials for stock car races—"Saturday Night! Saturday Night! Saturday Night!"—interspersed
with the croonings of Gene Pitney, Buddy Holly, Elvis and
Patsy Cline. Cousins visiting from Fort Worth and Dallas, from
Atlanta and San Francisco and New Jersey, enabled us to par-
ticipate, however vicariously, in an emerging world of juvenile

delinquents, beatniks, surfboards, then flower children and heavy-duty rock and roll. Our vocabularies expanded with *cool, boss,* and *far out,* and we learned about sex and drugs and even met some kids who had seen The Beatles live, been to a Cowboys' game, or flown on an airliner. We heard there were places with rivers you couldn't walk across and trees so abundant you couldn't see the forest for them. We didn't believe it. We also heard that people were orbiting the Earth, but I don't think we believed that, either. For us, West Texas, empty, vast, and hostile as it seemed, was vacuum enough. Who would blast off on a rocket merely to discover more?

Through these outsiders, though, "out there" forced itself into our consciousness. We imitated them and tried to make our place like theirs, and while we watched such programs as *The Andy Griffith Show* and desperately prayed that such hick-infested burgs as Mayberry weren't a reflection of our own rural reality, we knew all the while that they probably were.

But we tried. None of us was a cowboy—or cowgirl. We wore the latest fashions, as observed on *American Bandstand* and the Sears Catalogue, combed our hair in the style of our idols on record album and magazine covers, and talked with authority of the doings of faraway people and places most of us couldn't even imagine. We sensed that somewhere out beyond the buttes and prairies that blocked our view of "out there" there were places where people acted the way movie people acted, the way people in books acted, and we wanted to know them, to be like them, to know what they knew. Or some of us did.

I left when I was seventeen, and I was bitter: angry over slights, real and imagined, that I'd endured all my conscious life. I want to "show them"—although I wasn't sure, exactly, who "they" were—and I was insensitive to the fact that "they" couldn't have cared less, that less than a decade later most of them wouldn't recognize me on the street or have very much to say to me if they did. I didn't understand, then, that each individual has to find his own life, his own stories to tell, and that geography doesn't really have much to do with it.

What I eventually learned, though, was that for a writer, it's necessary to leave a place—not merely physically, but spiritually—in order to come back to it, to understand it, and to write about it. But there are many ways of leaving, and it's not until you turn around and look that you can appreciate how far you've come. For a writer, it's often not very far.

It wasn't until I had been away a decade that I found my-self drawn back home in a spiritual sense. At first, it was a kind of pedagogical thing. I wanted what I believed to be the uniqueness of my youth to be understood by those who had never experienced the isolation of a West Texas small town. I found myself wanting to write stories about where I was from, about the people I knew. Over the next several years, those stories coalesced into an idea, ultimately into a place that I eventually named Sandhill County. The name was not an accident, but it was important, and almost instantly, it became as real to me as the actual county in which I grew up. I had taken the first step: understanding that fiction is truer than memory, and in the long run, more important than fact.

A writer setting a story in cities as large as New York or Los Angeles—London or Tokyo, Dallas or Houston—has considerable license to manipulate geography and even people. But a writer who sets his story in a world no larger than that of my youth must imagine the whole of it. He must make that imagining fit the story he tells. And so I came home to Sandhill County.

The name was appropriate because the county I was writing about was bordered on the north by the Prairie Dog Town Fork of the Red River, one of the sandiest and most treacherous waterways in the Southwest, and on the east and south by the Pease River, which was smaller and less treacherous but no less sandy. Both flooded frequently, washing out bridges and fields. Lining both riverbeds were endless mounds of sandy diluvium hills covered with light vegetation at their crowns. These descended into labyrinthine loblollies and swamps filled with dark and dank plants, thickets of thorns, and dens of bob-cats and snakes. Among the few more naturally appealing fauna that farmers and ranchers hadn't hunted into extinction or killed out of pure meanness was the sandhill crane. These huge, graceless birds made an annual pilgrimage from points north each winter, camping out on their storklike legs on the river-beds, enticing the bloodsportsmen among us to—what else?— try to kill them.

As a youngster, I tried to hunt sandhills along with quail, dove, and rabbits, but the birds were skittish and elusive. Their preference was for the vast, sandy emptiness of the Red's or Pease's bottoms, which, when they weren't flooded, were truly just huge sandbars occasionally cut by shallow rivulets of briny water. To reach the browsing flock, I often crawled through a

frozen swamp—a quarter mile of mud, mesquite, and plum thickets—and endured thick red goo, horsefly and mosquito bites, sharp thorns and stings from a variety of nasty, ugly plants no one in his right mind would even touch. Finally, my stealthy companions and I would emerge onto the riverbed, wipe off the slime and ignore the pain, then trudge our way around quicksand bogs that would suck our shoes right off. When at last we were nearly in shotgun range of the tall, gray birds, we would stand there helplessly in our frigid, wet misery and watch them rush in an awkward gait down an icy sandbar, spread their huge wings, and take off, slapping and honking into the cloud-mottled blue of the West Texas winter sky.

I recall our trying to bag a sandhill crane maybe twenty or thirty times. Old-timers, who said they knew, assured us the cranes tasted just like turkey, but we never found out. The closest we ever came to them was still too far away to identify their coloring with the naked eye, and we never forgave them for waiting until we had labored so hard to come near them before taking off and beating, tantalizingly close, over our heads toward a safer haven, while we faced the discouraging return trip through the swamp.

So I named my county after those rivers and those obnoxious birds, and after the hundreds of fields of dry-land cotton that were plowed and churned out of the loamy soil of the bottoms, farms that were mostly abandoned to the Dust Bowl and Great Depression before I was born. Those fields—reclaimed by modern wells—provided my chief motivation to leave that gritty, biting, and stinging hell.

I remember one summer, hired at the exploitative rate of seventy-five cents an hour, I trudged row after row of cotton plants, technically charged to chop out the weeds that threatened the young cotton plants. In point of fact, we cut few weeds with hoes. The weed of cotton-field choice in that loosely packed soil was the careless weed, a tube-rooted, fuzzy-shafted vegetable demon that thrust its sticky leaves upward toward the sun from the shadows of the tender cotton plants. A careless weed could not be hoed out. If you chopped it off, it would merely grow back—overnight, it seemed. It had to be pulled, and in that field—which was irrigated—the roots ran deep. This meant stooping, grasping, and tugging until the tip of the root came reluctantly from the dusty sand, where it could then be unceremoniously dropped, exposed to the harsh sun and utter aridity of the West Texas summer that would, in a day's time, shrivel it to virtually nothing.

In an hour of this labor, my hands stung from the sap of the plant and its pointy, stickery leaves, and my back ached from the effort of tugging them from the soil. It was July, which meant it was yellow-grass hot (I never knew green grass was even possible in summer until I was sixteen and went with my parents to visit an aunt in Corpus Christi. I thought all grass turned yellow on the Fourth of July, just as the mesquite leaves fell in winter.) At the end of each row, I turned and went back up the next. But alongside the field at one end was a huge billboard designed to be seen from the highway some two miles away. Across the enormous blank white field of the sign swept a muscular arm and fist, and clenched in the fist was a frothy stein of FALSTAFF BEER, or such was the red-lettered claim. The foamy head of the brew swept out behind it in an icy contrail that splashed the hairy disembodied forearm that moved it as, I imagined, a bartender might sweep the beverage across a mahogany bar to sit in front of a thirsty customer.

In the history of the world, no one has ever been thirstier than a kid chopping cotton in a sandy river bottom in West Texas.

For half the time I trudged through the grasping, ankle-deep sand of those cotton furrows—bending and straining to jerk the tenacious careless weeds from their taproot hold on the soil that would, we knew, rise and blow taller than a building with the first norther next fall, turning the sky black and any standing water to instant mud—for half that time, I was confronted with that promise of permanently slaked thirst and icy, frothy wonder of pure refreshment. Although at that tender age of twelve or thirteen, I had never tasted beer—never even smelled it or been in the room where anyone had done so—I knew that people "out there" could taste it at will. They could walk into any saloon or bar—dens of sin, from my mother's point of view—plunk down a few coins, and for that minuscule amount be presented with this ambrosiac, golden liquid that I was sure had a bouquet and aroma that not even a Baptist god could resist.

From that agonizing week of summer on, I vowed I would never again live in a dry county where such liquid balm could not be had, even by a preteenager whose only barrier against grainy, sandy thirst was warm tin-cooler gyp water and a well-worn stick of Juicy Fruit.

Sand and West Texas, skin-scorching heat and bone-aching cold, then, had been inscribed on my experience from my youth. Some years later, when I worked on a farm and ranch near the Pease River bottoms, I discovered that cotton chopping wasn't the only mean and unforgiving labor that resulted from sandy-land farming, even without a torturous, taunting billboard. One incredibly hot afternoon, I cut the wheels the wrong way and buried to the axles a John Deere 4020 and the harrow it pulled in a fallow sand terrace. While I trudged in 110° heat through devil's-claws and Russian thistle—keeping a wary eye out for rattlers—to face the anger of my rustic employer, I felt the bitter disappointment of one who'd begun to realize that his entire life might be rooted in loose and shifting soil. And I vowed again to leave, never to return, but never to forget the clutching, choking sand of West Texas.

Thus, my relationship with the county of my imagination was initially one of antipathy for its ephemeral but somehow always painful and torturous nature, metaphorically represented in the baking dunes and blowing fields of sand and the icy misery of its swampy riverbeds. It had existed in reality, briefly, when I was a child in my own reality. But very quickly, it became a memory, and as a memory, it carried with it the trappings of both horror and humor. At first, of course, the humor somehow escaped me. Like most youngsters in their callow twenties, I was far more interested in outrage than in irony. But eventually I came to understand that both those elements were a part of who I was and who everyone who had ever lived there was. If I was going to tell stories about it, about them, then that had to be my subject, and the subject had to reflect, however indirectly, the gritty verity of a place called Sandhill County.

The name of the county came second, though, after the name of the town in which I determined to set my stories. I needed a name that seemed to say West Texas; Agatite did that, and more. It was, once upon a time, a real town in West Texas. Only a few people remembered it, and no one was sure exactly where it was.

When I was a child of no more than seven or eight, my grandfather, Joe Reynolds, who was the gyp mill's mule wrangler and postman and who lived in Acme, Texas, took me and another boy for a long walk out into a pasture. I don't remember who the other boy was, but he may have been an older cousin visiting from California. We tramped out there in the milkweed and salt cedar, mesquite and switch grass for a while, when my grandfather shouted for us to be careful. He told us there were old foundations and wells around, and we might fall into one, or possibly "run up on" a nest of rattlers or "mama bobcat." He then assured us that we were in the "smack dab middle" of where a town once stood. The town was called Agatite. It was nowhere visible.

Agatite was an interesting place in its brief history for a lot of reasons. For one thing, it was the terminus of the shortest independent railroad in the world, the Acme Tap Line, which ran from the Quanah, Acme, and Pacific junction in Acme, Texas—my father's birthplace—more or less north, for a mile and a half. The function of this one-track railroad was to haul gypsum ore and, I guess, the wallboard and plaster products manufactured from it, down to Acme, where it would then either be put to use at the Acme mill or shipped far away to build houses in cities in places I'd only heard of. It also carried mail and passengers, I suppose, in those days early in the twentieth century when trains were as reliable as UPS and Toyota pickups have become today.

Agatite was, from all I've been able to learn, a mill town, owned part and parcel by some company or other (possibly, the Wabash Plaster and Wallboard Company of Chicago, Illinois), and it didn't last for very long before fading away into the indefatigable and largely useless but nevertheless discomforting groundcover of West Texas. Acme was a much more important place, until it, too, was eclipsed by Quanah, some five miles to the east, which in turn would be eclipsed by Wichita Falls, which would be eclipsed by Fort Worth, etc., etc. The source of Agatite's name is a mystery. There is a street named that in Chicago (near the Wabash company's headquarters, by the way), but no one seems to know the word's etymology. I invented one in a later novel called *Franklin's Crossing*, which truly is the start of these stories.

Agatite was interesting to me, however, more because it was a place that might have been than because it was a place that ever was. The name sounded hard and harsh, flint-edged, and granite ugly. It sounded like the result of something, rather than the cause of something, and it seemed to suggest a difficulty that was as metaphoric as its definition or meaning was shrouded in the past. In many ways, that suggested West Texas to me. It was a place where people came more out of desperation than out of adventure, where they stayed more out of necessity than because they had grand hopes and dreams for anything like progress.

As a place, West Texas was hard to come to, hard to stay in, hard to be from. And it was hard to leave. Most of the people I met out there knew it only as a vast, empty nothingness they had to cross to get to the snowy slopes of northern New Mexico or Colorado. According to legend, the Comanche weren't very much interested in it. They visited from time to time, of course, for it was "theirs," and it was reputed to have places with medicinal properties. But it seems they spent more time scurrying across it than hanging around counting rattlesnakes, scorpions, and red ants. They were no more in favor of careless weeds than I was. They understood that virtually everything that grew naturally there stung, bit, clawed, or itched, and there wasn't much potable water around, either. They had better sense than to stay there long enough to be caught and trapped by the sandy soil.

So the names of the town and the county were born out of a real place and real experiences, and they connect to the whole. But towns and counties are really only spots on maps and lines in almanacs without the people in them, and it was in those people, or in my imperfect memory of them, that I sought my stories.

The people of my past and my imagination are vague things. They too often haunt that rare fog of the past. In my fiction, they take shape for me, become real. But they really are manufactured from the whole cloth of my own wonderings. In my first novel, *The Vigil,* I was initially interested in using this town and county only as a backdrop for one woman's ordeal. And I never thought anyone would read it, so I wrote it with unfettered honesty.

The incident that inspired the story didn't happen in my hometown, not even in Texas. I'd read about it in a newspaper, and my memory was vague, but I was still intrigued enough to want to tell the story. I set it in Agatite, Sandhill County, because it was the place I had been writing stories about for so long, although I had never published any or thought I ever would. Because I did set the story there, though, it became something more than the story of the character's horrible experience and what she learned from it. Maybe by using the town and the county as I had fixed them in my imagination and brought them to form in my words, it became the story of a place and the people who made it.

The Vigil tells a story about a woman, Imogene McBride, who loses something that defines her, her daughter. There may be all sorts of "subtexts" (oh, how I hate that word!) and literary layering involved in the question of whether or not a mother *should* define herself in her child, but I wasn't concerned with that. Truly. I was only concerned about what the impact of that kind of loss would be on an individual who experienced it. Originally, I didn't plan for it to be a novel. I planned for it to be a short chapter, part of something else; but it tended to grow a bit more than I thought it would, and by the time I was finished with it, it had become a whole story.

Fundamentally, I think, *The Vigil* is about the discovery of self. In that sense, it's no different from any work of fiction we have, dating back to Homer or Moses, in what we are arrogant enough to call Western Literature. When Cora, Imma's daughter, disappears, leaving her mother alone and distraught, Imma must confront herself. She is alone, utterly, and she has nowhere to turn, nowhere to go. At first, she does what anyone else would do: she looks to institutional authority, to tradition, to the values she has been taught will save her from her fate. In the novel, Ezra, the sheriff of Sandhill County, represents these. But Ezra cannot help her, because the limits of his practical authority hold him back from the metaphysical. Even if Ezra could find Cora, could return her to her mother, he couldn't help Imma find herself. No one but Imma can help Imma. That's sort of the point of the book, I think.

Along the way, though, I discovered that Ezra is also in search of self. He is a man whose life has largely been unremarkable. He has a history of honor, which he thinks is phony, and he has the respect of the town, which he thinks is undeserved. He has actually reached the zenith of his ambitions in life, but what he found when he arrived was no more satisfying or meaningful than what he had when he started out. The things that mattered to him—his wife, his child—have been somehow lost along the way. So, in some ways, Ezra is as lost as Imma. And like Imma, he must finally confront himself. He looks into the darkness of the abyss only to find nothing staring back: nothing that will help him, nothing that will harm him; nothing. He, too, seeks help in the common value structure—he seeks love, companionship, understanding. He, too, must face the reality that the only person who can help Ezra is Ezra. But the discovery that gives Imma the strength and courage to go on almost destroys Ezra.

And so *The Vigil* became the story of two people, trapped in the wilderness of West Texas where there is no hope, no reason really to be there other than it's where they are and there's nowhere else to go. They have a choice: to die or to endure. And while they look for help in one another, they discover, ultimately, that even that most fundamental of human yearnings is inadequate to answer.

Now, in that sense and to that point, I suppose *The Vigil* could take place anywhere. It could be in the middle of the Midwest or somewhere in the Canadian Rockies, or, for that matter, it could be in Central Park on Manhattan Island. But it's not. It's in West Texas, and specifically, it's in Sandhill County and in Agatite. And it is here that I think I inadvertently discovered something important in my writing. I discovered that there was a relationship between the town and the people who live there, or those who merely come there and stay. As the story developed, I realized that there was a symbiotic relationship developing between these two individuals, lost and helpless as they were in the cosmos, and this small, isolated town, lost and helpless as it was in the geography of West Texas. Like the two main characters, the town itself was staring off into the abyss, trying to discover something that would define it, but nothing was there. Instead, it was forced, like Imma and Ezra, to turn its vision inward, to seek within itself what it could not discover from without, not even in its history or in its collective faith.

Slowly, the town and its inhabitants swirl around the two bewildered characters at its center, trying to deny that Imma's and Ezra's crises are reflections of the meaninglessness of their own existences. In short, the town wants them to go away, to stop reminding them that the placidity and complacency of their lives are a façade, and that beneath the mask may be something dark and ugly and extremely frightening, even though it never quite comes into view.

The Vigil never quite reveals it, either. Rather, the town finds itself defeated by the determination of a single woman's search for self, by her insistence that she will defy convention and order and even reason; she will prevail by asserting her identity and forcing an awareness of her presence on all of them, a constant reminder of their truer selves, a constant temptation for them to face, and possibly to surrender to, their more genuine natures. Imma and the town of Agatite, then, come to represent opposing visions of one another, opposing interpretations of truth that undermine logic and common sense, perhaps, but that appeal to that universal *something* within every human being that responds to notions of faith, love, and above all, understanding—that impulse that finally apprehends that whatever evil we perceive in the world is truly within ourselves, as is the good, and it's the process of separating these that we call life.

When *The Vigil* was initially accepted for publication in 1986, I had no idea that I had embarked on the mapping of this place, this Sandhill County chronicle, or that I would become inexorably tied to it. I had merely made use of a fictionalization of memory, a falsification of factual matter that permitted me to manipulate and direct the background in a way that, I hoped, complemented the story I wanted out front.

In *Agatite,* however, I began to see the town and the surrounding county in a far different way. Again, I believe, the underlying theme is the same—a quest for self, a coming to terms with the face behind the mask, the admission of the truth of the nature of good and evil only when it refuses to be denied any longer (and before anyone says it, yeah, I'm aware this is hardly an original set of ideas for a theme). Yet *Agatite* differs from *The Vigil* in that the motivation for revelation is less public (even though its revelation is much *more* public) and in a sense, the result of a deeper self-deception and self-denial.

For a while, after *Agatite,* I tried to leave Sandhill County again, this time for good. But I was instantly drawn back to it, as a prodigal, I suppose, because I realized that in the course of working on the first two books, I had discovered a wealth of ignorance in myself about the very place I thought I knew so well. I had grown up surrounded by its history, by its past of which I was less than dimly aware—that elusive fog, again. In *Franklin's Crossing,* I tried to tell about part of that past, and about the founding of the county, but what I wound up doing was writing a kind of prequel to the county's history, a sort of prehistoric account of what had happened to give the place an identity, a chance to discover itself. I realized, somehow, that in the fabrications of my first two novels, I hadn't really accounted for the place's right to exist, and I needed a novel such as *Franklin's Crossing* to do that. It became a birth bathed in blood, one in which evil takes on a corporeal reality. But as any good Baptist knows, without being washed in blood, nothing can be saved.

My next attempt to break away was in *Players,* but even then I maintained a connection to Sandhill County that is so obscure no one I know has pointed it out. It was a far more subtle connection than exists between *The Vigil* and *Agatite,* more on a par with the connection between *Franklin's Crossing* and the first two books—and, not incidentally, a number of short stories that do not mention the name of the town but which, nevertheless, I will quickly admit are directly connected to or set therein.

After that, I rather gave up on escaping. *Monuments* represented a complete return to the town. Its connection to the first books, which I am now shamelessly calling a chronicle, is direct. It is Agatite, again, and it is Sandhill County, again. But this time, the story is far less about the people than about the physical town itself. I thought it was about time I brought the main character out front, gave it a spotlight, and allowed it to play all by itself, allowed its own search for self to be realized through the eyes of a boy.

Monuments, I knew from the outset, would be called a coming-of-age story. The central character, Hugh Rudd, is a youngster, a typical small town boy, and his foil and friend, Jonas Wilson, is an old man, a last vestige, perhaps, of the enduring spirit of the town, of the county surrounding it. The analogues to classical literature are not difficult to trace. But I think it is a mistake to read that novel as a simple story of one teenager's confrontation with adulthood. I think the true protagonist is a dying town in the middle of the vast, cruel nothing that is West Texas. In that sense, *Monuments* is about hope unfulfilled, promises unredeemed, and values and ambitions unrevealed. That sounds negative, but I don't think it is. I think it is real and about as positive as things ever get in West Texas.

I also think that, as with the first two novels, the point is to separate the perception from the reality of self through a process of confrontation—which is not unlike the process of trying to separate good and evil from within. Virtually every experience Hugh has that summer reinforces the notion that, ultimately, we are alone in the universe, and we must become self-reliant. I don't mean this in the Emersonian sense—not entirely—or even in the existential sense—not entirely—but rather in the sense that informs *The Vigil, Agatite, Franklin's Crossing* and, to a lesser extent, *Players* and a yet-to-be-told story, "Threading the Needle." By *self-reliance* I mean that humans often come to a point when they realize that all they can rely on is what they know, what they have learned, what they have experienced. And ultimately, this is all there is. This is the foundation of whatever hope and love and compassion we can find within ourselves. This is the stuff of life.

Monuments, then, represents a full return to Agatite, to Sandhill County, and I hope that it will not be the last. I want to tell other stories about it. I want to discuss the ramifications of teenagers' hopes and dreams, informed as they are by those outsiders—cousins or otherwise—who brought to the town the false prophecies, the "dirty words" and "nasty habits" of elsewhere, and sent them shivering through the innocent small-town souls of the West Texas young on the staticky strains of rock and roll. I want to recapture a time when the narcotics of choice were cheap beer, sweet liquor, sweaty backseat sex, and two eight-cylinder-driven automobiles shrieking demonlike through the night. Those stories and others continue these chronicles.

I think this is important work. That may be self-flattery, but I hope not. I hope that it has a broader context. Some more forward-looking writers and critics have averred that the "myths" of the past, the drama of the small town, are dead letters; that there is nothing left there of interest. I don't agree. I think that in the greater scheme of things the dramatic moments of these lives, caught in microcosm, as it were, fretted by the significance of exposure—exposure such as only a small town can provide—provide a closer and more cogent look at the truth of the human experience, of the human heart. And the human heart, after all, is the only genuine subject worthy of a fiction writer's attention.

What makes sense to me is to create characters, put them into situations that cause them to react in some human way, and contain the whole thing in a crucible of time and place. My time and place is Agatite, Sandhill County, and my characters come from the people who I imagine live there, either now or in the past. The situation in each of these novels is unique to the characters I created and has nothing but the most coincidental relationship to any other situation or characters, real or imagined. After the initial reaction, I think, the characters are on their own, just as the people of West Texas are on their own. As the writer, I can nudge them here and there, can throw more obstacles, opportunities, and circumstances in their paths; but how they find their way to some kind of resolution—some sense of self—is up to them. It's not up to me to conclude their stories. The characters must do that. And apart from reversing them if they make a wrong turn, an author really shouldn't—in my case can't—interfere with how things develop. To me, my characters are as real as my county and my town; in many, many ways, they're more real than the actual county and town and the people who inhabit it and its cemetery, who drift shadowlike in the gritty fog of the sandy past.

I probably will tell as many stories about Sandhill County as publishers are pleased to put into print. It took me a long time to realize it, but in truth, I suppose that everything I write will, in one way or another, be a part of the Sandhill Chronicles. I hasten to say, though, that I don't do this out of pure ego—although on at least one level, all writing is merely an exercise of one individual ego—but because this is ultimately what I know. It's the place I came from, came out of, and ran away from. It is the place I know. And it is the place I am somehow always drawn back to, at least in my fiction; for it is there that I can discover, to the extent that it's discoverable, the meaning of West Texas and, more importantly, my own definition of self.

Clay Reynolds
Denton, Texas 2001

For my mother and all who live for hopes
and dreams and faith

Hope is a thing with feathers
that perches in the soul
     —Emily Dickinson

PART
1

As *is* the mother, *so is* her daughter

Ezekiel 16:44

O N E

The August sun had already heated the seat of the concrete bench to an uncomfortable temperature when the old woman found her way across the courthouse square and wearily sat down. She had been serving customers breakfast since six-thirty that morning and had been up two hours before that making biscuits and gravy—a staple of Agatite early risers who regularly came by the Town and Country Dinette for their morning meal—and she was tired. Her faded pink uniform from the dinette had gotten egg on it that morning, and Dinah had suggested that instead of taking up her usual position on the park bench—*her* park bench, they had both corrected at the same time—why didn't she just go home and change, maybe take a little nap before noon and the lunch rush. But she had come out to the courthouse lawn like always. Poor Dinah, she thought. After all these years a body would think she'd understand.

Imogene McBride scooched her skinny bottom around on the concrete bench, testing it to see if it had cooled any from the protection from the sun her body offered, and pulled brightly colored yarn from a shoebox she had brought with her from the dinette. She had started an afghan the day before for the Sellers' new baby. It would bring her almost fifteen dollars after she paid for the materials, and with the three others she had yet to do this month, one more birthing and two wedding presents, she figured she might be able to squeeze out enough

3

money for a new uniform, certainly a new pair of nursing oxfords too. Her feet had been bothering her lately.

Her posture was rigid on the bench as she knitted, like a secretary sitting at a typewriter, and although the knitting occupied her hands, her eyes paid it no mind; they were focused on the line of stores and businesses on the block facing the courthouse. They might shift away from time to time, but never for long. It was a long-established habit they had, and Imogene was completely unaware of their movement.

She was nearly seventy, but from a distance she looked much younger, and up close there was still the hint of a beautiful woman who had once been desirable and happy. Now, however, her skin, weather-worn and pulled taut by a severe ponytail gathered high on her head, was rough and betrayed none of its original suppleness and youthful glow. Her eyes were gray and clear, and her hair, long since gone white with age and work and worry, had begun to thin out in front, leaving small bald spots wisping free of the ponytail's pull. She was thin and looked lean and tough, like a fence post that has seen too many seasons change but still has the strength to stretch the wire. Yet there remained a definition of a girlish figure, and she gently crossed her legs at the ankle, careful to keep her knees together in the uniform made for a much younger woman.

She came to the bench by the courthouse every day, winter and summer, regardless of the weather. She sat for about two hours every morning, longer when Dinah felt she could handle the noon crowd on her own, and two hours every afternoon. The dinner crowd was always too heavy for Dinah by herself, although the numbers of diners in the small dinette always seemed insufficient to keep the business out of debt. On pleasant nights, after the dishes had been washed and the preparations were made for breakfast, she would come out in the evenings too, sometimes sitting until past midnight, and on most occasions she would knit or crochet. Her habits were familiar to her, and she didn't think much about them. It was just what she did: she sat on the bench—*her* bench—between nine and eleven of a morning and between three and five of an afternoon, every morning and every afternoon.

She was waiting for her daughter to come back.

A lot of folks had decided a long time ago that she was crazy. She knew that, but she didn't think much about that either. She really didn't care. She never had.

A little over thirty years before, she had sat down like a normal person on a park bench on a small city's courthouse square, and her little girl had sat down on the green grass beside her for a while and then gone to the drugstore for an ice cream. And she had simply disappeared. Just like that, Imogene would have said, had anyone ever asked her about it. But no one ever did, and she never thought much about that either.

She had come to Agatite, Texas, thirty years before, driving her husband's bright green Hudson and carrying more than two thousand dollars of his bright green money. In the car with her was everything she owned or cared about in the world: clothing packed neatly in over-large, expensive traveling bags, her jewelry, an oil painting she had purchased on her honeymoon trip to Cuba in 1932, a rosary made of specially selected stones, mostly pearls and opals, but a couple of diamonds too, and Cora, her beautiful eighteen-year-old daughter.

The Hudson coughed and died two miles outside Agatite, and she gave the job of repairing it to Luke Short of Short's Garage and Gas. Whatever was wrong with it wasn't too serious, apparently, since Luke Short himself told her he could have her on the road again in a couple of hours, just as soon as he sent somebody over to Childress to the Hudson dealer to pick up some parts.

5

Luke's station was directly across from the Sandhill County Courthouse, and she and Cora strolled over to the lawn. It was spring, April, and they took seats on and around the brightly colored wooden benches that invited weary pedestrians to sit and take off their shoes and wiggle their toes in the soft Bermuda grass of the courthouse lawn.

They sat there watching some birds fly back and forth along the lawn and idly commented on the people and traffic that passed in front of them along Main Street. Both were a little nervous, and both were wondering how things would be at Aunt Mildred's up in Oregon.

Imogene didn't mind the breakdown nearly as much as she'd thought she was going to. They had been traveling straight through from Baton Rouge, stopping only by the side of the road for an hour and a half while Imogene slept, washing up in filling stations and roadside cafés. She wanted to get to Oregon by the end of the week, so she could settle in with her sister and then call that son-of-a-bitch Harvey and tell him she would never speak to him again.

They had left Atlanta, her home for the past twenty years, the previous weekend, and then they had driven to Baton Rouge, checking into a motor court and waiting for Harvey to come and get them. Leaving him had been a very hard thing to do, and she should know. She had tried to do it twice before and lost her nerve. Her courage usually played out just after she packed, but this time she was gone, and gone for good. She had hoped for a scene in Baton Rouge, something climactic to convince herself and, of course, Cora, that it was really over between Harvey and Imogene McBride. But naturally, he refused to oblige.

Well, she insisted to herself on that bright April day, there would be no divorce. She didn't believe in divorce, and even if she did, she wouldn't give him one. The bas-

6

tard could go on with his fooling around with every slutty little secretary he met if he wanted to, but he wouldn't be marrying another Mrs. Harvey McBride. That was one thing of which she was certain.

Cora was so pretty, she noticed, sitting in a beautiful white-and-pink cotton dress on the green grass. The morning sun made her golden hair shine brightly. She had cried most of the way since they left Atlanta. She missed her daddy, Imogene supposed. Well, she'd get over that. Out in Oregon she could be told what a disgusting man her father really was, how he had made Imogene's life a living hell with his mistresses and his drinking. But she didn't want to tell her yet. Let her get all the tears out first, Imogene thought; then there would be none left for Harvey at all.

From an outsider's point of view, Imogene's life wouldn't have appeared to have been anything short of wonderful. The McBrides lived in a large mansion in a fashionable neighborhood in the "best part" of Atlanta. Harvey McBride, a big, handsome Scot with a winning grin and red, curly hair, had taken a beaten-up old sawmill and converted it into a thriving lumber business in spite of the Depression and war shortages. From the time he first met Imogene, who was working as a secretary in her father's business in Memphis, they had looked like a perfect match. She had actually defied her father and moved down to Atlanta to be near him two years before they married. But she often wondered if he would have married her at all if she hadn't discovered that she was pregnant with Cora.

She had had an easy time with Cora's birth, but she was a long time getting over it. She had hated the way she blew up like a balloon and couldn't get out of a chair without struggling like a floundering walrus. She hated the whole experience, from morning sickness to labor pain, the maternity clothes, the confinement, the probing icy hands of the doctor, and the sheer humiliation of the whole process.

She knew of Harvey's cheap little affairs even then, and she excused him, even if she didn't forgive him, on the grounds that sex was the one thing she didn't want or need in her frame of mind. Although her body mended quickly, her mind healed slowly, and by the time she wanted him to come to her bed again, he did so grudgingly, and finally he stopped completely. He spent his time and pleasure in the company of bleached blondes and trashy redheads he picked up at conventions and in his customers' offices. No better than whores, that kind, Imogene thought with a dark hatred. He fathered at least one child by one of them, and he'd had to pay her off royally to avoid a scandal.

Still, he provided a comfortable life for Imogene and his beautiful daughter, Cora. They had two maids, a chauffeur, a cook, and a gardener. Imogene's dresses as well as Cora's were all handmade, and they were permitted to go on long, expensive vacations, although Harvey rarely went with them, to California, New York, even once, before the war, to Europe. Cora became a debutante and a very sophisticated beauty by the time she reached the climax of her teenage years. She had wanted to enter the Miss Georgia contest that year, but Imogene refused permission. It wasn't dignified.

As the years went by and Cora grew, Harvey's flings became more frequent and less discreet. He was getting older, fatter, balder, and the girls seemed to become cheaper in proportion. But he was also getting richer, so his relative attractiveness continued. Imogene endured well-meaning friends who told her "quite confidentially" that he had been seen with another woman on several occasions, visits from the parish priest who attempted to console her without revealing Harvey's confessions, and the pitying looks of almost everyone she knew, most of whom thought she only suspected things, almost none of whom knew how well she was informed.

Finally she decided she had had enough. She made preparations to leave him, carefully and completely. When she had tried before, she had just thrown a few things into a bag, bought two train tickets, and usually dragged Cora as far as the train station before panic struck and she raced back home, unpacked, swore Cora to secrecy, made it to table in time for Harvey to come swinging in, half stewed from his double martinis at the country club, and managed to smile while he shoveled food into his mouth, made lame excuses about some extra work he had to do or a client he had to meet, and lurched out before dessert was served. Then she would spend the rest of the evening crying into her pillow more over her own cowardice than Harvey's infidelity.

This time, however, she started planning months in advance. She made Gregory, the chauffeur, teach her to drive Harvey's Hudson. It was a big, heavy car, but she wanted something substantial to take her to Oregon. She threatened to tell Sid Howard's wife about his and Harvey's little after-hours meetings at the bar of the Bledsoe Hotel if he didn't use his legal powers to alter the title of the car into her name. She packed everything in new and expensive luggage, and she simply got the money by walking into Harvey's office, the loaded Hudson parked down the street, and asking him right in front of his partner and new secretary—the one he hadn't had a chance to conquer yet—if he could spare some cash for new drapes for the front hall. She explained in elaborate detail how they were to be handmade, and the man wanted twenty-five hundred dollars in advance, in cash. Harvey had too much pride to turn her down right in front of these people, so he immediately wrote her a check, which she cashed at his own payroll window, and that was the last she saw of him for a long, long time.

Cora stood up and brushed loose grass from her dress. "I want an ice cream, Mama," she announced, looking over across Main Street to a shop that offered a sign, PETE'S SUNDRIES AND DRUGS, and boasted a large cardboard ice cream cone in the window. "You want one?"

Imogene fished a five-cent piece out of her coin purse, "No, honey, but you come right back, hear?" She looked over toward Short's Garage and Gas. "The car should be ready soon."

She watched as her daughter strolled across the lawn to the corner and waited before crossing the dusty brick street. Imogene frowned. Cora had a way of walking that bothered her. It was as if she were wearing spiked heels instead of the flat-soled oxfords. Her hips undulated as she moved from step to step, and her breasts seemed actually to rise and thrust forward. It wasn't walking, really; it was almost prancing, like a show horse. Watching her from behind and then from one side, Imogene found herself wondering if Cora wore any underwear under her modest, white-and-pink cotton dress. Then she shook her head, passing her hands over her eyes briefly. It was a ridiculous thought. The dress was lovely, that was all. It had been specially made along with a dozen others by the best seamstress in Atlanta. It just looked so very nice in the morning sun, and as Imogene watched her daughter cross the street, she smiled with pride at the beauty of her only child. She would have to do something about that walk when they got to Oregon, she reminded herself.

A 1932 Ford with AGATITE EAGLES printed on the door passed behind Cora, and the two boys in the seat stared at her. They were too old to be boys, Imogene thought, and she started to rise and call to her daughter, but Cora went on her way, swishing her hips a bit too much, and looked back over her shoulder at the Ford with a big, toothy grin. Then, to Imogene's horror, she winked at the boys. But before they could respond or Imogene could get to her feet, Cora disappeared inside the drugstore.

She's too much like her father, Imogene thought, scowling at the green courthouse grass, and then tried to relax and lean back on the bench. She wears too much makeup for a girl her age, and she's always wanting to fix her hair like those trashy movie stars. She wants to be more than she is. But why? She's already the prettiest girl ever, much prettier than her friends, and naturally pretty. She didn't have to bleach her hair or pull out her eyebrows the way they did. Imogene smiled when she thought of Cora's one disastrous attempt to give herself a home permanent. Her hair had turned orange, and she had cried for three days straight. She had been only fourteen then, Imogene remembered, and it had seemed an eternity before her hair all grew out and returned to its natural, golden sheen.

But lately Cora had been talking about cutting her hair again, about possibly dying it dark just to see what it would look like, and she had taken to buying all sorts of cheap perfumes and wearing bright, printed scarves and heavy imitation pearl necklaces and other junk that made her look tacky and—Imogene winced at the thought—of easy virtue. Cora had spent a whole week's allowance just before Christmas on a dozen peasant blouses, which she started wearing low on her delicate shoulders and would have continued to wear that way if Imogene had not put a stop to it by giving them all away to a charity drive.

Well, there would be none of that in Oregon. There would be no money for extravagant allowances, for one thing. And for another, Imogene had made sure that none of the cheap clothes and perfumes and makeup were packed in their luggage. Aside from whatever Cora carried in her purse, in fact, none of the miserable traits of their past life had come with them. In Oregon things would be better, back to normal, and Harvey would be a distant, unpleasant memory.

Imogene wanted her daughter to have a normal life, to marry, to live a happy and long life with a man she loved—and who loved her, Imogene added quickly—that was the important thing. She didn't want Cora to fall for the first glad-hander with a pocket full of promise and a mouth full of sorry who came her way. She didn't want her to become a man-hater either, though, or even to hate Harvey. Not really. She just wanted her to know enough to be careful, not to make the same mistakes Imogene had.

She had mixed feelings about taking Cora out of high school so close to graduation. She would be exempted from final exams in all but two courses—algebra and French—and Imogene had arranged for her to take them by mail under the supervision of a Portland school. The last month of senior year was all parties and fooling around anyway, and while it might be unfair to deprive Cora of those things, it would serve the purpose of keeping her far away from Joe Don Jacobs.

Joe Don was college-bound and a good athlete. He would only break Cora's heart or, worse, leave her pregnant while he went off with some cheerleader, Imogene thought. Cora had no thought of college, although the McBrides could well afford it and she was smart enough. She had announced that she wanted to go to secretarial school! Well, that was one thing she would not do, Imogene promised herself. Imogene had a few thoughts about secretaries these days.

She sat on the bench patiently, now vaguely uncomfortable in the bright sunlight, and waited for Cora to emerge from the drugstore. Ten minutes went by, then fifteen. That was well nigh long enough for an ice cream cone, Imogene calculated, even if she sat down and read a magazine while she ate it. She was probably lost in one of those cheap, trashy movie fan magazines all drugstores carried.

Imogene wanted to get up and go see what was keeping her daughter, but she had told Luke Short she would be on one of these benches, and she didn't want him to come looking for her and find her missing. She could go tell Mr. Short that she had gone to look for Cora, but Cora might come back and find her gone and panic.

She began to squirm on the bench, then she rose and walked up and down in front of it. She began to perspire in the sun. She needed a bath, she thought. She hadn't had one since they were in Baton Rouge.

After they checked into the motor courts, Imogene had patiently waited until Cora settled herself into the room's bathtub and closed the door. Then she called Harvey. "I've left you," she told him matter-of-factly. "If you want me to come back, you've got to give up—you've got to stop what you're doing. Change your life. I can't live like that anymore." He had said nothing, but she could hear him breathing, or so she thought, on the other end of the line in Atlanta. "Well?" she finally asked when she had endured all she could of his silence.

"What about Cora?" he answered. She hung up on him. That was that. It was on to Oregon and Mildred's.

An hour had passed since Cora went in for an ice cream, and Imogene was angry. She could see the Hudson in Luke Short's garage. He had the hood up and was leaning over the engine compartment. Finally she made up her mind and walked purposefully toward the corner, across Main Street, and into the drugstore. Inside, her eyes had difficulty adjusting to the dimmer light, but when they did, she saw an older man puttering around behind the drug counter. The fountain, the magazine rack, the two booths in the rear of the store, the jukebox, the perfume counter, all stood alone and empty. No one but the man was in the store.

"Excuse me," Imogene said, and the older man, Pete Hankins, looked up from the prescription he was filling. He had apparently not heard—or had decided to ignore, Imogene said to herself—the bell attached to the door that jingled when she came inside. "I'm looking for my daughter. She just came in here for an ice cream."

Pete scanned the empty store. "I haven't seen her, ma'am, but if I do, I'll send her right home. What's her name?"

"Cora," Imogene said automatically, tapping a polished nail on the soda fountain counter and glancing behind to see if her daughter was crouched down, hiding from her and waiting to jump out and shout something silly. "Cora McBride. But you don't understand. She came in here about an hour ago for an ice cream, and she's never come out. She must be here someplace."

"Hasn't been nobody in here this morning," Pete said, still concentrating on the pills he counted into a small bottle. "Not since Mrs. Thompson came by for her husband's medicine. Nope. No kids in here during school hours. Sheriff don't like that. Now, later this afternoon—"

"No!" she said emphatically. Then she caught her breath and calmed her voice. "You still don't understand. We're not from here, from . . . what's the name of this town?"

"Agatite," Pete said as if only a complete fool wouldn't know the name of the town she was in.

"Agatite," Imogene repeated. She really did feel stupid as well as foolish. "We're from Georgia. Atlanta. We're passing through, uh . . . on vacation. Sort of. And our car broke down, and while we're waiting on it to be fixed at Mr. . . . uh, Short's garage"—she pointed vaguely out the window—"Cora wanted to come over here for an ice

14

cream." She waited, studying the stained smock of the druggist. "And she did. But she never came out."

"Nope." Pete thoughtfully put a hand up to his red chin and rubbed it. Imogene noted that his face looked scraped raw, as if he had shaved too close. "I ain't served any ice cream today at all."

"Well, maybe she didn't have an ice cream." Imogene felt herself becoming exasperated with this doddering old fool. "Maybe she had a soda"—Imogene looked around the small store—"or a Coke or a . . . or something else. She only had a nickel, so she couldn't have bought much of anything other than ice cream."

Pete looked around, following her gaze at the cheap perfumes and fingernail kits on the counter. "Maybe she changed her mind and went down to Central Drugs," he offered. "They got ten flavors of ice cream, some with nuts."

"No." Imogene forced herself to be patient and to speak slowly so he would understand her. "I *said* she came in *here*! I saw her. She never came out. I was sitting over on the lawn there, on a bench." She pointed again. "The red one. Right in front of this store. And no one has come out since she went in."

"Nobody come in, neither." Pete sensed her patronizing air and wanted to let her know his resentment, but he saw something glint in her gray eyes, and he softened his face and came from behind the drug counter, scratching his white hair. "What's she look like?"

"She's blond, eighteen, very pretty," Imogene listed categorically. "She had on a white-and-pink dress and was wearing a pink ribbon in her hair and—oh—" Imogene broke off, realizing that the old fool was humoring her. "Do you have a back door?"

"Sure," Pete replied, pointing to a small door almost concealed behind the shelves of drugs. "But she ain't back there."

15

"Did she *go* back there?" Imogene felt a scream trying to take over her vocal cords and forced it away.

"I told you," Pete said, pulling a pack of Chesterfields out of his stained druggist's smock and lighting one with a Zippo lighter from one of the displays, "Ain't nobody been in here since Mrs. Thompson come in about nine-thirty for her husband's pills."

Imogene suddenly felt the desire for a cigarette creep all over her. She had quit smoking when Cora was a baby and grabbed a lit cigarette from her mother's mouth and burned herself. After all these years she shouldn't still want one, Imogene thought; in fact she hadn't thought about wanting one until this very moment. She brushed the sensation aside. "May I look?" She nodded toward the small door.

Pete hesitated, she thought, for just a moment. "Sure, go ahead."

Imogene walked back through the shelves and pushed on the door. It wouldn't give. It was locked with a sliding bolt she had to stand on tiptoe to reach. Cora could never manage this, she thought. She's a head shorter than I, especially when I'm wearing heels.

Finally she threw the bolt and pushed the door open. It was black as pitch in the room, but she went on in and fumbled around in the dark until her hand struck a pull-string that turned on a single hooded bulb overhead. The room was stocked with boxes of drugs, fountain materials, bottles of cola syrup, and every other conceivable kind of notion and sundry the store might carry. A sink and toilet were buried under an ordered cascade of cardboard and wooden crates against the wall, and Imogene turned a wrinkle in her nose at the sight of a small puddle of water beneath the rusty porcelain.

She spotted the back door in the center of the rear wall, and she went over and inspected it. It opened to the outside, but she couldn't get to it because of a stack of large boxes that almost completely blocked it off. She tried to move the biggest of the boxes, but it wouldn't budge, and she backed off and chewed on a fingernail as she studied the rest of the room. A safety razor and a bar of hand soap were visible in the damp sink well, and a bottle of cheap cologne was stuffed into the torn corner of a box atop the toilet. An open pack of Lucky Strikes rested on a stack of boxes on the wall opposite the sink and commode. It was half empty, she noticed as she picked it up. Once she had caught Cora smoking out in the greenhouse. Was it Lucky Strikes she had? Imogene couldn't remember.

After a few minutes she came back into the front of the store where Pete was mixing a Coke at the fountain. "You sure you don't want a Coke or cup of coffee or somethin'?" he asked. "You look kind of peekid."

"No." She forced herself into a polite tone once again, "Thank you." She moved toward him. "I couldn't open the back door."

"Nope." Pete sipped his Coke. "Neither can I. Lock's busted. Has been for years. The only way to fix it is to put in a new door, jamb and all." He rose from the stool behind the fountain counter and came around and leaned against the front of the counter. "That's why them boxes full of magazines and school supplies and stuff are piled up there." He hesitated, rubbed his raw jaw with one finger, and seemed to calculate. "I figure it'd take two, maybe three good-sized men to move all of them, and the door's small enough that it'd be too much bother for no more than I keep around here worth stealin'."

"You have drugs," Imogene said flatly, surveying the store once again in the incredible hope that she might yet spy the figure of her daughter.

"Oh," Pete said, sipping his Coke again, "I keep that kind of stuff locked up in a safe. Everybody knows that."

"Are these yours?" she said quickly, holding up the package of cigarettes.

"Nope," he replied. "I smoke these." He fished the pack of Chesterfields out of his smock pocket.

"Are you *absolutely* certain you didn't see my daughter when she came in here?" Imogene's eyes narrowed, focusing to detect a lie. She felt she was an old hand at detecting men's lies.

"Look, Mrs. . . . uh—"

"McBride!"

"Look, Mrs. McBride, I told you ain't nobody been in here since Mrs. Thompson came in for—"

"I know!" Imogene screamed suddenly, "For her husband's goddamn pills!" And she rushed past him and slammed the door behind her, listening to the ring of the door's tiny bell as she ran out onto the sidewalk.

T W O

Up and down the street the people of Agatite bustled about their downtown business. It was a small downtown district, with a single street and a couple of side streets where shops and businesses thrived. Imogene stood in front of the small drugstore and stared hard at the moving knots of people in the bright April sunlight. Two blocks down she could see the corner of the railroad depot, and in the far distance of the other direction the street faded into the intersection where it met the main highway. She walked back and forth in front of the drugstore, becoming more and more angry. This was a nasty trick, Cora, she thought, nastier than the time last winter when you stayed out all night with those girls without asking our permission or even letting us know where you were. You will be punished for this, Imogene thought darkly.

Finally she could stand it no longer, and she struck out in the direction of the depot toward the central district of downtown. Maybe Cora had gone into the shop, found the old man busy, and then slipped out while he wasn't looking. Maybe she was window-shopping. She didn't have any money. Imogene had been careful not to give her any, although she hated to admit she was afraid Cora might sneak away and call Harvey or, worse, run back to him.

She stopped briefly in front of every store and shop on Main Street, even the hardware store, peering carefully into each window. At the Ben Franklin store she walked in and made the rounds of the aisles, checking for a glimpse of the white-and-pink dress or yellow hair of her daughter. But Cora wasn't anywhere. Noon came, and people were walking up and down the concrete side-walk, a few looking curiously at the fashionably dressed woman with the firmly set jaw and fierce gray eyes who seemed to be searching every store for something she couldn't find.

When another hour had gone by, she went back to the courthouse and crossed the lawn to the bench and sat down. She was very upset, but she was determined to wait for Cora to come back, no matter how long it took. She lit a cigarette from the pack of Luckies she had dropped into her purse when Pete had denied they were his. It made her cough at first, but she smoked the ciga-rette down to a stub and dropped it into the grass, and in a few minutes she lit another. After another hour she promised herself that if Cora would just call off this silly, cruel game and come laughing back, she wouldn't pun-ish her after all. They would just forget the whole thing. Then she breathed a silent prayer and made the same promise over again, just to make sure.

About two-thirty a tap on her shoulder made her jump. She had been carefully scrutinizing every vehicle that passed down Main Street, hoping that Cora had somehow been picked up by some local boys or someone else and was out enjoying a ride and attention from strange admirers. But it was Luke Short who tapped her. He had parked the Hudson, she noticed, on the street beside the courthouse, a fact he was remarking on as her heart returned to its normal rate. He added with a slight grin that it was now in the shade and wouldn't be too hot when they got in. The bill, he sheepishly muttered, was $35.50.

She counted out the money from her purse, and suddenly a hopeful thought struck her. "You haven't by chance seen my daughter, have you?"

"Sure, ma'am," Luke said, his chubby face grinning under smeared grease.

"Really!" She felt delight swim up through her body. "Oh, wonderful! Where is she?"

Luke's smile evaporated when he realized that she meant had he seen her recently. "Why, ma'am, I seen her this mornin'. With you. When we towed in the car." He saw her face fall and suddenly felt as if he had just played a cruel joke on her. He noticed her eyes flick across Main Street again. "You ain't lost her, have you, ma'am?"

She looked at this simple mechanic in his greasy jeans and dirty shirt, standing awkwardly in front of her, shifting his weight from one bandy leg to another. He was hardly the type of person to become a friend, but she didn't see that there was much choice. He was the only one, other than Pete, of course—the senile old fool—who had taken any interest in her problem at all, so she poured out her dilemma to him.

Luke listened carefully to her story. He immediately recognized that there was more to this than some silly girl out skylarking with a bunch of boys just to devil her mother on their vacation. But like most small-town people, he had a strong respect for other folks' business, and the more Imogene talked about her daughter and her odd disappearance, the more uncomfortable he became. He decided that a well-placed lie might be in order. It might get him off the hook, too.

"Well, hell, uh . . . heck, ma'am. You know how kids are. She'll probably turn up in a little bit full of Cokes and hamburgers. I had a niece did the exact same thing to my brother's wife one time when they was visitin' out in Arizona." He looked into her gray eyes to see if she could sense that he was making the whole incident up. "Worried Bessie, that's my sister-in-law, sick. She run into a bunch of kids and they had went off to get some hamburgers and Cokes, that's all. She showed up two hours later, and, boy, her mama gave her hell, uh . . . heck." He grinned, pulled out a toothpick from his shirt pocket and jammed it into his molars, where a stubborn piece of meat from his noon sandwich remained.

Imogene realized that Luke Short was to be no help at all, and she forced a smile and thanked him for his work and his comforting words. He told her to be sure to call him if she had any more trouble with the Hudson, and that he'd be sure to send Cora to her if he saw her. Then he strolled bandy-legged back to his garage, where he had a Chevy waiting to have the wheel bearings packed.

Imogene lit another cigarette and paced for a few more minutes in front of the red bench. Then she decided to make one more pass through town. This time she stopped in every store and shop and asked anyone she found if Cora had come that way. Everyone was nice and polite, and everyone offered to help by sending Cora to her mother should she turn up, but no one had seen her. Cora simply was not downtown.

Finally Imogene went back to Pete's Sundries and Drugs. It was full of high school kids playing the jukebox, drinking sodas and Cokes, and eating ice cream.

Pete was in back of the fountain, mixing drinks and sundaes, and he smiled broadly when Imogene came in, hardly noticing that she was studying the faces of every blond or partly blond girl in the shop. "Hi!" he boomed over the music. "Did you find her?"

Imogene retained control of herself. Panic was welling up in her like a flood, and she could feel her heart pounding in her ears. "Look," she said in what she hoped sounded like a calm, reasonable voice, "are you absolutely certain that my daughter hasn't been in here, that this isn't some kind of joke?"

Pete shook his head slowly, the smile remaining on his lips. "It's like I told you this mornin', Mrs. . . . uh . . ." She didn't help him this time. "Mrs. I ain't seen her, not so as I'd know it was her, anyhow. A lot of these kids look alike to me." This brought a giggle from the group at the fountain counter. "But nobody came in here before you did, except for Mrs. Thompson."

Imogene leaned against the counter and felt exhaustion and frustration draining away all of what remained of her energy. She felt dirty, tired; her feet hurt from walking up and down the concrete sidewalks and in and out of stores, and, she suddenly realized, she was hungry. "Very well," she sighed out. "We'll play it your way. Maybe she offered you something to hide her or to lie to me or something. Well, whatever she offered to pay you, I'll double it. No. Listen, I know she hasn't any money, any cash, and she can't get any, either. I'll give you a hundred dollars, right now, cash! Just tell me where she is."

Pete's eyes widened, and several of the kids looked around. The jukebox had fallen silent after the last record, and her words carried through the entire shop. "Lady," he said, "I don't know what's goin' on between you and your daughter, if there *is* any girl and *if* she is

22

your daughter, but I'm here to tell you that I think you're nutty as a fruitcake!"

Several of the kids broke into laughter at this, and more of them focused their attention on the well-dressed woman who stood at Pete's soda fountain offering him something that sounded like a fortune just to find some girl.

"All right!" Imogene said in a voice that began to crack a bit. "Five hundred dollars." There was only silence. "A thousand!" she shrieked. By now all the kids were staring at her in wonder. Pete shook his head again and opened his mouth to speak, but Imogene put up her hand. "Very well. You *ain't* seen her." She mimicked his accent and fought for control. She needed to go to the bathroom, she suddenly realized. "What if I call the police? Would that make her magically appear?"

"That'd be Ezra Holmes," Pete said in a flat voice, then he perked up. "Why don't you call him over? His arthritis prescription's ready anyway." He enjoyed his joke, and there was a chorus of snickering among the kids, who felt the release of tension. "But he ain't no police. He's the sheriff."

She took a deep breath to face the sea of faces that now either openly gaped at her or peeked from behind soda glasses. "My name is Mrs. Harvey McBride," she began in what she hoped was a sane and reasonable voice. "My daughter, Cora McBride, came into this shop about ten-thirty this morning to buy an ice cream cone. She never came out, and I haven't seen her since. I have been unable to find anyone who will admit that he's seen her either." She glanced at Pete.

"Lady," Pete said, growing hot about being made out a liar in front of all the kids, "I told you I *ain't* seen her, and I ain't! Pete don't lie!"

She ignored him. "She's blond, eighteen years old, and

very pretty. She is wearing a white-and-pink cotton dress, black-and-white saddle shoes with bobby socks, and . . ." She hesitated for just a moment. "And I am prepared to pay five hundred dollars, cash, to anyone who brings her to me or tells me where I can find her. Cash! I strongly suspect that she is hiding from me as part of a cruel joke, and I'm frankly tired of it. If she's not hiding, then perhaps she has met with some sort of . . . of mischief." She wanted to look at Pete in the worst way, but from the corner of her eye she saw him stiffen and thought better of it. "I'm going to wait on that red park bench over on the courthouse square"—she pointed out the window, and the kids all strained to see the bench, as if they hadn't seen it a thousand times before— "and I will pay whoever comes up with her first. No questions asked."

Imogene closed her speech and turned on her heel and walked out of the drugstore. She crossed the street at the corner and seated herself on the bench. Very well, Cora, I can play this game as well as you.

At five-thirty, when the shadows of the courthouse brought an unseasonable chill to the shade that now draped over that portion of the courthouse lawn where Imogene waited on the bench, she crushed out the last of the Luckies on the grass in front of her and went inside to seek out a rest room and Sheriff Holmes.

THREE

At better than fifty-nine years of age, Sheriff Ezra Stone Holmes of Sandhill County was still very much a man to be reckoned with. He had a long-standing reputation for courage and strength, and he had been reelected sheriff every year for as long as most could remember. No one

24

ever stood against him, and he was as widely known and respected as any small-town sheriff ever could hope to be.

As a younger man his reputation had grown steadily as he practically built a wall around the county and stopped the flow of bootleg liquor from Oklahoma. Like most small towns in the rural Southwest, Agatite sat in the middle of a vast emptiness, pockmarked by the odd agricultural center—a store, gas station, and maybe a barbershop—but Ezra had made them all his personal headquarters. He seemed to be everywhere during the dusty Depression summers, and even in the bone-cold winters his car was a familiar and comforting sight as he prowled the county's back roads, keeping a lawman's eye out for mischief or genuine crime. He was a serious man, soft-spoken and steady in his manner, but few men had ever found it worthwhile to rouse anger in him, and while almost no one in Agatite had ever heard him yell at anyone, those who had never forgot it sufficiently to want to hear it again.

Arthritis had settled into his knee some years before, and while the medication he took for it, along with the occasional hot-water bottle, kept the pain down to a bearable level, he had already recognized that retirement was soon coming. And he truly didn't mind. But there was one more election coming up for him, and the absence of an heir apparent to his office and badge, someone he felt was worthy of the trust and respect he had earned for the sheriff's office, caused him to stand again for the spring primary—a formality, really—and to postpone retirement for another term.

He discovered that his abilities and energies were only somewhat limited by his advancing age and aching knee, but he still cut a good figure of a lawman in his butternut khakis, brightly shined black boots, and felt Stetson, all complimented by the heavy .44 Colt that comfortably graced his hip almost all the time. He was a familiar and reassuring sight to the citizens of Agatite.

He was sitting at his desk under a cloud of pipe tobacco smoke when Imogene knocked firmly on the open door jamb and interrupted his report on an assault that had taken place in the colored section of town the day before. It had been a minor skirmish, a gambling debt quarrel, from what he could learn, and the victim was only slightly less injured than the accused after the victim's wife got into the act with a pair of knitting needles and, of all things, an old croquet mallet. Ezra had almost chuckled at the look of terror and relief in the suspect's eyes when he spied the sheriff approaching. The small black woman had already taken a couple of chunks out of his arm with the needles, and if Ezra had not shown up when he did, she would have for sure pulped his skull with the wooden mallet.

He glanced up and assessed the well-dressed woman standing in his doorway. "Can I help you?" The question came from Dooley, Ezra's part-time deputy and most-time go-fer who was in his semi-permanent home, the office's holding cell, washing out the coffeepot in the cell's sink.

"I'm looking for Sheriff . . . uh, Sheriff . . ." She put her hand to her forehead and trailed off. She looked to be in great pain, and Ezra was about to rise when she recovered herself and stared at him with the most piercing gray eyes he could ever remember seeing. "I'm looking for the sheriff," she said.

"I'm Sheriff Holmes," Ezra said, standing and gesturing toward a creaky chair adjacent to the desk. "Sit down. Can I help you?"

She blurted out her story, and Ezra refired his pipe as he listened. He had been aware of her all day. Little happens in this town I don't know about, he contentedly thought. He didn't know about Cora or Pete, and he

26

raised his eyebrows in wonder as she described the odd details of Cora's disappearance, noting with a bit of shock that the woman was barely restraining herself from accusing old Pete of kidnapping, or worse. As she spoke, he noticed that her voice gained control. Most women would be losing their composure, he thought, but not this one. She was cool, careful, and gave off no visible signs of the frustration and near hysteria he sensed were boiling just beneath her calm surface. He watched her hands. They lay neatly folded around her purse. There was no clenching of fists, no digging of nails into the purse's leather. She was totally in control.

As she finished, Ezra's pipe went out and he reached for a knife to clean out the bowl. "Well"—he tried to sound serious but really unconcerned—"I expect she'll turn up directly. Kids do this sort—"

"Damn it, Sheriff!" she burst out, and Ezra immediately caught sight of her hands going into a white-knuckled clench of the purse, and the panic he had sensed burst forth with a volume he had not anticipated. "I don't need any more lectures on how kids behave. I've gotten it from everyone I've talked to all day long, and I didn't come in here to hear it again!" Her gray eyes flashed, and Ezra saw the glimmer of something he truly didn't like behind them. He couldn't put a name to it, but it made things in the back of his mind stir, and he felt suddenly uncomfortable.

"I don't mean to sound like I don't care," he said, "but really, ma'am, this isn't hardly a—"

"I want you to go over to that drugstore and find my daughter!" she ordered, standing up suddenly and pointing a finger right at the sheriff's badge on his shirt. The hysteria and loss of control were gone, he noticed, but in their place was something terrible and strident, something awesome.

"I ain't likely to do anything unless you calm down."

Ezra felt a mixture of resentment and fear growing inside him. He didn't like people to talk to him that way, and he didn't intend to put up with it. "Suppose you sit down and tell me what happened again."

"I've already told you—" she said, then she paused, caught her breath, and looked deeply into his eyes. "Would you please go over there and find out where my daughter is?"

"You've already told me she isn't there." Ezra calmly refilled his pipe from a canister of tobacco he kept on his desk.

"Well . . ." She finally sat down and regained the cool composure and control over her voice and manner she had brought into the office with her. "She *was* there. And that . . . that Pete there, he knows about it. He knows about her! He was the only one in the store when she went inside!"

"Start from the beginning," Ezra said as he applied a match to his pipe and blew out billows of smoke over the bowl. "I want to hear it one more time."

She went through the story again, this time adding small details and minor recollections that added nothing of substance. What became disturbing to Ezra was the utter simplicity of it all. He had dealt with runaway kids before, many times, but the fundamental conviction this woman had that something odd had happened to her daughter in the drugstore overrode any hysterical conclusions or wild imaginings runaways' parents usually came up with. Something in Ezra told him that there was considerably more going on here than he, or possibly than she, knew. But he had no idea what it might be.

Agatite was what is often called a quiet town. It was a small, out-of-the-way place where crime was not much of a problem. Ezra knew that the image of a crime-free Norman Rockwell picture of pastoral America was not exactly the truth, however. He made an average of four arrests a week, and while most of them were for minor infractions of the law, he was enough of a realist to know that people, even "good" people, often broke the law, sometimes for good reasons, sometimes not, and unless the small crimes were controlled, the bigger ones usually followed. There was the odd burglary, confidence game, or marital quarrel that escalated into assault. Livestock thefts weren't uncommon, and vandalism often cropped up, especially toward the end of school or around Halloween. Every now and then there would even be a murder or a rape, but the former were usually passionate affairs, more accidents than actual homicides, and the latter were hushed up pretty much unless they were brutal and violent enough to make the local news. For the most part his job during the past ten years or so had centered on traffic problems, many of which came as the result of the new highway bypass, car wrecks and the like, and on keeping bootleggers from bringing beer and whiskey into the dry county and peddling it to kids who were too timid to go over to Oklahoma on their own. In fact, there had been quite a bit of teenage drinking and other nonsense of late, and his mind groped for a connection.

"You say you're from Atlanta?" he asked as she concluded the second account of Cora's disappearance.

"That's right," she shot back, and he sensed the panic rising again, along with that indefinable something that made him so wary and uncomfortable. "And my husband, Mr. Harvey McBride, is a very influential man there. And all across the South."

Resentment flooded Ezra's mind. He didn't like people with money much in the first place, and he especially didn't like people who tried to use it to throw their weight around. He fought down the bitterness the remark brought up in him, and asked, "And you know no one in town here?"

29

"No one at all," she answered quickly. "except people I've met today. Luke Short, for example."

Ezra tamped down the burned tobacco. "Is there anything else, anything at all, you think you ought to tell me?"

She pulled herself up even more erect in the creaky old chair. She took a breath and looked him squarely in the eyes. "Only that I truly think your duty calls you to go over there and talk to that druggist, uh . . . Pete."

Ezra fished out a pocket watch. "Well, ol' Pete's about to close in fifteen minutes. I don't guess it'd hurt to go over and have a chat with him." She looked relieved, and he could see a mocking satisfaction in her eyes. "But I don't mind telling you I've known Pete most all my life, and if he's mixed up in anything crooked, I'd be more than a little surprised."

"Stranger things have happened," she said matter-of-factly.

"Yes, ma'am," he responded, and he mentally acknowledged that she was right. But not this time, he silently added. "Dooley," he said without taking his eyes off her gray stare, "watch the phone and the radio. I'll be across the street." He continued to sit, not moving but simply studying the woman across his desk.

"Well?" she asked at last. "Are we going or not?"

"I think you ought to wait here."

"I will not!" she announced, rising and clutching her purse to her stomach. "Cora's my daughter, and if something's happened to her, I want to know about it!"

Ezra sighed and jammed the pipe between his teeth. "All right," he said as he rose and moved around his desk. "Let's go."

F O U R

The damn fool of a sheriff had been no help at all, Imogene thought bitterly to herself. He had refused, at first, even to go talk to the old fool in the drugstore. But she had insisted, firmly controlling the growing sense that something was terribly wrong with Cora, and he finally had strolled across the street with her at his heels.

Pete had stuck to his story—she'd known he would—and the stupid sheriff had seemed to believe him! He refused to search the back room or scour the town for Cora, telling Imogene that he had dealt with runaways before. They usually came back home, he said, especially when it got dark and they got hungry enough. Imogene hadn't had the courage to tell him that Cora's going home was the one thing she was afraid of. Then the sheriff, who was almost as old as Pete, if not older, left her in the charge of a drooling semi-idiot named Dooley whose chief function, it seemed, was to chew tobacco and try to spit within a narrow ring of near misses around a filthy spittoon. She abandoned the office and returned to the park bench on the now dusky lawn.

Downtown was all but deserted by seven-thirty, leaving only an occasional passing automobile to distract her from her continuing stare at Pete's Sundries and Drugs. She saw Pete himself lock up and walk down the sidewalk about ten minutes after she returned to the bench, and she toyed with the idea of going over and breaking in and giving the small store a thorough searching. She knew Cora was no longer in there, but there might be something there, something to prove to the stupid sheriff that she wasn't crazy. But she didn't know what.

She also knew that staring at the shop wouldn't take her back to the morning when the sun was shining and Cora had looked so beautiful sitting on the green grass, and she recognized that her continual gaze wouldn't bring her daughter out of the shop at this late hour. But she didn't know what else to do. She groped around in her bag and found the empty cigarette pack and wadded it up in a tightly clenched fist and tried to ignore the hunger pangs that were attacking her stomach.

F I V E

Sheriff Ezra Stone Holmes was home eating a tasteless meal he had cooked for himself. His wife, Hilda, had died six years before, and he was thinking how much he hated eating alone, a thought he now had every night without really thinking of Hilda at all. He was also thinking about his retirement, about taking a permanent fishing vacation. He certainly couldn't survive too many more years of his own cooking, that was for sure, and a county sheriff couldn't afford to plan extensive retirement vacations while he was eating expensive restaurant food.

He was having trouble getting the woman—what was her name? McBride, Mrs. Harvey McBride, Imogene—out of his mind. She had seemed more than a little desperate, and he figured that there was more to this than a simple missing child case. He had been a law officer for more than thirty years, and he could spot a case of a woman running away from her husband a mile off. He had looked over the Hudson carefully as she fished out a copy of the girl's high school yearbook. Those suitcases had been packed for more than a vacation. He knew a foul ball when he saw one.

As he washed the dishes, he flipped on the radio and tried to relax, but his mind just wouldn't let it go. After a bit he pulled on his boots and took a drive downtown, just to check and see if she was still there.

She was, perched on the park bench the same way she had been when he first noticed her that morning. He parked the car and walked over to her, feeling his arthritic knee complaining with every step.

"Not back yet?" he asked as he got closer. She looked weak and a little pale.

She turned her head slightly toward him. "Don't tell me you're concerned."

"Look, Mrs. . . . uh . . . McBride," he said as he took his pipe from his shirt pocket and began to work the partly burned tobacco down, "it's my job to be concerned. I, uh, I had to come back over here tonight anyhow, so I thought I would ask you about your daughter. There's no reason to get snooty with me."

She looked him up and down. He *was* an old man, she realized, and she was reminded of her father suddenly, a man who had had the sense to hate Harvey McBride from the day he met him. The sheriff was being polite, he had been polite all the while she was ranting at him and old Pete. He had a point, too. "I'm sorry, Sheriff. But it's so—so *damned* exasperating!" Suddenly, in spite of herself, the tears came, welling up inside her and making her choke and shake all over.

"Hey! Now!" he said, and he came and laid a horny, knobby hand on her shoulder, which was heaving with the convulsions of the sobbing. "I'll do what I can, Mrs. McBride, but I got to have something more to go on."

She pulled a handkerchief from her purse and began wiping her eyes. "Oh, I'm sorry, Sheriff. It's just that I love my daughter so much, and I'm so worried about her. She's a good girl, really she is. We've never had a cross word between us. I know this looks just awful. Like we had a fight or something. But it was nothing like that. She's just gone, and I really do suspect, uh . . . I suspect *mischief.*"

Ezra sat down beside her on the bench. He didn't think

there was any foul play at all, but he sensed an opening in her, so he asked his next question gently. "You say you're on a vacation trip to Oregon? That right?"

She nodded, wiping her eyes with the handkerchief. "To visit my sister, Mildred, in Portland."

"And your husband, Mr. McBride, he knows about this trip? That right, too?"

"Of course, he does," she said too quickly. She could see his face illuminated in the white streetlamp's light and knew he sensed the lie. Suddenly she decided to be truthful with him. What the hell, she thought, I'm expecting him to be truthful with me. "Sheriff," she began, "I've . . . I've left my husband. He's an adulterer—worse, a drunk. He knows we were on our way to Oregon, but he has no idea of how we would go, what our route would be, so if you're thinking he showed up to take her away from me—well, that's just impossible!"

Ezra nodded and let go a silent sigh. So, he thought, there it was, out in the open. It'd been like pulling teeth. But he knew that he actually had less information than before.

"How could he possibly know that our car would break down here, in Agate, Texas?" she asked, looking with a searching stare into Ezra's eyes.

"Agatite," Ezra corrected, pulling on his pipe and realizing that it wasn't lit.

"Agatite," she repeated, choking back another bout of sobs. "No, I'm not sure she—Cora—even knew where we were. She slept all the way from Fort Worth." The crying took over again.

"Listen," Ezra said, rising, "I'm going to make some calls, neighboring sheriffs and the like, and I'll be back in a little bit. Or do you want to come inside? It can still get chilly here at night."

She shook her head. He leaned down and patted her shoulder, feeling strange and out of character in making

34

the gesture. He caught the faint smell of body odor stain-
ing the spring air. Was it him? No. It was her. A thought
came to him. "Say, you had anything to eat today?"

"Not since breakfast, early this morning," she said,
pulling the tears and sobs back inside her.

"Well, why not go down to the Agatite Hotel and
check in. They got a nice little café there, too. It's open
till ten."

"No!" She sat straight up, and he noticed the now familiar strangeness come into her eyes. He was startled.
"I'll stay right here until she shows up!"

"Okay," he said softly, drawing back from her. He
turned and started across the lawn to the steps of the
courthouse.

"Sheriff?" she called to him after he took a few steps.
"Have you any cigarettes?"

He held up his pipe. "No, I'm afraid not," he replied.
She was silent, and he went on inside.

S I X

Once behind his desk, a cup of Dooley's thick coffee in
front of him, he placed a call, not to a neighboring sheriff
but to Atlanta, Georgia, to Mr. Harvey McBride. Ezra explained the situation at length and waited for a response.
After a spell McBride spoke. "Well, what is it you want
me to *do*, Sheriff?"

"I thought—" Ezra started, then paused. What was it
he did want McBride to do? "I thought you might have
an interest in these developments," he concluded. He felt
uncomfortably like a hick county sheriff trying to sound
like a knowledgeable city policeman.

"I *am* interested," McBride stated flatly, "but I fail to
see what I *can* do about the situation." He had a habit of

35

punctuating certain words in every phrase he spoke, usually some word other than the one Ezra expected him to emphasize, and the sheriff found it annoying.

"Listen, Mr. McBride, it's your family, and I just thought—"

"Now hold *on*, Sheriff." McBride cut him off. "It *was* my family. I *loved* my wife and dearly *love* my daughter, but this past week has been very *hard* for me. Imogene *stole* my car and over two thousand dollars *in cash* from me, not to mention *some* very expensive jewelry and personal items. She *took* Cora, willingly, I assume, and they *departed* for parts unknown, although I suspect they are off to visit Imogene's *demented* sister in Oregon. I expect that after a few *weeks* of that, she'll be running *back* home. My main *interest* is in Cora's well-being, *naturally*, but taking some action to save my wife from some *sort* of embarrassment is—well, it's *out* of the question! She should count herself *fortunate* that I am not filing charges and asking *you* to arrest her for grand theft!"

Fat chance, Ezra thought. "But what about Cor—what *about* your daughter?" Ezra cursed himself for imitating the odd speech pattern McBride used.

"Cora will turn up," McBride said confidently, and Ezra got the mental image of a man polishing his fingernails on his coat lapel. "I'm *certain* of it, either here or *back* there. But even if she doesn't, she's *eighteen*, free, and capable of *making* adult decisions—possibly *more* capable than her *mother*, for *that* matter. I don't see *there's* a cause for alarm, that is, unless *you* suspect something has happened to her . . . of an, uh . . . *unpleasant* nature."

"No," Ezra admitted. He was finding his dislike for McBride enjoyable, the way he disliked mongrel dogs and snakes. "There's no evidence of anything like that. Not yet."

"Well, then," McBride summed up, "I'm *very* sorry to disappoint you, Sheriff, but it seems that the *problem* is yours and yours alone. Imogene is apparently in *your* backyard, for a change, and *you're* stuck with her. *Do* call me if Cora shows up, however. I'd like to talk to *her*."

Ezra broke the connection as McBride hung up. The sheriff began tooling the tobacco around in his pipe with his knife and thought carefully. "Dooley," he called to his assistant, who was working a large piece of wood with a sharp carving knife, "go over to the hotel café and get a chicken-fried for the lady outside. Bring it back and give it to her, and let her pay you for it if she's a mind to. If not, just leave it there. Also, tell whoever's on the desk tonight to hold a room for her, one of the big ones near the street so she can see the square." Dooley spat, missing the spittoon again, and pulled himself up to leave. "Oh, yeah," Ezra continued, "get her a pack of cigarettes, too."

"What brand?" Dooley asked as he pulled suspenders up over his shoulders from their usual dangling position around his knees.

"Huh?" Ezra was lost in thought. "Oh, uh, Luckies, I guess. And ask for fried potatoes with the steak instead of mashed. She's outside." Dooley sauntered out, spitting once more with no better aim than before.

This was something he didn't really need, Ezra thought. He pulled the girl's yearbook over to him and opened it to a marker where her class picture was. She was damn pretty, that was for sure, about the prettiest girl in the whole class, maybe in the whole high school. This was a yearbook for her junior year, and he flipped idly through it. Something didn't quite make sense.

She was clearly prettier than the "Most Beautiful Girl—Junior Class," and her picture didn't appear as a blowup for any of the other awards for which she was eligible either. Well, Ezra mused, these are mostly popularity contests—maybe she just wasn't popular. But that didn't jell. Pretty girls were always popular, weren't they? He turned back to her class picture. Even the small shot showed a beauty that far surpassed the Homecoming Queen, Prom Queen, and School's Favorite Gal photos of other girls that were blown up to eight by tens. Even the runners-up for each contest couldn't hold a candle to Cora's almost mystical beauty. Under her class picture Ezra read the list of organizations to her credit: Pep Club, French Club, Typing Team, Poetry Club. That was it. He suddenly realized that she had been a member of these clubs but never an officer. Never a leader. That was odd. Officers were popular kids too, but never as popular as the big award winners. He knew that. And, he persisted, pretty girls, especially very pretty girls, were always popular, very popular, *too* popular. Yet she wasn't an officer in any club, not a member of the student council, not even listed as a member of the Junior Prom Decorating Committee. This was wrong, he knew, but he refused to think about why.

He got up and went out to his car. She was still sitting on the bench, rigid as a goddamn flagpole, he thought. She had mentioned two men, boys really, in a 1932 Ford with AGATITE EAGLES printed on the door who had given Cora the eye when she crossed the street. That would be Nolan Talbert and his brother, most likely. Not exactly a logical pair of suspects for abduction, since Nolan had declared for the ministry and was home on spring vacation from the Baptist Seminary.

Ezra drove over to the Talbert place, anyway, but Nolan didn't remember seeing the girl. His brother, Gary, remembered her, he thought, but he recalled that she had red hair, not blond. Cora was blond, Ezra knew; the black-and-white yearbook shot even showed that.

Ezra made the rounds of houses belonging to one or two others he knew had been downtown that day, and he even drove out to Luke Short's ramshackle house and questioned him. Nothing. No one but Luke had seen

Cora to know who she was, and while everyone remembered the mother's frantic questions, no one except Luke was even completely sure that Cora McBride existed anywhere but in her mother's mind. The gossip had already started. "She's tetched," Lucy Holloway told him. "Scared the dickens outta my boy Fred when she came inta the drugstore!"

No, Ezra thought as he drove back into town, she's not "tetched." She's tired, dirty, scared, and probably a little bit lost, but she's not crazy. Not yet.

He turned back onto Main Street and parked the car at the courthouse and killed the engine. She still sat on the bench, staring at the darkened drugstore. It was almost nine-thirty, and most of the cars on Main Street had long since gone home. Only the railroad crews and some kids moved around after nine o'clock during the week. Agatite was, Ezra thought, a quiet town all right. People didn't just disappear here, not without some kind of reason.

One thing McBride had said bothered him. He was *certain* that Cora would turn up. He had emphasized the word more than the others. Ezra's mind had already decided that there was something the girl's father knew, or thought he knew, that Imogene McBride didn't. Maybe McBride had found a way to slip his daughter some money for a bus or train ticket. Two passenger stops had taken place since noon, although one of them was westbound, and she would be able to pay her way by just getting aboard and buying a ticket at the next station. It would have been easy if she had the money. But how could she? McBride couldn't pull something like that off without somebody in Agatite helping out. Ezra knew his people, especially Pete. Pete wouldn't do something crooked if it would save his mother's life. He was *too* damn honest sometimes, Ezra thought. Still, every man has a price, Ezra believed; that's the first thing a lawman

learns. But not old Pete. Hell, they'd gone swimming together as kids, fished every other weekend, known each
other all their lives. Pete wouldn't sell anything for
money if he thought somebody wanted it bad enough
and it was his to give away. But maybe Cora hadn't offered him money. She didn't have any, Mrs. McBride
had said. Pretty girls were popular unless . . . unless
they had a *reputation*. There. The thought was out. But
Ezra squelched it immediately. Not old Pete. That was
impossible. Hell, he's older than I am. No. Her father
must have gotten to her some way.

Ezra got out of his car and lit his pipe. But how could
McBride plan such a thing? Luke had said that the fuel
pump had gone out and the carburetor needed overhaul-
ing. That's not the sort of thing you can count on or fix to
break at a specific place. Maybe he had some kind of private detective following them. Yeah, maybe. But Agatite
was small enough that a stranger stuck out like a sore
thumb. Four people called to tell him about her breakdown before Luke even got her back to town. Ezra was
bothered. This was an itch he couldn't scratch.

Walking across the lawn, he noticed the smell of spring
in the air, flowers and bushes around the courthouse.
The stars were out, clear and bright, and the air carried
only the slightest chilly suggestion of the brutality of
Texas winter as it reluctantly gave way to spring. It was a
beautiful night. She noticed him coming and raised her
hand in greeting.

"Sheriff, I want to thank you for sending the meal."
She smiled as he approached. "It was delicious! I'm
afraid I was hungrier than I knew I was." The plate and
napkin from the hotel café were on the bench beside her.

"Well, I couldn't let you starve yourself to death." He
uncomfortably puffed.

"And you didn't!" she said brightly. "Mr. Dooley is *so*
nice! Do tell him how much I appreciate his trouble."

"I think he'd be sufficiently obliged if he never heard you call him *mister*." Ezra smiled. She was pretty, too, he thought. It was easy to see where Cora got her beauty, for although she outstripped her mother in every specific department, Ezra was keen to notice Imogene's shapely legs and clear, almost transparent skin, which caught the streetlamp's glow.

"Did you make your calls?" she asked. "Has anyone seen her?"

"I called," Ezra said, "but nobody's seen her." He felt uncomfortable about the small lie. He really had meant to call some other sheriffs. "I checked out those boys in the Ford, too, and there's no worry there. Nolan Talbert— that's the driver—he's going to be a preacher, and he couldn't even remember watching her the way you said."

"Oh, he remembered." Her mouth became a pencil-thin line. "But I doubt that he knows anything."

"Mrs. McBride," Ezra began, knocking his pipe out against the metal arm of the bench, "is there any chance your daughter could have gone back to her—to your hus-band?"

"No," she said quickly and quietly. "I mean, no. There's no way she could. She only had a nickel, and a train ticket costs a bit more than that, a bus too." He nodded in agreement. "Sheriff"—she had a lilt to her voice and raised her chin a bit, making him aware of her attractiveness once again—"have you spoken to my hus-band?"

He couldn't lie. "Yes, ma'am."

"And did he say that she had run away to go back to him?"

"Not exactly."

"But that's what you think, isn't it?" She almost sighed the question.

His knee was bothering him suddenly, and he shifted

his weight. "Ma'am, to tell you God's truth, I don't know what to think."

"What else did my husband—did Mr. McBride say about me?"

"Well—" Ezra hesitated. This was none of his affair, this divorce, if that was what it was. He didn't really want to get involved in a marital problem. But, he realized, he already was involved, so he took a breath and plunged in. "He said you stole his car and some money and other stuff, jewelry, but he wasn't going to press charges."

She laughed, a mirthless, dry cackle that seemed so odd coming from such a pretty woman. It was, Ezra realized, almost hysterical, and he recognized once again the indefinable quality that he had seen lurking behind her gray eyes so often that afternoon. He found it disturbing and vaguely frightening. "That's rich!" she said, wiping the tears from her eyes. "Well, Sheriff, the owner's papers in my name are in the glove compartment of the car, if you'd care to see them. I took care of that before I left, and let me tell you, it wasn't easy. But it *was* legal! The money he gave me freely, in front of witnesses. As for the rest of the things—well, you'll just have to take my word for it. They're mine!" She was speaking too loudly, Ezra knew, speaking out of weariness and desperation, but he didn't know how to stop her.

"Yeah, well"—he paused—"I don't want to see nothing. If you say the stuff's yours and he don't want to make a case out of it, it's none of my business."

Suddenly she calmed down, visibly gained control of herself once again, and Ezra found himself amazed again at her ability to harness her emotions and display complete calm in the face of panic and worry. "Yes, Sheriff, of course. I'm sorry. You've tried to be kind to me, and I've done nothing but yell at you and cry all over you. I do appreciate all you've done, really! I'm just a bit tired, that's all."

"Well, that's all right, about the crying, I mean. You've been through a rough day."

"Still"—she held up a hand, and he noticed how long and graceful her fingers were, the nails perfectly manicured and lacquered with red polish—"that's no excuse for being a crybaby. I swore I'd never cry again when I left Atlanta." This last was said hard, but her gray eyes immediately softened, and she looked up at his fumbling with his empty pipe. "Have you a match?" she asked.

He handed her a box from his pocket, and she lit a cigarette from a new pack, the one Dooley had brought her. She took the smoke in deeply, exhaling it through her nose like a man, but not without a certain style that made Ezra's heart jump suddenly. He shook his head when she offered him the box back, and she dropped it into her purse.

"Yeah," he said finally, "I'll bet you are . . . tired, that is. Listen, I had Dooley make you a reservation down to the hotel, a big room that overlooks the square. Maybe you want to go over there and check in, freshen up, maybe get some sleep. Maybe tomorrow . . ." He trailed off.

"Thank you, Sheriff, I'll think it over, really I will." She folded her hands in her lap, one holding the cigarette away from her skirt, and resumed her stare at the drugstore across the street. It's like somebody watching a movie show, Ezra thought.

"Well, good night," he said, and he walked back to his car. He was perplexed and more than a little attracted to her. Suddenly he turned, and without thinking, he strolled back and asked her, "Uh, Mrs. McBride, has Cora ever done anything—this sort of thing, before?" It wasn't the question he wanted to ask, and he was relieved when her only answer was to smile brightly and confidently and shake her head.

"She's a good girl," she said, and she resumed her stare, and he turned and started again for his car.

Hell, he thought, cursing himself, there's twenty years' difference between us, at least. But she seemed so help-less and determined. He realized suddenly and with a shock that he was about to ask her to come home with him. What could he be thinking of? Something in the back of his mind stirred uncomfortably, and Hilda's face suddenly swam before his eyes. Only it wasn't Hilda's face, not exactly. It was hers, Imogene's. He rubbed his eyes briefly, and the image retreated. He started to load his pipe and then thought better of it and put it in his pocket. His hands were shaking a bit. Gaining control of them, he bent his arthritic knee and got into the car and started it. As he drove slowly home, the face came to him again in his thoughts. Her face. She is pretty, he thought.

S E V E N

Imogene's first night on the park bench was horrible. She hadn't spent an entire night outdoors since she was a little girl and had gone camping with her mother's brother and his brood of children. That had been a ter-rifying experience, and she had wound up in a smelly canvas tent hiding under a mound of old quilts, trying to escape the mysterious night sounds coming from the for-est around her. From that time on she had hated being alone in the dark, and even in her room at home—not *home*, not anymore, she reminded herself—she kept a night light on except when she was too exhausted to stay awake and listen to the outdoor sounds of night.

After the sheriff left her, heavy silence covered the entire downtown area. Because a new highway had recently bypassed the main business district, almost no traffic at all came around the courthouse square after ten o'clock, when the last of the high school kids went home.

She heard the distant sounds of trucks and cars out on the bypass, but they were muffled and remote from the oppressive quiet of the small downtown district, and she found herself studying the silent, darkened storefronts along Main Street. As midnight came and passed, even the highway sounds diminished, and she found herself completely alone. Even the noises of her breathing seemed to penetrate the blackness around her and bounce off the buildings across the street from the courthouse.

"Where did you go, Cora?" she asked aloud after a while, and the sound of her voice, although whispered, seemed deafening. She even looked quickly up to the darkened window of the sheriff's office to see if Dooley or anyone else was looking out to find out who spoke. There was no one, and the lights of the office stayed off.

But the question hung in the atmosphere of the small town, and she thought she could almost see the words she had spoken floating around in the glow of the streetlamp. Frustration welled up in her again, and she felt tears coming to her eyes, but she fought them back and lit a cigarette. This was an impossible situation, she admitted, just impossible. Every minute she delayed could mean Cora was getting farther and farther away, maybe running back to Harvey, maybe—but she didn't have another alternative to suggest. There just wasn't one. She shook her head. This couldn't be happening. It was too much like a nightmare, too much like a dream that she fervently hoped would suddenly end and find her and Cora sitting in a roadside park somewhere, stopped to rest for a few hours before going on to Oregon.

It wasn't a dream, and she knew that. But there had to be some alternative she hadn't thought of, some *logical* explanation for it all, something that was right in front of her nose that she hadn't or couldn't yet see, like a puzzle or a mind twister that they ran in the funny papers. "Find Six Presidents in This Picture." "Find the Missing Daughter in This Town." It was like a mystery story, but then again it wasn't. Mystery stories always worked out; there was a "who" to be discovered that "done it," but here in this godforsaken town there was no "who" but Cora, and Imogene wondered and worried over how she "done it."

She was prepared to take whatever drastic measures presented themselves to get Cora back and go on, but no measures at all seemed to come forth. There wasn't even an unreasonable action in a final, desperate move to recover the sense of escape and freedom she had enjoyed up until the damned car had broken down in this horrible wide spot in the road in the middle of nowhere. She didn't know what else to do but sit here and hope and pray for a miracle or at least for enough insight to let her understand what had happened to her daughter.

She got up and paced a bit back and forth in front of the bench and noticed that her feet were wet. She took off her shoes and squished her stockinged toes into the moist grass now becoming increasingly heavy with dew. Soon, however, she began to feel chilled, and she put her pumps back on, noting that her feet were more than a little swollen and hurt. In fact, she thought as she mentally catalogued the areas of her body, she felt pain from every corner of her being. The emotional pain that was actually on the rise with every passing moment was only barely offset by the physical discomfort that also seemed to increase as the night grew darker and more quiet.

And, she thought with a disgusted wrinkle of her nose, she could smell herself. She was dirty. And the thought made her want to cry again. "Oh, Cora!" she said, hearing her voice crack with tension. "Why are you doing this to me?" But, she almost thought out loud, and the idea completely drove the weakness she was giving into from her mind, did *she* do something, or was *something* done to her?

Imogene was a worldly woman. She knew what happened to girls who were kidnapped, abducted. She didn't have to imagine too much to think what some perverted mind could find to do with her beautiful, innocent daughter. She—but the rest of the thoughts wouldn't come, and the horror they suggested even as they rested in the corners of her mind made her shiver and quake all over.

A locomotive whistle came from a distant crossing, punctuating the silence of downtown Agatite. Then she heard it again, closer. She checked a tiny wristwatch on her arm, holding it high and squinting to read it in the dim streetlamp's light. It was twenty-five of three, and the train was coming from the east. Maybe Cora would be on it. Maybe she had really found the money to get on a train somehow, and once away for a few hours realized how foolish her actions were. Maybe she got on the next train back and would soon come up the street, running to her mama and begging forgiveness.

As the train's whistle sounded again, even closer now, Imogene gave in completely to her fantasy. She saw herself standing over the kneeling Cora, the girl weeping and hugging her mother's legs as she pleaded for understanding. Imogene wouldn't scold, she told herself, but she would make Cora promise and swear on the rosary never to do such a thing again. Never again. And she would never let her out of her sight again. Never again. Then they would embrace, both crying by now, she thought, and go get into the Hudson and go. She wouldn't tell that sheriff anything about it. Let him stew in his juices, she thought. Big help he had been.

As she reveled in her fancies, a pickup truck pulled onto the street in front of her. In the back she recognized the overalls and curious flat, striped hats so common to railroad men that the five or six occupants wore. Replacement crew, she realized, and she waited as they went to meet the train that she now was certain contained her prodigal daughter. As the truck disappeared down Main Street, she opened her purse and pulled out a brush and a compact. She needed to go to the rest room, she realized, but she didn't dare leave, not until Cora came bounding down the street and into her open arms.

In a while the train's whistle sounded again, this time very close, and almost immediately Imogene's ears were met by the curious collage of sounds that accompany a locomotive pulling into a station. Screeching brakes, steel on steel, the protesting escape of steam, the bells, the thuds, the bumps of station activity were all drowned out by the final blast of the whistle. She remembered that the depot was a mere two blocks from her bench, and she adjusted her clothing and waited. It was best for her to appear just as Cora had last seen her, sitting primly and patiently waiting for her to return. The way a lady should.

Time ticked by, and Imogene's apprehension grew. The station sounds began to subside, and then the departing whistle screamed. "Any second now," she said, and stole a glance at the corner of Main Street around which she fully expected to see Cora run.

She heard the steam again, then the slow chugging of the engine as the wheels sought purchase on the steel tracks. Slowly the chugging increased and the whistle blew again, and in her mind's eye she saw the engine gathering speed as it pulled its load away from the station. Soon it was growing distant, and she heard the whistle announcing a crossing, then another, and another as it faded into the darkness of the west.

The same pickup she had seen delivering the replacement crew emerged from the buildings on Main Street and turned the corner. In the back the weary men from the arriving train swayed with the truck's motion. The vehicle pulled up in front of the Agatite Hotel, and she watched as the men climbed down, toting their lanterns and lunch pails. Their voices lit the night air as they disappeared into the hotel's lobby, and soon the pickup started up again and moved out onto Main Street once more, finally disappearing up the street.

The train's whistle was now just a faint vibration from far off in the night, and downtown settled into its cryptlike silence once again. Imogene visibly collapsed on the bench; her shoulders seemed too heavy to hold upright any longer. She couldn't bear the weight of her own head.

She couldn't understand anything anymore. She wanted to cry, but there simply were no tears available. She wanted to think, but her mind wouldn't function. She just sat on the bench, her head down, almost reaching her lap, concentrating all her thoughts on keeping her back alive, keeping it from just folding forward and spilling her onto the dewy grass in front of the bench. Cora didn't come. Of course she didn't. She didn't come. Her mind went blank.

She must have slept a bit. Her first thought upon sitting erect again was of Cora in a pretty slacks set at a picnic they had gone on the summer before. She didn't feel rested, however, just cold. She hugged her body to her and suddenly became aware of all sorts of nocturnal sounds she hadn't noticed before. Bullfrogs from far off someplace called to one another in a symphony of eerie, deep-throated gurgles, and night birds sang across the business district's few trees. The sounds were frightening, but she was too miserable and cold to really feel afraid.

She got to her feet and felt the stiffness in her legs and back protest any movement at all. Except for the new sounds of night, nothing had changed since she had last looked up. She strained her ears and caught the noises of a switching crew working on the railroad somewhere to the west, and she flushed at her stupidity in thinking Cora would magically appear from an eastbound train. I didn't even know if it was a passenger train, she thought. How silly of me, how really silly of me. She peered at her watch and noted that it was after four.

All at once an incredibly loud series of cries and screams struck her ears, and she instinctively moved around behind the bench and almost crouched down. The horrible noises came from across the street, from behind the drugstore, which in its darkened façade suddenly began to resemble a great face, the door an open maw, a devil's mouth, Imogene thought with creeping terror, a great devourer of children!

Her ears strained to sort out the screeches that rose in intensity and seemed to come directly from the drugstore's black front, completely shadowed in the streetlamp's glow. The light hit the inset threshold of the door at an odd angle, and a series of sharp, razorlike teeth emerged in the patterns of light and dark. Some of the screams were panic-stricken, there was no doubt about it, Imogene deduced, and some of them were definitely aggressive and terrifying. It's not a store! she screamed to herself. *It's a monster, a devil monster that captures and tortures children!* As the cries continued, she said, "Cora!" but her voice was croaky and dry, and she swallowed painfully and said again, "Cora!"

The cries crescendoed, and she took a tentative step toward the street away from the bench. "Cora!" she called louder, and she heard her voice echoing off the downtown buildings. All those kids in the store weren't kids, Imogene thought as panic filled her mind and she

50

moved more rapidly to the curb; they were imps, demons, and that old man, that Pete, was the Devil! Now she was running to the street, calling, "Cora! Cora! Mama's coming!"

She put one foot onto the bricks of the street, but her heel caught in a crack, and her ankle folded beneath her, wrenching itself and making her cry out. "Oh, God! Cora! I'm coming!" Gaining her balance again, she limped painfully to the center of the street, the heel trying to collapse again. She had to reach that door, that gaping mouth, get inside and save those children being tortured inside. She felt for the rosary in her skirt pocket, but it wasn't there; she'd left it in her purse. No time to go back; she had to reach the door. Pain made movement almost impossible, and she cried out again, almost screaming, and this time her voice sounded off the buildings several times before dying away.

Suddenly movement in the shadowed doorway made her pause and freeze in the center of the street. She put up her hands to block whatever might emerge from the horror she had conjured inside the mouth/door she now perceived clearly in front of her. Then she saw them. Three cats ran out of the door's shadow and raced up Main Street, away from the screaming woman in the middle of the street.

"Cat fight," Imogene said aloud to herself, suddenly feeling giddy with foolishness, more foolish than she had felt even under her uncle's quilts all those years ago. The sounds that had been so familiar were of cats battling in the predawn hours, something she knew well. As a child she had grown up around cats, and even Harvey liked them and kept several big ones around the house. Their fights had awakened everyone more than once.

She turned and limped back to the bench, casting her eyes back toward the drugstore monster that suddenly seemed as harmless as any closed business awaiting the owner to come and light the morning with overhead bulbs. She shivered from the perspiration that had come forth in her terror and pain, and she noticed that a light breeze had sprung up and made her downright cold and uncomfortable. At the bench she retrieved her purse, found her keys, limped painfully over to the Hudson and opened the trunk. She found her fur coat packed away in a large suitcase. Pulling it out and putting it on made her feel instantly better. She got inside the car and moved it to a Free Zone nearer the bench, then locked it and went back and took her seat again.

"Cat fight," she said again, pulling out a cigarette and lighting it, luxuriating in the warmth she now felt from the large fur coat. She shook her head and laughed a bit, realizing a marvelous relief in expressing even an ironic display of humor. It was a good thing, she thought, almost giggling, that no one saw me or—and she glanced at the still silent and darkened window of the sheriff's office in the courthouse—heard me. Any doubts they had about my sanity would have been dispelled completely.

She finished the cigarette and dug her hands into the pocket of the coat, listening again to the call of night birds, crickets, and the distant bullfrogs. She tried to see the drugstore's front as she had visualized it before, as a monstrous mouth of evil, but it remained a drugstore, and the contours she had seen only a few minutes before eluded her imagination.

After a long while she realized she was seeing things more clearly, and a milkman's truck passed by. She could hear another train coming, this time from the west, and she checked her watch: five-fifteen. Morning was coming, she thought, and she felt more relieved than she had ever been in her life. Her first night on the bench was over.

E I G H T

That morning Sheriff Ezra Stone Holmes rose at his customary hour, five-thirty. No phone calls had awakened him to report prowlers, cattle or chicken thieves, or—praise God—a car wreck, and he had slept deeply. He had dreamed about her, Mrs. McBride—Imogene—but the dream faded as soon as he bathed and shaved, and it was completely gone as soon as he hard-fried some eggs and bacon. He enjoyed breakfast at home. It had always been a quiet time for him and Hilda, and since she died he had unthinkingly continued the tradition, even though he never could get the eggs just right, and his coffee resembled crankcase oil.

Pipe gripped firmly in his mouth and steaming in the cool air of morning, he turned the corner onto Main Street just as the sun broke over the horizon, and he grimly smiled as he looked over at the courthouse square. She was still there, just as he'd known she would be.

Some time during the night, he noticed, she had moved the Hudson. She was also wearing a fur coat, an expensive one from the look of it, too. But he was sure she hadn't gone to the hotel. She still had on the same flowered print dress she had worn the day before, the same little hat with a veil. She waved briefly to him as he parked and went up the sidewalk to the courthouse. It was sad, he thought, and it made him sad.

Dooley had just made coffee when he walked into his office. Dooley's coffee was the only brew he had ever tasted that was worse than his own. "Go over to the café and get her some breakfast," Ezra said, and he sat down and made the calls to neighboring sheriffs that he had promised to make the night before. He also called the Highway Patrol and the Texas Rangers. He would wait a couple of days before alerting the FBI, since they normally required a three-day waiting period unless there was clear evidence that a felony had been committed, and, Ezra thought to himself as he waited for the operator to connect him to another sheriff's office, there was no evidence of that at all. In fact, there was no evidence at all. None.

As he hung up the phone, he shook his head. That was all he could do, not just for now, but at all. He could go over and talk to Pete again, but later, when maybe she just couldn't stand it anymore and went over to take a bath and rest awhile, and he could see Pete without her knowing.

He hated to think what he should be thinking about Pete, and somewhere deep inside him that part of him that wasn't a lawman told him that to even consider such thoughts was ridiculous. Pete was his old friend, one of his best friends if the facts were told, and to suggest such things was almost obscene. But there had to be an explanation somewhere. People didn't just vanish into thin air. He really didn't believe Pete knew anything he wasn't telling, and he had questioned him very closely.

But another part of him that was all lawman told him that even if he did know something, it was going to take more than close questioning by an old friend to get it out of him. *That* sort of thing wasn't something you told even God, let alone your old swimming hole and fishing buddy, even if he was the high sheriff.

Ezra had morning patrol to do, and he was wasting time with this McBride thing. He strolled out of the office down the hardwood floors of the courthouse, noting with some disgust that local chewers had missed more often than not in their attempts to hit strategically placed spittoons. The glass door of the Highway Patrol's local office was dark. They hardly used the place, Ezra thought, again feeling a bit of disgust when he considered the arsenal of weapons and stock of equipment they stored inside the locked room. He passed through the heavy doors and stood for a few moments at the top of the steps leading down to the square. It was a beautiful morning, he thought. The rain would come in a month, but for the next week or so Agatite would enjoy a bona fide spring. Flowers seemed to be blooming everywhere, and the traffic that now had picked up along Main Street seemed to flow with a freshness to match the clean, crisp air and floral scents of April. "Comanche Spring," he said as he descended the steps. "That's what they used to call it."

He moved down the sidewalk, trying not to look over toward the bench where Dooley chatted amiably with the woman from Atlanta. The mystery of it all ate at him, and he tried to push it back into the storage space of his mind where he kept all his memories. But it wouldn't go, not yet.

At his car he stared hard at Pete's Sundries and Drugs, then he got inside the car and started the vehicle up. It was indeed a beautiful day, he thought again, and it was too bad this had to come up and spoil it. He drove off to make his morning rounds.

N I N E

Imogene sat on the bench until late afternoon, when she found herself going to sleep sitting straight up. Thus far she had remained awake just by force of will, but the warmth of the April sun was now making her too drowsy to maintain her resolve. The sheriff had sent her breakfast, and twice Dooley brought out some horrible excuse for coffee, but she knew the head lawman was losing patience with her. She could sense it when he passed her going from his car to the office or out again. He barely spoke or nodded when she waved, and she knew he regarded her as an embarrassment.

She had made three trips to the courthouse to use the terribly filthy toilet, but on her last trip the grimy walls and fly-specked seat had been bested by her own body smell, and she had gagged. She just couldn't stand it much longer. Cora had to show up and end this misery.

About four-thirty she rose and slowly walked over to the hotel, looking back over her shoulder every few steps, expecting, improbably, for Cora to come laughing and yelling out of the drugstore, hollering, "Alley Alley in Free!" and thrilled that she had bested her mother at this horrible game. Imogene really didn't believe it would happen, but she was too tired and too emotionally drained to think of much else.

She stood for a long time outside the hotel lobby, feeling the exhaustion and pain from her ankle throbbing through her body. Finally she forced herself to go inside, to lose sight of the square and the drugstore, and she hurriedly checked in. She could see the whole area clearly from her room, and she raced through a bath, coming back to the window in time to see Dooley picking up the cigarette butts she had littered around the bench.

She couldn't stand to climb into the same clothes again, so she called down and had the desk clerk send someone to the Hudson for her luggage. A pimply-faced boy soon appeared at her door for the keys, and she eyed him suspiciously, wondering if he knew anything about Cora. But she kept herself from asking. She was already considered crazy; there was no point in attacking every person she met.

While she waited for her bags she tried to pace the room, but she was too tired, and she soon sat on the edge of the bed, feeling a swooning sensation overtake her. Although clean, she still felt an oppressive weight on her entire body, as if her weariness had become a heavy wool suit or a coat, and she lay back, unable to sit up any longer. In seconds she was asleep.

She awoke in a panic at six-thirty. Her luggage was in the hall, and she dressed quickly, never taking her eyes off the square. What if Cora had come back while she had been asleep? She'd never forgive herself. She should have left a note.

She raced down the hotel's stairs, not waiting for the ancient and semi-operative elevator, and onto the rapidly emptying streets. The sheriff's car was gone, for the night, she assumed, so she couldn't count on Dooley's bringing her any supper. She stopped by the Hudson and got some crackers from a box on the front seat, and then she took up her vigil for the night. Cora would have to come back tonight, and then they could go on to Oregon and put this horrible farce behind them. She had to come back, Imogene insisted. She just had to.

T E N

The phone jangled him awake. It was still the middle of the night, or, more accurately, the early morning. His alarm clock told him that it was nearly three. The phone rang again, and he waited until his pulse stopped pounding in his ears before he answered it. One of these nights a phone call's going to kill me, he thought. He interrupted the third ring and put the receiver to his ear.

"Sheriff?" Dooley's voice cracked through the receiver. It sounded rough. He'd just been awakened, too.

Who the hell else would I be? Ezra asked himself testily. "Yeah, Dooley, what is it?" He always liked the way he could sound clear and calm even during an emergency phone call in the middle of the night.

"We got an auto accident out on 287, about to the lake cutoff." Dooley sounded matter-of-fact. He always said "ot-tow" accident instead of auto accident or car wreck or anything else.

Ezra felt his stomach turn over. He hated car crashes worse than anything else. "How bad?"

"Pretty bad, from what I can tell," Dooley replied. "Looks like two dead anyhow, and they're gonna have to cut somebody out. I done called Luke Short, and he's coming in to get his ex-cet-a-leen torch."

"Any locals involved?"

"Nope, looks like a bunch of tourists. Looks like they got hit by a big truck head-on."

"Damn," Ezra said under his breath, and he was silent for a moment. The car would be smashed into the front of the truck like somebody had melted it and then thrown it haphazardly across the truck's grill. There would be glass and twisted, sharp points of steel everywhere. Arms and legs would be lying around, maybe even a head cut off, sitting on the goddamn road and looking surprised and lost in the red glare of the emergency lights and flares. He didn't want to go out and face that. And there was that poor bastard trapped inside, probably screaming and crying. His stomach turned over again.

"They got Leroy Walker from over to Vernon handling it," Dooley said at last, as if he could read Ezra's thoughts.

Walker was Highway Patrol. Good. That got him off the hook. "Get him on the horn and tell him to shout if he needs any help," Ezra said. "I'll be here."

"Right, Sheriff," Dooley said, and hung up.

Ezra had made it an unofficial policy not to go out on traffic accidents unless people from the county were involved. He felt faintly guilty about not going out, but too many years of seeing people, especially little kids, chopped up like dog meat in a broken and twisted car had soured him. It made him sick. Hell, he thought as he turned over and tried to go back to sleep, he could remember when the first car came into the county. Then, investigating a minor squabble between two drivers who smashed into each other was just a matter of deciding whose fender was dented worse. But these modern cars were big and heavy, and they went too damned fast. He thought to underline the last assessment as he considered his worn-out Dodge down in the driveway: too fast for me to catch, anyhow. He'd been a kid when he saw his first real car crash, but now he was an old man, and he'd seen enough blood and guts for one lifetime.

He tried to concentrate on going back to sleep, but he couldn't. He had been dreaming about her again, he suddenly realized. Silly, stupid woman. Two weeks had gone by, and she still spent all day, every day, sitting out on that damn bench. She sat there until ten or eleven some nights, he guessed, since she was always there when he got back from night patrol and checked in and went home. And she was back at dawn. He had stopped sending Dooley out to get food for her, and he guessed she went back to the hotel café on her own, if she ever went anywhere. One thing was sure, that damned old Hudson hadn't moved. It was still parked in the Free Zone, so he couldn't even ticket it. Already one tire was flat, and another was looking low. A dust storm on Sunday had coated it with a layer of red dirt, and it looked lonely and pathetic. Like she was, he thought suddenly—abandoned. But it was dead, sure as hell; battery was gone by now. She was alive, and she showed no signs of stopping.

The dream glimmered faintly in the distance of his mind, but he couldn't recall it. He remembered being disturbed by it, and he wondered if his racing heart and distress had been caused as much by the startling sound of the telephone as by the dream. After ten minutes he cursed and got out of bed. He fumbled around for his clothes and got dressed. Maybe he'd go down to the office and monitor the accident by radio. They might need his help after all.

The FBI had sent down an agent to talk to Imogene. He'd talked to her for about an hour, then had gone over to see Pete. After that he left town without so much as a how-de-do to Ezra. The sheriff had never liked those prissy G-men anyway. They dressed too well for lawmen. Made too damn much money. He did finally get a preliminary report two days later, and it all but shut the door on the case of the missing Cora Lee McBride. She was eighteen. There was no reason to suspect that she had been abducted or harmed in any way. She was apparently fleeing an intolerable family situation—maybe an insane mother—but the report had only implied this, and she'd most likely turn up in Atlanta or someplace else. So that was it. Case closed.

Ezra filled his pipe and got into the car, wincing as his knee pained him from having to bend it under the steering wheel. He knew but wouldn't admit that his real reason for going downtown was that he was curious about whether she'd be there at three in the morning or not. As he turned onto Main Street and his headlights picked out the square, he felt a sense of relief.

The bench was empty, of course. She'd *have* to be crazy to keep watch all night, two weeks later. But she was there all day, that was for sure, and she'd become the object of quite a bit of gossip around town. He'd already had to stop some kids from driving around and around the square and yelling names at her. "Crazy Daisy" and "Loony Tunes" had been some of their kinder catcalls. But he'd put an end to that by speaking to some key parents.

As he parked the car and got out, he thought he saw

someone coming out of the courthouse. It was her! She must have gone in to use the toilet or something. She walked primly over to the bench and sat down. It was a warm night, and she made a pillow of her coat and lay down on it. He could arrest her, he supposed, for vagrancy, but, he corrected himself, that was stupid. In the first place she had ready money, more than most folks around here had in cash, in fact. She paid for everything up front, even the meals Dooley had brought out to her. She was bathing and changing clothes regularly, and she had sent some things to the laundry and dry cleaners over on Potter Street. She had stopped wearing makeup, and Ezra could see that she was indeed just under forty. But she was still very pretty.

He pulled out his pocketknife and began working the tobacco in his pipe, and he coughed loudly, but she apparently didn't hear him, or if she did, she wasn't going to look around. He tramped on up the steps into the courthouse and into the office where Dooley was asleep on the cot in the holding cell. He poured a cup of coffee into a cracked mug and turned on the radio.

It was apparently quite a wreck. The guy they were trying to cut out might lose his leg. Two were dead, and the ambulances were bringing in two more who were likely to die. The coffee tasted like acid, and Ezra poured it into the toilet bowl in the holding cell. Dooley snored on. He never woke up unless the phone rang or the fire alarm went off. Maybe I should drive out and see if they need any help, Ezra thought. Hell, why not? That's my job, ain't it?

P A R T

2

A prudent man foreseeth the
evil, and hideth himself:
but the simple pass on, and are
punished.

—Proverbs 22:3

O N E

After another week, Sheriff Holmes found himself becoming more and more upset over the situation involving the "crazy old lady on the courthouse bench"—for so Imogene was referred to all over town. He had been seriously unnerved by his discovery that she stayed out all night every night, and he found that she was on his mind almost every waking minute of his day.

The dreams had continued as well, and each night they seemed to become more graphic, more violent. But one dream in particular finally motivated him to do something more than wait for news of the missing Cora Lee McBride to surface or for the girl to simply appear. One night's dreaming, in fact, had disturbed him more than all the rest put together.

He came in from patrol later than usual one evening, and, after eating his favorite snack, Shredded Wheat crumbled into a glass of sweet milk, had undressed and gone to bed. He couldn't stand being alone in the house anymore, not since Imogene had appeared in Agatite, and the discomfort he felt made him even more upset with himself.

He fell asleep quickly, a habit he had acquired long ago to guard against exhaustion caused by duty calls late at night and sometimes days gone without more than a few hours' rest, but it seemed as if he had just closed his eyes when a jangling awoke him.

At first he thought it was the telephone, and he was

groping for it blindly in the dark when he noticed someone standing at the foot of his bed. Rubbing his eyes and
sitting partly up in the bed, he tried to focus in the dim
illumination of a streetlamp that crept into the bedroom
window, but he couldn't make out the figure.

"What do you want?" he croaked, surprised at how
dry and dead his voice sounded. Each syllable was a trial
for him to make, and when he tried to swallow, his mus-
cles wouldn't function right. "Who are you?" he tried to
say, but the figure remained silent and stared at him
through a quasi darkness. He then noticed that dangling
from one hand was a set of keys, a large antique key ring
with four or five small keys on it, moving from one finger
to another in a teasing, mocking fashion.

Gradually his eyes began to focus, and the figure took
shape in the gray light. It was a woman, a girl really,
dressed in a white dress, a summery dress. He couldn't
see her face, but long strands of blond hair fell casually
across her shoulders and moved lightly as she shifted the
key ring from one hand to the other. Cora! his mind said
to him, and he was about to ask the first of a thousand
questions that were trying to gather themselves into co-
herent organization in his mind, when she turned and
walked out of the room, easily passing through the open
bedroom door and silently leaving him raised on his elbows in the bed.

Painfully aware of his knee, Ezra eased out of bed and
groped with his toes for his slippers, which were not under the bed as they usually were. He felt the hardwood
floorboards give a bit as they always did when he put
weight on that spot, and he staggered a bit as he came to
his feet. Barefoot, he padded out of the room and into
the hallway after the girl. He followed the empty hall into
the living room, which was awash with lights from every
lamp he owned. Cora wasn't there, but the brilliance of
the light hurt his eyes, and he lowered them as he moved

through the dining room and past the swinging doors into the kitchen. There he spotted her standing at the stove with her back to him, fussing with a coffeepot.

"Cora?" he asked stupidly, still trying to form questions and amazed at how fuzzy his mind felt. Nothing seemed to come in the order he wanted, and he stood there in his long drawers, barefoot in his own kitchen, improbably talking to the missing daughter of the crazy woman on the courthouse bench.

Instead of answering him, the girl turned and brought the coffeepot over to the kitchen table, where she poured him a full cup into a china cup she had apparently set especially for the purpose. She ladled sugar and cream into the black liquid, something Ezra never took, but before he could protest, she returned to the stove, replaced the pot, put both hands on the appliance's top, and leaned forward.

The kitchen seemed larger than ever to him, and the lights were blindingly bright, making everything appear in black-and-white contrast to his burning eyes. He took an unreasonable three paces from where he stood over to the coffee cup and, without thinking about what he was doing, lifted it to his lips and sipped it. Something told him that the warm liquid would loosen the thickness in his tongue and throat, but the coffee was cold. Rock cold. And the combination of cold coffee and cream and sugar made him gag a bit.

The girl, her back still to him, giggled, and she started out the kitchen door to the driveway. Ezra set the cup down. He still hadn't seen her face. When she'd come over to pour the coffee, she'd kept her head down, and her blond hair, white in the brilliance of the kitchen lights, cascaded down and covered her features completely, but he did see a burning cigarette in her mouth, and he distinctly recalled seeing the circular brand stamped on the paper: Lucky Strike. He replaced the cup on the table and called after the girl, who had now disappeared out the kitchen door. "Cora? Is that you? Where are you going?" The questions took a tremendous amount of energy, and he stumbled after her.

It took ten paces to reach the open kitchen door, and once over the threshold, he seemed to take forever to descend the two steps to the driveway. He peered into the backyard, then he heard the jangling keys again and swirled around to see her standing at the end of the driveway, a cigarette glowing from her darkened face, and the keys passing from one hand to the other in the same teasing fashion.

"Wait," he said, moving toward her, but she turned, and without hurrying began to move down the sidewalk, swishing her hips a bit and casting a teasing glance back over her shoulder at the barefoot man in his underwear who was coming toward her.

Suddenly a sharp pain shot up from the sole of his left foot, and Ezra stopped and stuck out a hand to lean up against an elm tree that lined the driveway. Goatheads had cropped up in the cracks of the cement driveway, and with Hilda gone, no one had the time or interest to chop them out. The small, hard sticker was imbedded in a crease in his sole, and when he plucked it out, he could distinctly see a bubble of blood where it had stabbed him.

"Just a minute," he called to the retreating figure. She continued to move down the sidewalk, her dress a swash of white in the streetlamp's light. "Let me get my shoes." He turned back to the kitchen, which was dark, although he couldn't remember turning out the lights, and he moved through it toward the living room, which now was also without any light at all.

Reaching his bedroom, he found his pants and shirt and tumbled them onto the bed. He grabbed his boots from under a chair where he had left them and fumbled in his mind for where he had dropped his socks.

He sat on the edge of the bed and began an absurd mental debate over whether he should get a clean pair from the bureau or search around for the ones he had taken off before going to bed. His mind weighed pros and cons, and he found himself growing incredibly weary with the internal, silent argument. As he lay back on his bed to settle the matter, his eyes glanced over at his alarm clock face, which read twenty after two. Suddenly he was very tired, and the sheets of his bed seemed so cool and relaxing that he closed his eyes. He dropped the single boot he had held in his hand onto the floor beside his bed and remarked as he drifted off that it hadn't thumped loudly enough to have hit the hardwood floor.

When he woke up, it was after four, and his knee was giving him hell.

He struggled up to a sitting position and ran his hand over his face. He felt wide awake, and a sense of urgency overwhelmed him. He reached out onto the bedclothes and discovered his pants and shirt, and then he remembered. Cora! She was here! I've got to do something, he said to himself.

When his feet hit the carpeting on the floor, he suddenly realized what had happened. It was a dream. All of it. A goddamn dream. Every night he dreamed of that damn fool woman, and now her missing daughter was haunting him as well.

But dream or not, it was more than a little disturbing. He couldn't get it out of his head. Slowly, as if carrying out a reenactment of his somnambulant wanderings, he stood up and recalled the feel of the hardwood floors in his dream. Hilda had covered them with carpeting years ago, and he hadn't thought of the creaky spot beside their bed for over a decade. He shuddered.

He pulled on his clothes and gun belt and moved out into the hall and down to the living room. All was as it should be, he noted, taking his pipe from the ashtray next to the radio. The lights were out, and a stream of white from the streetlamp crossed the worn carpet of the room. He moved through the swinging doors into the kitchen, and suddenly he caught his breath. Even in the dark room he noticed the china cup, full of coffee, sitting on the kitchen table next to a sugar and cream set he hadn't used in months, not since he'd had a small meeting of civic leaders in the house right before Christmas.

Ezra put out a hand to steady himself on the door jamb. His eyes swept the kitchen, but nothing else was out of place. He examined the cup and sugar and cream set, noting that both were full, and then passed through the door onto the driveway. The door was shut but not locked, he noticed as he squinted into the backyard and then turned to look down the drive into the street. The Dodge sat squarely in the middle of the drive, but he couldn't recall it being there in the dream, and he began to relax. The streetlamp glowed brightly, illuminating the early morning gloom around the very spot where he recalled Cora standing in almost total darkness, smoking a cigarette. The night sounds of crickets and other nocturnal creatures seemed deafening, far too noisy not to drown out the sound of jangling keys.

He went back into the kitchen. The coffeepot, he learned by hefting it, was half full of yesterday's makings, and he lit the burner under it to reheat it. He poured the cup's contents down the sink and carefully washed it and replaced it on the sideboard in the dining room next to the others that matched it. The cup was part of a cherished set of china Hilda had received from her mother. They'd never used the dishes or cups much even when she was alive, and after she died, Ezra never touched them at all except to dust carefully around them from time to time.

When the coffee boiled, he rose from a chair where he

had been musing over the dream and poured himself a steaming cup. He kept trying to piece together the dream, separate what had happened from what had not. I've been sleepwalking, he said to himself as he gingerly sipped the burning coffee. I got up, came in here, poured myself a cup of cold coffee, sugared it, creamed it, and then—His mind raced down to his foot and, almost upsetting the coffee cup on the table, he reached down and jerked off the left boot and sock. Sure enough, a small, almost invisible wound was angrily red inside a crease of his sole. It didn't hurt, but he squeezed it hard to see if it was indeed as fresh as it looked. Blood bubbled between his fingernails in a tiny spurt. It was fresh, all right.

He couldn't stand to be alone in the house for another second. Rising quickly and thrusting his foot painfully into the boot, he stumbled to the kitchen door and slammed it shut behind him. He got into the car and drove quickly out onto a spur of road that used to be the highway before the bypass came through. Pressing the accelerator down and rolling down the window, he allowed the old Dodge to speed up past the limit, to seventy, to eighty. The speedometer pegged at one hundred miles per hour, but he kept pushing the old car, trying, it seemed, to press out the memories of the dream that had made him get up in the middle of the night and move around like a damn fool.

He knew he was going too fast, and he sensed the thrill of danger that comes from excessive speed, the excitement that drives teenagers and drunks to kill themselves in nightmares of twisted metal and broken glass. He had arrested many a would-be dragster for doing what he was doing right now on this very stretch of highway, but he had never really understood what made them do it, not until this very moment.

He didn't slow down until he passed the triangular sign that warned HIGHWAY INTERSECTION 1000 FEET, announcing the point where the spur rejoined the main highway, and then as he pressed hard on the brake and clutch pedals, he found himself enjoying the pain that raged from his knee and the agonized whine that came from the engine as it wound down.

He remained at the stop sign of the intersection for what seemed like a long time, then he slowly steered the car back toward town. "What is happening to me?" he asked himself in the weak yellow light of the dashboard. He knew he had been dreaming about Imogene, but he hadn't yet dreamed of Cora, and he had never sleepwalked before—or had he?

After the Dodge crossed the city limits line, Ezra turned into the parking lot of the Holiday Motor Courts, Agatite's only motel. He parked and got out, moving over to a metal staircase that led up to the flat roof over the driveway in front of the office. The owners, Mary and Buddy Spradlin, had put down a tile floor on top of the carport roof, and guests were invited by an arrow-shaped sign to go up on sunny days and sit on canvas lawn chairs and drink Cokes from a dispensing machine they had installed. Mary, a beautiful young woman of about twenty-five, was the most frequent sunbather, however. It was a place where she could get out of sight of the traffic on the highway and take the sun without every kid in town driving by to gawk at her.

Ezra looked into the vacant office and noted that the NO VACANCY sign was on. The Spradlins had obviously filled up and retired long ago, no doubt relieved that they wouldn't be disturbed until early morning checkouts began ringing the office bell. Ezra climbed up through the small opening trap in the roof's ceiling and seated himself heavily in one of the canvas chairs.

As he pulled out his pipe and began to refill it, he tried once again to analyze the dream. Need to bring it out front, he told himself, turn it over, look at it. He recalled it vividly. It was not like a dream at all, but more like

72

something that had really happened. The details stood out in sharp black-and-white contrast in his mind. It was all too real, he thought.

He recalled with a shiver the specter of Cora standing at the foot of his bed. He could almost smell her, he remembered, the freshness of her youth. He mentally traced the dream's action: He got up, followed her through the house, sipped the coffee, gagged, then followed her outside and hurt his foot. Then he went back to the bedroom. He even remembered the absurd argument he had with himself over the socks, and he remembered looking at the clock. It was so damn real, he thought.

But there were things that didn't fit, he recalled. The carpeting on the floor was missing, for one item, and the bright lights in the living room and kitchen. If every lamp he owned was on, it wouldn't be that bright, he knew, and Hilda had complained for years about how dim it was in the kitchen's single overhead light. Also he remembered that he was wearing long underwear, not the boxer shorts and undershirt he had worn to bed.

Again he traced the steps of the dream, disturbed not only by how easily it all came back to him, but also by the familiarity of it. Was it a dream or not? he demanded of himself. Then other problems cropped up in his memory. The Dodge hadn't been in the driveway, he thought. But it was there when he came out later. And the tree! Hilda had mowed down that old elm with her car on V-J day. It was the first and only time she had ever tasted anything alcoholic—a bit of champagne poured into her cup by a celebrating mob downtown. She had gotten tipsy—she claimed anyway—and run right over that elm. Ezra had spent three days digging out the stump, but he distinctly remembered putting out his hand and leaning on it when he stepped on the sticker. Of course! It had to be a dream. Nothing more.

73

But the discovery of sufficient errors to discount the reality of the experience did little to comfort Ezra. It was disturbing enough to have a nightmare, he knew, and it was even more disturbing to have one over a case he was working on. It showed too much personal involvement. It was unprofessional as hell, as a matter of fact, he told himself. But to discover that he had gotten up in the middle of the night and poured himself a cup of coffee and gone chasing around outside in his underwear was far more serious than unprofessional involvement in a case. It showed a darker thing that his conscious mind refused to admit. But then he recalled something that made him more upset than ever. This had *not* been the first time.

When Hilda died Ezra stored away three things. First, and obviously, he stored away Hilda herself, burying her in the Sandhill County Memorial Cemetery. And with her body Ezra had buried his grief. The mourners who stood beside him as the preacher droned the final prayers could not see the invisible body of grief that the sheriff placed beside his wife's coffin. He knew he couldn't carry it with him, that if he tried to keep it secretly stored inside him, it would eat away at his confidence, at his ability to do his job, at his very life until there was nothing left. So he put the grief right into the grave and admonished it to stay there, not to come out until he was ready to join his wife in the ground beside her. Then, he reasoned, it couldn't hurt him.

The second thing he stored away was the array of things in the house that were completely Hilda's. With the exceptions of the china, one or two odd pieces of furniture, and a box of small, personal things, he gave away or boxed up everything that reminded him of his departed wife so the grief would remain where he had put it. To be surrounded by her things, he thought, would be to tempt the monster grief to come out of the grave and stalk him like a beast of prey. And he intended to keep the temptation away.

Thirdly, and most importantly, he stored away his memories. He and Hilda had been partners in life, shared a bed and a home for almost thirty-five years. There had been painful memories, and there had been so many pleasant ones that he couldn't always sort them out as well as he wanted to. So he stored all of them, collected in small bundles, labeled and carefully tucked away in the back of his mind. There they rested, away from awareness, away from the trigger that also might cause grief to stir in the cemetery, to come out and hunt up the spirit of Ezra Stone Holmes.

It was a special talent, and he was somewhat proud of it. He had placed many memories in such storage bundles—seeds, he thought—and it was a comfortable way of storing away Hilda's memories as well. And it kept things even, cool, collected. They waited quietly there, and they didn't stir.

There were times, of course, when the memory seeds stirred themselves and threatened to break open. When he ate a meal alone or tried to cook something he liked that Hilda had prepared so lovingly for him so many times, he could feel it moving the way any seed might move before sprouting. But he could control that sort of movement, and he did. He was proud of that also.

And there were times when he took the seeds out deliberately and examined them. Once or twice a year he would go out to the cemetery and sit beside Hilda's grave and take them out that way. He was not reluctant to open them at such times, indulge himself in their nostalgic warmth, inventory their contents, then repack them, restore them in the back of his mind and try to forget they were there. Never, never had he feared that the monster grief would disturb the grave's grassy mound. Ezra had never cried over Hilda's grave.

It wasn't that he hadn't loved her, that he *didn't* love her. But he knew he couldn't love a memory, that soon that sort of love would stir the monster grief and consume him. He had never cried because to cry would be to give in to a kind of weakness that Ezra Stone Holmes had never admitted to his character. Before this night he would have said to anyone, especially himself, that the stored memory seeds remained where he put them, that they never emerged of their own accord.

But now, sitting on the motor court's carport roof, his unlit pipe in his bony fingers, he suddenly and shockingly recalled one horrible night when they stirred themselves, and this was the first time in his recollection that he had ever thought of it.

Substantially it had been the same dream—or event, or whatever it was—the major differences were incidental. It had been Hilda standing at the foot of his bed that time, not Cora, but like Cora, his dead wife's shade had wordlessly left him and gone into the kitchen, where, he discovered when he followed her, she offered him a cup of cold coffee in one of the china cups. She had left him alone then, just as Cora had, ignoring his calling to her, and when he followed her out the kitchen door, the ghostly shape was gone. He remembered going back to bed, awakening the next morning with bright sunlight streaming into his bedroom, his feet still on the floor and his body awkwardly sprawled across the bed. But he had shut out the dream then, refused to acknowledge its presence or its relationship to reality. Even now, vivid as it seemed to be in recollection, he couldn't recall whether or not the house had been bright with light, whether it had been so starkly black-and-white as had the Cora dream. He had shoved it into his storage place for memories so abruptly and roughly that some details must have spilled out and been forgotten forever, and try as he might he could not recover them.

Even now, as the colder if not clearer light of day was finally graying the skies of the Texas east, now, as his mental fingers probed the memory seed and looked for the lost details of a long-ago nightmare, now, as he sat stock-still and watched the traffic pass below him on the highway, Ezra felt totally abandoned and miserable. So much of the first dream had been exactly the same, but there was one big difference. That had been Hilda. This had been Cora, or at least the mental picture he had from the missing girl's yearbook. But what about the sugar and cream, the keys, the lit cigarette? What did it all mean? Or did they mean anything at all? This time he had gone further into the dream, following the girl until the sticker in his bare foot stopped him. What if he hadn't stumbled over a loose goathead? It was deep, Ezra thought, too deep for an old man to delve into, and it scared him.

Idly he pulled out his watch. It was nearly six, time for breakfast. A passing truck blew up a swirl of dust in front of the motor court's parking lot, and Ezra bent over to shield a match over the bowl of his pipe. Quietly and deliberately he replaced the first dream back in its seed and stored it again in his mind. But the second one, he decided, he must keep out for a while. He wasn't ready to put it away just yet, not until he found some answers. But, he also reluctantly admitted, he hoped that by keeping it out, alive and in front of him, he might avoid having it again.

Ezra didn't believe in visions or premonitions. The Hilda dream had come shortly after she died, and maybe that was why he could forget it—store it, he quickly corrected—so easily, rationalizing that it was caused by the monster grief fruitlessly trying to break free of the grave. And this dream, he was sure, was because this case was

77

constantly on his mind, because Imogene had somehow gotten inside him and disturbed those stored memories in a jostling way, not intentionally, not even violently, but accidentally. Still, he wanted it out, in the open, in the daylight where he could see it and use it if he could, if not to solve the case, then at least to keep in touch with the reality of it.

He stood and stretched. The sky was fully light now, and the trucks and cars that occasionally whizzed by on the highway looked odd as they poked their lights into the gathering brilliance of a bright spring day. Mary was sweeping in the office as he descended the stairs, and she held up a coffee mug in one pretty hand in a gesture of welcome. She and Buddy were used to Ezra's nocturnal visits on their carport roof, although they had never mentioned them to him or anyone else, as far as he knew. It was just the whim of an old man, he guessed they imagined, and perhaps it made them feel safe to know a lawman was standing watch over them as they slept.

Ezra shook his head and moved over to his car. I've had one too many cups of coffee poured for me this night, he thought. Breakfast is what I need now. Breakfast and then—he paused before he went ahead with the thought—and then Pete. Again. There's too much here I don't know, too much, maybe, I know but don't want to know.

He started the car and headed for home.

T W O

It was a lazy morning outside, and Imogene's figure seemed to dominate Ezra's view of the courthouse square. She sat like the Civil War statue, silently vigilant,

78

staring at the drugstore. Ezra felt bile from his breakfast rising as he opened the door and stalked in under the tinkling of Pete's bell. No goddamn wonder I have bad dreams, he thought acidly, with her sitting out there and ruining what little good digestion I've got left.

Pete wasn't in sight, but Ezra had hardly adjusted to the dim light inside the store when the druggist emerged from the back room, carefully sliding the bolt home to secure the door.

"Ezra!" Pete said, indicating both surprise and delight at an early morning visit from the sheriff. "Got some fresh coffee on. Want a cup?"

"No thanks," Ezra said, pulling his pipe out and stoking the tobacco in the bowl. "Just wanted to talk."

"That's funny," Pete said, pouring himself a large cup of coffee that looked so good and rich compared to the gook Dooley cooked up that Ezra almost changed his mind and asked for some. "I been wantin' to talk to you too." Pete ladled a large spoonful of sugar into the cup and followed it with a healthy dollop of cream from the counter pitcher, and Ezra felt himself go cold all over. Pete pulled a Chesterfield from the pocket of his druggist's smock and lit it with a Zippo from a display on the counter. The smock was stained, but it always was; the sheriff couldn't ever remember seeing Pete in anything but a stained smock all the years he had known him. It was like his unshaven face, a sort of trademark.

When they had been kids and waiting forever, it seemed, for whiskers to sprout on their young chins, Pete had vowed to grow a beard. He never had, but he also refused to shave regularly enough to keep stubble from his cheeks. He managed to scrape it off for Sundays or special occasions, such as marriages and funerals, and once in a while Ezra recalled catching him with a clean shave in midweek for no reason at all, but for the most part Pete sported a perpetual three-day growth.

79

Had he been cleanly shaved the day Cora disappeared? Ezra heard a voice ask somewhere inside him. He rubbed his own chin and shook his head. Got to stop thinking this way, he thought. Got to.

"Listen," Pete said, smiling broadly, exposing yellowing dentures, "I got a call from Howell Gibbs over to the sportin' goods department at Monroe's, and he told me my boy was in there buyin' one of them fancy-dan rod and reel setups."

"So?" Ezra climbed up onto one of the counter stools opposite Pete and examined his friend's eyes. Pete was older than Ezra by only two months, but he hadn't aged gracefully. Something in life had been hard on him, and he seemed more grizzled and gray than anybody Ezra knew of their age or some older. He had been widowed almost twenty years before, Maureen dying in a car wreck down around San Antonio, where she had gone with her sister to visit some kinfolks of theirs, and while Pete had managed to take widowerhood in stride, Ezra wondered how much boiled beneath his affable surface and calm exterior.

"So?" Pete repeated, laughing out a cloud of blue smoke and smacking the counter top with the flat of his hand. "So? Tomorrow's my birthday!"

"Is that a fact?" Ezra asked, genuinely surprised. He usually remembered such things. "I forgot."

"The hell you did," Pete said, pretending to be hurt. "Well, my boy didn't. And he was out buyin' that rod and reel for his daddy!" Pete sipped his coffee and lustily drew in on his cigarette. "You better believe it!" he concluded.

Ezra had serious doubts that Pete's son, Dub, had spent his hard-earned money on a gift for anyone, least of all old Pete. The boy spent what he made mostly over at the Oklahoma river joints, and when he did buy something special it was usually to impress some woman or other. He was next to worthless and had just about drained old Pete dry, borrowing money when he couldn't find work, which seemed to be just about all the time. He held a variety of odd jobs around town, usually hard, dirty work no one else wanted, and as soon as he made enough to get whatever he was after that week, he would quit whether the job was done or not.

"So, you dumb son-of-a-bitch, so how about you and me and maybe Dooley or somebody gettin' together and haulin' out to the lake for the weekend?"

"You going to close up?" Ezra asked, only half listening to the proposition, his eyes wandering all over the store, inventorying everything in sight as if he'd never been there before. He knew the inside of Pete's store as well as he knew his own office. Pete had been running it for more than thirty years, and Ezra often said he wished he had a dime for every hour he'd logged on one of the counter stools in Pete's Sundries and Drugs, for if he did, he could retire in style.

"Hell, yes! I mean, a man don't turn sixty but once, does he?" Pete crushed out his butt and lit another, bobbing the cigarette on his lip as he talked. "And I ain't had me a vacation in about a hundred years, so I thought you and me and—"

"I want to look in your back room," Ezra said all of a sudden. The statement had come logically out of his mouth, the normal conclusion to his eyeing the store and coming to no firm decisions about anything. It was the next step in the process. But he realized as he said it how rude and abrupt it sounded. Pete had been unaware that Ezra was in the store on business, and he had no idea of the horrible thoughts that were creeping around his best friend's mind.

"What?" Pete's eyes were wide with surprise.

"I want to have a look in your back room," Ezra repeated, stepping down from the stool.

81

"What for?" Pete's eyes narrowed with suspicion.

"I got to have a reason?" Ezra asked, hating himself for sounding official and testy about it.

"Uh . . . no. Of course not, Ezra. I just wanted to know why." Pete opened his hands wide. Then he tensed a bit, shifting his arms to his chest and folding them tightly. "Fact is, I got a right to know why. Don't I?" Ezra nodded and started to speak, but Pete cut him off. "It's about that gal, ain't it?"

"Could be," Ezra answered, moving slowly toward the back room's door.

"I told you I never seen her!" Pete said, and Ezra turned to look at him.

"Pete," Ezra said calmly, "she came in here."

"No, she didn't." Pete's voice rose. "I'd have known if she did, and she didn't!"

Ezra said nothing but waited for his friend to go on. "Who says she did? That crazy old woman over there. Shit! Ezra, who're you gonna believe? Me or her? She's crazy as a loon! We been friends all our life! Who're you gonna believe? Tell me that!"

"She says she came in here," Ezra repeated flatly. "I got to tell you I believe her when she says that." He held up his hand to stop Pete from protesting. "I ain't saying you saw her, and I ain't saying you're lying. You say she didn't come in here, and to tell you the truth, I'd rather believe you. But you both can't be telling me the truth. Somebody's lying, that's for damn sure! Maybe it's her. Maybe she is crazy. I don't know. But I got to find out, so I got to look in your back room."

"Well, I'll be goddamn!" Pete growled, and he moved quickly from behind the soda fountain and past Ezra, almost shoving him aside as he passed him in the narrow aisle.

"It's my job," Ezra said, again keeping his voice as flat

and professional as he could. God, I hate this, he thought.

"Yeah, yeah." Pete growled again, shoving back the sliding bolt and opening the door wide. "The light pull's in the center of the room," he said, moving away from the door and turning his back on Ezra.

"I remember," Ezra said, and he moved toward the dark, small room and entered it, sticking out his hand to find the pull string for the overhead.

Even with the light on, the room was filled with shadow, and Ezra's eyes had a bit of trouble adjusting to the darkened storeroom. Around him boxes and cartons and jugs were methodically arranged in every nook and corner. He noted the toilet and sink, moist, but covered with boxes and papers and other junk, almost as if it had been thrown there carelessly. He spotted a razor and some soap, and noted that both were dry. Ezra was aware of Pete's form looming in the doorway, the smoke from his cigarette trailing eerily over his head. He admitted that it made him uncomfortable, and the admission as much as the discomfort made him feel guilty about what he was doing.

"What's behind these?" Ezra asked, pointing to a large stack of boxes against the wall.

"The door," Pete said in a voice that accused the sheriff of base idiocy. "You know it's been busted for years."

Ezra recalled something about it. He hadn't been in this back room for more than a decade, and now that he was again inside the small storage area, he felt as if he hadn't ever been there at all.

"Let's open it," Ezra said, taking a box off the top and noting that it was empty.

"What the hell for?" Pete asked, not moving from his doorway position.

"Because I'm asking you to," Ezra replied.

"I'm not gonna do it!" Pete said, firmly and too loudly, Ezra thought. "That door's been busted Lord these many years, and if you start monkeyin' around with it, I'm gonna have to call somebody and have a new lock put on. Maybe a whole new jamb, too. It's fine the way it is. I don't want— Hey! Watch it!"

The largest box was stacked on two smaller cartons, and Ezra made the false assumption that it was just another empty piece of cardboard. He pulled too hard and the thing came down on him, bringing with it a shower of other boxes and cartons, some full and some only half full. Ezra staggered back under the weight of the avalanche and felt his knee bump against something hard before he hit the floor on his back.

"Goddamn it, Ezra!" Pete shouted as he pulled the cardboard pile off the sheriff. "See what you done now?"

Ezra found his feet and stood knee-deep in cartons and boxes. "What's in that?" he asked, pointing to the large, full case that had caused the confusion.

Pete shrugged. "School supplies, mostly," he said. "You know, notebook paper and shit."

Ezra poked the corner of the box with the toe of his boot, and a feeling of horror and revulsion swept up from the black point at the end of his foot. He swallowed and, finding his mouth dry, nervously ran his tongue over his lips. "Open it," he said, and he moved slightly away from it. Something seemed to be crawling up his spine, and he shuddered, although the room was almost too warm for the outdoor weather. He didn't want to know what was inside. But he knew he had to find out, and he didn't think it was school supplies at all. "I said open it," he repeated, trying to deep his voice steady.

"The hell I will," Pete shot back with a sudden fierceness that caused the cold Ezra felt in his back creep to his throat. "You caused me enough mess here already, goddamn it!"

Automatically Ezra felt his hand go down to the butt of the .44 Colt on his pistol belt. A wash of shame flooded over him, driving the cold back down, and he fervently hoped Pete hadn't seen the gesture. "If you can't get what you want by askin'," he remembered a fat old sheriff saying somewhere in his memory, "then *ask* again, polite this time," and the fat hand of the old man fell to his own gun and he drew and cocked it smartly.

But that wasn't the kind of sheriff Ezra had ever been, and it wasn't the kind he intended to be now. Besides, this wasn't some bootlegger or bank robber—a thought ran through Ezra's mind, and another convulsive shudder came involuntarily as a long-stored memory seed stirred—it was Pete. Druggist. Friend. Fisherman. Pete.

"Look, Pete," Ezra said quickly, moving his hands in front of him and opening them in a helpless gesture. "I got to ask you to open this and let me look inside. If you don't, then I'm going to do it myself, and I'll likely mess it up worse."

With a sigh Pete moved past Ezra and waded into the fallen boxes. He knelt down and pulled at one seam of the box, ripping open the masking tape that held it shut. Under the hooded overhead light the contents were revealed to be exactly what the druggist said they were: paper, notebooks, pencils, and other school supplies.

"It just seemed heavy," Ezra muttered quietly, more to himself than to Pete.

"Nothing heavier than paper," Pete said matter-of-factly, "Except glass. I got a box with spare soda glasses around here someplace. You want to open it too?" The sarcasm in Pete's voice cut deeply into Ezra's heart, but he tried to ignore it and moved through the pile of boxes to the door.

It was stuck tight, all right, but Ezra put his shoulder against it and turned the antique knob and shoved. His knee protested and the door squeaked loudly, but with a splintering crackle it finally opened out into the alley, flooding the interior of the back room with bright sunshine.

Ezra stepped over the threshold, noting that the lock had been sheared away by his push, and he shielded his eyes against the sun's glare. It was painfully bright, brighter than anything he could remember except . . . *except the lights in the house in the dream,* he thought. He peered up and down the alley. He didn't know what he expected to find, but whatever it was, it wasn't there. Two blocks down, the depot was visible as it sat beside the railroad tracks. In the other direction the alley faded into the distance, where, Ezra knew, it would terminate at the highway a mile and a half away. Pasteboard trash containers lined the backs of the buildings on both sides of the alleyway, and Ezra moved up and down, casually glancing in them and noting the commercial refuse of the stores on the two streets parallel to the narrow passage in back of them. Pete's own bin, he noticed, was half full.

"Thought you never used that door," he called back into the darkness of the storeroom.

"Don't."

"How do you take your trash out?" Ezra asked, poking around and discovering a newspaper from the day before and some other fresh-looking garbage.

"Carry it around from the front, smart ass," Pete quipped. "What do you think? I toss it over the roof?" He was clearly angry, and Ezra felt terribly sorry for all this. If the girl had come out this way, he reasoned, it was one hell of a lot of trouble for her. And she couldn't have done it without Pete's knowing about it and—he hesitated, then went ahead and thought the word—without his *help.* But why should he help her? Ezra asked himself, glancing again at the two possible escape routes. What could she offer him that would make a man of almost sixty help a teenager run away from her mother?

Ezra went back inside and pulled the door to. It shut with a click in spite of the busted lock and splintered wood, and he tried the knob. It seemed to be holding just fine, but he didn't want to antagonize the druggist further with more speculation and silly questions. Pete was bent over, trying to rearrange the cartons and boxes, and as soon as the door was shut, Ezra began helping him restack them against it.

"I can do it," Pete said irritably, but the sheriff worked alongside his old friend, trying to repair the disorder his stupid investigation had brought.

The shambles caused by the avalanche of boxes was hard to straighten out. Pete kept moving boxes up and around, but they couldn't get the puzzle quite as it had been before. Suddenly he moved a box from a stack that hadn't been disturbed, and Ezra noticed the corner of a mattress sticking out.

"What's this?" He tried to sound merely curious and free of suspicion.

"Oh!" Pete laughed. "I forgot about that." He turned over a couple of boxes and revealed a small cot buried under them. An antique mattress rested on the cot, and a set of sheets made up tightly was visible under an army blanket. "I used to sleep here," Pete said, pointing to the small cot. "You know, on slow afternoons, before the school kids came in. The bell would wake me up if somebody came in, and I'd just grab forty winks. And then, back before Central Drugs opened up, I had to come down here once in a while at night, you know, in case somebody needed somethin' emergency-like. Then the next day I'd be bushed. So I'd sneak back here and get some shut-eye. It don't do for a druggist to be draggin' his ass around when he's mixin' perscriptions."

Pete patted the top of the mattress with his hand in an almost loving way, and Ezra turned off the suspicion buzzer that was going like crazy behind his eyes. He felt a headache coming on, and he wished he had the courage to ask Pete for something for it.

They were replacing the cartons on top of the cot, while Pete muttered about having to take it down someday since he never used it anymore, when the bell out front jangled, and Pete disappeared.

Ezra worked over the remaining boxes and finally had them all stacked in what he hoped was an acceptable order for Pete's inventory. He stood, hands on his hips, and looked at the small room. It wasn't that big, he thought, just a storeroom. But there was something sinister about it, something threatening, and he shuddered at the thought of sleeping back here. That would cause some dreams, he mused.

He reached for the light cord and pulled it, but just as the room went black, something registered in the sheriff's brain, something that he caught a glimpse of as the light snapped off. He fumbled in the dark for the dangling string and finally found it and jerked it too hard, making the hooded bulb sway eerily in the gloom of the small storage space.

His eyes searched the wall next to the stack of cartons in front of the door, and then he spied it. He felt sweat bead on his forehead as the cold creeping sensation again spread like electrical current all over his body. It was a horror he never had felt before, and it was hanging there on the wall like a taunting finger. Just about eye level, but almost obscured by an old calendar with a picture of a blond, smiling girl on it, was a small nail. And on that nail hung a ring of keys. A ring of keys just like the one the girl in the dream had been playing with. A ring of keys just like the one that had "awakened" him into the nightmare, the dream, the event of the night before.

Ezra stared at the key ring for a long moment, then slowly and reluctantly he walked over and stuck out his hand to touch it, almost afraid the key ring would disappear or, worse, be white-hot and burn him. But it wasn't and it didn't. It was just a ring of keys.

One of them appeared to be the right size and type for the back door, and he moved around to the other side of the stack and inserted it into the ancient keyhole beneath the automatic lock. It turned easily, and he distinctly heard the lock open smoothly as the key operated the tumblers.

He must have seen the keys when he was in the storeroom years ago, he reasoned with himself. Possibly even Pete didn't know there were any keys here. The calendar was fifteen years out of date, and they almost fit behind it. His mind raced for explanations, but suddenly swimming above it all was the girl in the dream, the girl whose face he never saw, the girl whose long, feminine fingers had dangled these keys at the foot of his bed the night before.

He shook the ring and the jangling noise the keys made was exactly the same as in the dream. He sat down on a stack of boxes and ran his hands over his eyes. His head was aching full force now. His eyes blurred and his head swam. Behind him in the drugstore he could hear Pete amiably chatting with someone, and Ezra fought for physical control. "God in heaven," he whispered. "Pete! What did she offer you? What did you do?"

"Nothing!" he said almost too loudly. "He didn't do nothing." A set of old keys, a rusty cot and old mattress. An old door that about half worked right. All of it. None of it. Nothing made any real sense. That girl might never have come in here. Imogene McBride might be crazy, like Pete said she was. The whole thing could be the fancy of a crazy woman's mind. But Ezra didn't really think so. He just didn't know.

He got to his feet and slowly replaced the keys on the nail. What he did know was that none of this was proof, none of it pointed to anything, at least not to anything he could allow himself to actualize into concrete images. He had had a dream, he thought. A dream came to him about a girl, about keys. There was a back room, a cot covered with boxes that looked like they hadn't been moved in years. There was no evidence, no proof of anything at all.

He turned off the light and went out of the room, pausing to throw the sliding bolt home. Pete was mixing a drink for Mrs. Hightower, who was clutching at a prescription bottle and making noises with her mouth that Ezra dimly realized were words.

"Why, hello, Ezra!" she said, surprised to see him coming out of the drugstore's back room.

"'Lo," Ezra automatically responded, moving to the counter and holding onto it to steady himself. The headache was receding, but slowly.

"You found that woman's girl yet?" Mrs. Hightower asked, reaching for the Coke Pete handed across the counter to her. Ezra distastefully reflected on the woman who sat looking at him. She was a busybody and a snoop, and everyone in Agatite would know he had been poking around in Pete's back room before they had their lunch if she had her way about it.

"Not yet," he said, and then turned to Pete as quickly as he could without appearing to be abrupt. "Listen, Pete," he said, "I don't think they can get in that door, but if you think there's any more fooling around with it, you let me know."

Mrs. Hightower's eyes widened in curiosity, her attention immediately diverted from gossip to a possibly more interesting set of events. Pete picked up Ezra's cue with a grateful look. "Okay, Ezra," he said. "Whatever you say." Then in a darker tone he added, "You're the sheriff."

Ezra looked at Mrs. Hightower with what he hoped was a resigned sigh and explained, "Pete thinks somebody tried to break in here last night. I was checking it out."

"Oh, I see!" she said in a voice that said she wasn't buying one ounce of this bullshit. "Local boys, you think?"

"Might not be boys," Ezra said, and he quickly walked by her, noting that the headache was now merely a dull throbbing somewhere in the back of his brain, uncomfortably close, he noted, to the memory storage department, uncomfortably close to reality.

"What about that fishin' trip?" Pete called to him as the sheriff reached the door, and Ezra turned, unable to conceal his surprise. He doubted that Pete would ever want to see him again, let alone go fishing. But he could see in Pete's eyes that there was no sincerity in the invitation. The druggist was baiting him, that was all.

"Not this weekend," Ezra said, glancing one more time around the store. "But happy birthday, anyhow."

"Oh, is it your birthday?" Ezra heard Mrs. Hightower say as he passed through the door and into the morning sun.

T H R E E

Imogene saw Ezra go into the drugstore, and she waited with increasing anxiety. Normally when he dropped by the store, he would be out quickly, after, she imagined, a cup of coffee or a cold drink. But this time he stayed inside an awfully long time. She went through almost half a pack of cigarettes before he emerged.

She was terribly disappointed, crushed with disappointment, that he hadn't brought Cora out with him. She still felt that somewhere inside that store her daughter was hiding, waiting, covered up until this stupid, sadistic ruse was over. But he hadn't brought her or anyone else out with him, and he now stood on the sidewalk opposite where she sat, lighting his pipe and seemingly thinking about nothing at all.

She lifted her hand in a half wave, which he did not acknowledge; then she lit another cigarette. Slowly he walked down to the corner and crossed the street. She could see he was coming her way—she could almost feel it—but for some reason he was delaying. Why? She couldn't imagine unless he had found out something horrible, something that might have happened to Cora that he didn't want her to know, something—but her mind wouldn't allow the possibilities to form themselves into thoughts. So she continued to wait. It was something, she often thought, she was becoming good at.

He finally made his way across the grass to the bench and stood there a moment. "Mrs. McBride," he said in greeting, and she nodded. He continued to stand and smoke and rock on his feet in silence. The suspense was overwhelming.

"Did you learn anything, Sheriff?" she asked as modestly as she could, trying to keep anticipation out of her voice.

"Uh . . . what?" Ezra asked, confused.

"I have no idea 'what.' That is your job."

"Yes, ma'am." He puffed on his pipe a few more seconds. "I didn't find out anything I didn't already know." She thought she saw something sad in his face, but it disappeared behind the pipe's smoke.

"That man—that Pete—he still contends that my daughter never came into his store?"

"Yes, ma'am," Ezra acknowledged, and she again saw something pass behind his face. "He says he never laid eyes on her."

"And you still believe him?" she asked, keeping her gray eyes riveted to his.

"I don't see as I've got much choice, ma'am," he said. "I've known him all my life and—"

"That, my dear Sheriff, is a *non sequitur*," Imogene announced firmly and with a delightful sense of satisfaction. "I rather suspect that many of the people you must arrest around this town are people you've known most of your life."

"Yes, ma'am, but—"

"The point is that you think he's telling the truth and that I'm out of my mind. Isn't that it?" She smiled as sweetly as the bitterness in her mood would let her.

"Listen, ma'am," Ezra said, and she noticed that he was sweating, although the temperature outdoors was comfortably cool for the time of year, "I got to ask you something."

"Yes?" She smiled again, this time masking anxiety with her best ability.

He sat down and pulled out a knife to work his tobacco. "This is a hard question. And I really don't know how to ask it except straight out." He concentrated on working on the pipe and kept his eyes away from hers.

"Go on, Sheriff." She scooched forward a bit, trying to see his face. "If it will help, I'll answer anything."

"Was your daughter . . . uh, is your daughter . . ." He trailed off helplessly.

A sudden suspicion revealed itself around the edges of Imogene's gray eyes. "What? Sheriff, *what* was my daughter?"

"Well, you see, Mrs. McBride, it's like this. I looked at her yearbook, and I noticed her pictures and all. . . ." Ezra paused again, and he stared hard at his hands, struggling for the right words to make her understand. "Uh . . . well, she's very pretty—"

"Thank you, Sheriff," Imogene interjected, and leaned even farther out on the bench. What could this man be getting at? she wondered.

93

"And . . . pretty girls are, you know, popular." He began to speak faster, and she felt her heart skip a beat.

"Yes," she said, nodding. "And Cora was—*is*—very popular. She's one of the most popular girls in her school."

"Uh . . . well . . ." He paused, then said flatly, "Maybe not." Their eyes met and locked.

"What are you getting at?" Imogene felt the hackles of the protective mother rising and tried to fight them down. Logic told her not to stand against this line of inquiry, but she couldn't help it. She could hardly believe what he was suggesting.

"Well"—Ezra took a deep breath—"popular girls are, you know, usually *voted* popular, you know, in the yearbook stuff. They're officers, and they're leaders. Pretty girls are usually popular, and popular girls are usually pretty . . . unless . . ." He stopped again.

Her eyes widened and she fought to control her voice to keep it from becoming a scream. "Unless *what*?"

"Unless they have a . . . a reputation." The last word was spoken so softly that Ezra could hardly hear it himself. He wiped his eyes with his hands and tried to avoid Imogene's fierce gray stare. Incredulity invaded her face, and she gaped at him, unable for the moment to say anything at all.

Ezra seemed to relax once the horrible word was spoken. His shoulders slouched a bit, and he replaced the pipe between his teeth. For a long moment silence prevailed in the courthouse square.

Imogene's fists slowly clenched until her nails bit into her palms. Her teeth were locked together, and she found it impossible to open her mouth, so great was her rage. With the greatest of efforts she fought to control her voice, trying to make it sound reasonable and light, but in spite of all she could do, it hissed when she spoke, like a snake poised to strike. "Tell me, Sheriff," she spat out,

94

"is your . . . uh, Mr. . . . uh, Pete . . . is he a philanderer?"

Ezra clearly had not expected such a response to his line of questioning, and he was thrown. His eyes raced around the square to see if she was changing the topic of conversation because someone had come within earshot, but they were alone. His mouth widened into a smile, and he almost laughed. "Aw, Mrs. McBride, I don't think so. I never heard him say anything original or anything. But I guess you don't live as long as he has and work in his kind of business without having some kind of phil—"

"Not a *philosopher*, you idiot!" she screamed at him. "A *philanderer*! A whoremaster! A womanizer! A lecher!" Imogene was almost beside herself with anger.

Ezra put his hands up in front of him to ward off her personal, verbal attack. The misunderstanding came crashing down on him all at once, and his foolishness registered in his eyes. "Oh," he said, interrupting her list of synonyms, "I see! No. No, ma'am! Far as I know he's straight as an arrow. And like I said, I've known him—"

"*All your life!*" she brayed into his face, and Ezra's eyes fled to the sidewalk where passersby had stopped to stare at the pair of insane people screaming at each other in the middle of the courthouse square. "And you haven't known me more than a few days! And why shouldn't I lie to you? Do you think this is some kind of stupid joke? Are you out of your mind?"

Ezra reached out for her to try to calm her, but she jerked back from his hand. She got to her feet and began pacing in front of the bench. "I didn't mean it like that," he said, his head swiveling to follow her movements.

"Like what?" She stopped for a moment to stare at him, burning a hole through him with her gray eyes. The exhaustion and frustration of the past weeks now was welling up to a crisis, and as she began walking again, back and forth in front of the helpless sheriff, she felt the dam break and the flood begin to roll. "You have the nerve to come out here after . . . after *analyzing* a high school girl's yearbook and accuse her of being some sort of *slut*! Is that right?" Ezra sat silently and watched the rage build to a high point. There was nothing he could say that would stop it. Imogene's heart was racing wildly with the free feeling of finally letting go.

"You *assume* that because my daughter is pretty and not elected to every stupid, silly contest that comes along she's a tramp! Is that right?" Ezra said nothing. "If anything happened to her in that drugstore, I mean if anything like *that* happened, then you had better look to your lifelong friend instead of to the innocent doings of a teenage girl!" The climax was coming. Her voice was cracking, and she felt her legs going wobbly and her head beginning to spin. "I am *fed up* with being looked at like a lunatic around here!" Her eyes began to fill with tears. "My daughter walked into that drugstore with a nickel in her hand to buy an ice cream cone, and she never came out! I *know* that. I *saw* it happen!" The high point was reached and the tears gushed forth. "Now," she sobbed, "what I want to know . . ." She reached out and grabbed the metal arm of the bench and lowered herself onto it, gulping and crying as she spoke. "What I want to know is what are you going to do about it besides come out here and cast aspersions on the character of a young girl you do not know and have never met?" She gave him one last fierce look through her tears. "Who, in fact, you really do not believe ever existed. . . . Oh, God!"

Imogene leaned forward and began to retch. Nothing came out of her mouth, but her body shook with violent heaves and convulsions. She desperately wanted vomit to flow from the sick fear she had kept inside her. Ezra laid one bony hand on her shoulder, but she apparently did not notice his attempt to comfort her.

After a few moments she raised up, took a hand-kerchief from her purse, and wiped her face.

"I'm sorry as hell, ma'am," he said quietly. "I really am."

She looked at him with her penetrating eyes, now rimmed red with the strain of her outburst, and searched him for truth.

"What are you going to do now?" she asked.

"I don't know, ma'am," he replied flatly. "I honestly don't."

"Yes, you do," she said without any apparent emotion at all, and she turned her face toward the drugstore again and said nothing else.

"All we can do is wait," he offered as he stood and relit his pipe. "That's all I know." She remained silent on the bench, and Ezra turned away from her and started back to the courthouse.

F O U R

It's been one hell of a morning, Ezra thought as he went up the courthouse steps and looked back at Imogene's rigid figure on the bench. He fought back the temptation to turn and yell, "She ain't never comin' back, lady!" at her, and the effort it took him to resist brought back his headache with a sudden hammering. I'm too damn old for this kind of crap, he thought, reddening under the memory of her attack on him.

It was about the hardest question any lawman ever had to ask a parent, and in the whole of his career Ezra had had to ask it only once or twice. Those times the answer had been so obvious that it hadn't hurt much, but this time, he thought, turned out to be as bad as asking such a thing was supposed to be. Pardon me, his mental voice mocked him, is your daughter a whore? Does she fuck

97

around? Was that why no one would vote for her in high school? What is she, lady? A round-heeled hooker with ball bearings in her ass?

He felt so ashamed of himself for bringing it up. He had to. There was the dream. That was no innocent girl in his dream. That was a woman! Ezra recalled the way she moved, like silk, her hips swinging provocatively as she beckoned him to follow. But, and he rubbed his forehead, that was a *dream*. He had no right to ask Mrs. McBride about Cora's moral background, no right at all. He had nothing to go on. Nothing, he thought, except an old cot and mattress and a back room that seemed to be the perfect—he choked off the thoughts and ended the series of questions that began to form in his mind once again.

It had already gone too far, he reasoned. He had already made an enemy out of one of the best friends he had ever had, and now he had given this lonely, abandoned woman another worry to fret over. But—he tried to avoid the thought—but then how *did* she get away? The question hung hot and angry in the spring noonday.

For a moment the fleeting idea of calling Harvey McBride and asking him the same question came to Ezra, but he quickly squelched it. He could see in his mind's eye the potential disaster in the making. "Oh, *yes*, Sheriff," McBride would say, Ezra ironically imagined. "How *nice* of you to *ask*. My daughter *used* to fuck *the* socks off *every* hard dick who came *around*. The high school *boys*, the *gardener*, the *butler*! Why once, she *even* pulled a train for *my* lodge. We were *so* proud of her! Do *you* think it *had* anything to do with her *disappearance*?"

The sheriff spat in disgust into the plants alongside the courthouse steps. No, he answered his version of McBride's question, it probably didn't. And even if it did, I couldn't prove that it did. Maybe this is an end of it. The girl's gone, and that's that. One thing for sure, he resolved, I'm not going to worry about it anymore.

By a force of will so strong that it brought his headache to a crescendo of pain, he took the dream of the night before and compressed it into a fine little seed of memory. He deliberately forced it back into his mental storage area and placed it carefully and quietly next to the other stored memories. He was dimly aware that next to it were other seeds of Hilda and Hilda's dream, and there were other, far more sinister seeds. Car wrecks, for one thing, and terrifying chases through back county roads, and suicides, and murders, and one particular seed that he dared not disturb, but that he felt stir from time to time when he talked to Imogene McBride. Those seeds he kept buried as deeply as the grief out in the cemetery, and he had no intention of opening them.

Suddenly he began to feel better. The headache receded, and his knee even stopped throbbing. He felt tired, weary. He hadn't done a good thing all day long, and he knew it. He felt stupid. He wanted to go inside and lie down on the holding cell cot, but he had a pile of paperwork on his desk, and Dooley would be clucking like an angry mother hen over the sheriff's neglect of office duties. He sighed and reached for the heavy courthouse doors. Maybe tonight, he thought, I can get some sleep.

F I V E

Imogene remained on the bench every day and most of every night for the next month. The weather was warming up, and a long dry spell spared her any danger from rain or hail. The local paper, the *Agatite Eagle*, did an article on her vigil, and it was picked up by wire services and run all over the country. At the end of the month a reporter from *Time* came down with a photographer and did a feature article on her—"The Woman Who Waits"—and soon other reporters followed. But nothing changed her routine. She would just keep sitting there from dawn to dusk, watching the drugstore and waiting for Cora to come back.

Some people began to feel spooky about it and wouldn't go into Pete's anymore, although they never admitted to anyone why they started taking their business exclusively to Central Drugs down the street. The kids also stopped coming by after school, and when a teenager did go inside the shop, there usually was a group accompanying him or her, and none of them stayed long. Pete complained to Sheriff Holmes, but there wasn't any law against a person sitting on a park bench and staring at a place of business, and Imogene had been careful in all her interviews and public statements never to do more than imply that Pete had had anything to do with her daughter's disappearance. She still insisted, of course, that Cora went inside the shop and never came out, but she never mentioned Pete at all, and she responded to direct, prying questions from reporters with a secret smile if they tended to suggest that the old druggist had anything to do with Cora's mysterious dropping from sight.

Finally Pete complained to her, too. But she remained silent through his tirade, waited for him to finish and quit blocking her view and go away, which he eventually did. Women from the community came in small groups to talk to her, and five or six churches were represented by ministers who came to reason with her, pray with her, or whatever, but she remained on the bench. She would leave for a short while, sometimes, maybe to take a bath, get something to eat, or pick up her laundry, but she was always back within half an hour, watching and waiting for her daughter to come back.

By the end of May the novelty had worn off. A few

tourists who had seen the story in a magazine or newspaper would drive by and gawk if their travel routes took them through Agatite, but even these began to fall off after a bit. As June came the rains came, and she caught cold, which soon became pneumonia and almost killed her. She was in the hospital for a week, and Doc Pritchard had wanted her to stay another, but she got back to the bench during the day again by the end of seven days. She took to the hotel more and more at night, sometimes even spending the whole night in bed or sitting at the room's window, looking incessantly at Pete's drugstore.

When she got back from the hospital, she augmented her routine by taking a quick stroll through downtown, using the same route she had taken when she had searched for Cora on the first day. She wouldn't go inside any store but the Ben Franklin, and usually she would buy something there—a stick of gum or a sweet from the candy counter. Sometimes she would duck quickly into Central Drugs, also, for some tooth powder or other personal needs, or for a pack of Lucky Strikes and some matches. And then she would go quickly back to the bench—*her* bench, folks had already begun to call it—and smoke the whole pack, one right after another, putting the burned stubs in a rusty coffee can Dooley had brought her.

Another month passed, and her cash began to run out. She put a handmade sign advertising the Hudson for sale on its front window. It was now a hulk of a car, covered with dust, with four flat tires and a thoroughly ruined battery. It had become a sort of monument to the ruination of her life, she sometimes thought, and she would be well rid of it. Luke Short offered her five hundred dollars for it, mostly out of kindness, but she turned him down and held out for a man from Altus, Oklahoma, who spotted it and gave her eight hundred and fifty.

She moved out of the Agatite Hotel and into Mrs. Sweeney's rooming house, a place where road workers and construction people stayed when they were in town on a temporary job, and she kept her meals down to cheese sandwiches and bowls of soup or chili from the Town and Country Restaurant Frank Godwin had just opened on Second Street behind the courthouse square.

By the end of July the car money was almost gone, too, and she placed an advertisement in the *Agatite Eagle* to sell her jewelry, all but one of her fur coats, the painting, and anything else she had of value. A few people stopped by her bench to haggle, but most just came and quietly paid her whatever she asked for her goods. In mid-August a traveling salesman bought her luggage and trunks, and she put her good dresses and shoes into the Methodist Church's secondhand shop on consignment.

Reporters from papers and magazines still came from all over the country to talk to her, and she treated them all the same, speaking in low, polite tones, explaining that Cora would come back as soon as she got tired of playing this silly game, or continuing to imply that old Pete had had some sort of hand in her disappearance or was hiding her, and chastising Harvey in the most severe tones. She would tolerate no word of pessimism, and if any of them suggested that she might need to see a "doctor," she would laugh.

"You mean a psychiatrist, don't you?" she would ask them, and enjoy their red faces and false protests. "I'm not crazy," she would patiently explain, as if she were addressing children instead of world-hardened reporters. "I'm just waiting for my daughter."

Days passed into weeks, weeks into months, and Imogene's resolve to stay on the bench seemed to increase with the August temperatures. An occasional thunderstorm would send her scurrying for the shelter of the courthouse lobby, but other than rain and hail, no climatic discomfort seemed to diminish her determination to sit and wait for Cora's improbable reappearance.

She would politely get up and move about when the groundskeeper, Haskell Johnson, mowed the grass or came with his clippers to trim around the bench, and she would stand and lower her head when a funeral procession drove by, but to most of the citizens of Agatite she had become as much a part of the downtown scene as the broken Civil War statue opposite her on the square. Gossip even began to subside as her familiar form continued to keep vigilance on Pete's Sundries and Drugs, which had fallen on hard financial times with the continuing decline in teenage soda-drinkers, and while the phrase "Crazy as Imogene McBride" had become more or less regular in many Agatite households, few people really thought very much about her at all.

The boys at the municipal fire station got up a pool, picking days off a calendar when they thought she might give up and move on, but when they asked Ezra if he was interested in buying a date or two, the sheriff spat in disgust. "You're wasting your time, boys. She ain't never going to leave." And most of them recovered their money, nodding in agreement with the sheriff's wisdom.

Pete and Ezra no longer went fishing together, and the old druggist found himself more alone and friendless than he had ever been before in his life. He continued to profess his total innocence in the matter, and most who heard him believed him, but they didn't make much effort to spread their conviction around, and he was often seen walking down the street muttering to himself and shaking his head in confusion.

All in all, Agatite, Texas, continued to go about its business, enjoying a rare prosperity that years of wind-blown, dusty Depression had made untrustworthy. The picture show on the corner changed features weekly, a new county library opened as a result of the death of a prominent citizen who left enough books to stock several dozen shelves, and a new, oversized water tower was erected in the downtown area. And Imogene waited.

S I X

It took Ezra a long time to bring himself to go back and talk to Imogene after her outburst following his questions about Cora's morality. But as time passed and he became convinced that nothing would move her from the bench, he took to stopping by for a few minutes on the way into or out of the courthouse. He never stayed long, but he found that he had grown fond of their brief, directionless chats, and if his day did not include one, he felt incomplete. So dependent had he become on seeing her daily that on more than one occasion he had arrived at home only to get back into his car and drive back downtown just to spend a minute or two on some pretext or other in his office so he could sit beside Imogene on his way in or out.

The problem came, however, when he left the bench and the woman who had become so much a part of the downtown life of the small city. In spite of the sense of need that stopping by her bench fulfilled in him, when he departed he felt as if there were still something he should have done or said to her, something vague that kept flitting around the edges of his consciousness and never emerged during one of his visits. This gave him an uncomfortable sensation, but it was less uncomfortable than if he didn't see her at all.

They rarely talked about Cora specifically at all, not since his questioning had led to her near hysteria when he tried to probe her daughter's character. He was wary of prying questions, and the topics they discussed were often so general and common that they bordered on gossip. He would point out various people as they passed and "introduce" Imogene to them, describing their quirks and habits and telling their family histories until she knew most people in the town as well as if she had lived there all her life.

And they frequently laughed or joked about this or that individual or happening that appeared in their talks. Ezra knew that, in spite of his mixed feelings about her, the visits were a wonderful source of pleasure for him. And, he admitted darkly to himself, his dreams seemed to be less vivid after a particularly entertaining chat with Imogene.

"How long have you been a widower?" Imogene asked him one afternoon as the sky was growing dark with thunderheads coming out of the northwest and the air was heavy with ozone and humidity.

"Long time," Ezra said, suddenly and for the first time since Imogene had come into Agatite aware of a vague sense of guilt. It was a strange and entirely unpleasant feeling. "Six years, more now." What was wrong with him? he wondered, and he grasped his pipe tightly to keep his hands from shaking. "She died right after the war. Her heart." The words seemed heavy and hard to articulate; when they left his lips they wanted to hang in the air in front of him like accusations. What the hell is wrong with me? he demanded silently.

In the back of his mind he felt a familiar rustling of Imogene's image as it brushed less gently than usual against the seed with Hilda's memories stored so tightly. Ezra placed a mental hand on top of the seed to quiet it.

"Were you married long?" Imogene asked. She had found a topic she was pleasantly surprised to discover warmed her.

"Next month would be our fortieth," he said, and suddenly he choked and began coughing violently. As if in mocking reply, the sky lit with silent lightning, the storm remaining far away, although its forewarnings visibly echoed across the downtown area. "Smoke went down the wrong way," he choked out when he got his breath. He hoped she hadn't noticed his pipe was out.

Imogene, however, ignored the coughing fit. "You must have loved her very much."

Ezra dreaded the dream this conversation might summon tonight. "Yes, I did," he declared simply. "We didn't think to do anything else." He saw the indefinable something he always recognized behind her eyes, and he sensed danger, but he didn't know from where it might come.

"Did you have any children?" she asked, pressing a topic she must have sensed he was uncomfortable with.

It was an odd question, somehow, framed oddly, in spite of its innocence. Why did she say "did"? Ezra wondered. Why not "do"? Then before he could prevent it, a memory burst forth and began to take shape in the darkening atmosphere around him. He had thought it was long ago forgotten, not even stored, but there it was, and he felt powerless to do more than allow it to sweep over him and carry him along.

His eyes suddenly saw a floral wallpaper pattern and black-and-white portraits of his parents. In the middle, between the distinctive pattern and the small portraits, a window revealed a raging storm outside, lit by frequent flashes of lightning and vibrated by huge crashes of thunder. He moved through the conjured room and looked out the window at a model-T pickup with a large white sheriff's badge painted on the door. Its rear end had been jacked up onto wooden blocks, and pieces of its axle were dismantled and lying about in the mud and deepening puddles, glaring in the lightning light.

His memory-self turned and left the room and entered

another, where Hilda reclined under a blanket and pitched and moaned in the pain of childbirth. He looked at his hands and saw the sweat standing out on them, and then he heard her screams again, and he felt the frantic storm outside underscoring the anxiety that was greater than any emotion he had ever experienced.

He moved past the bed, replaced a wet washcloth on his wife's brow, and looked out the window, vainly hoping to see the head lamps of the model-T belonging to Dr. Cooper, lights that would indicate that he was there, that the hours-ago message had been delivered and that he would emerge from the black rain to save his wife from the pain that wracked her body.

The images blurred for a moment, then Ezra's memory-self was scalding his hands with water heated on a wood stove. He saw himself ripping sheets into strips when he couldn't find the prepared linens Hilda had set aside. She was a month early, and she was having what women sitting around church suppers referred to as "a hard time."

As a lawman, even a young one, Ezra had dealt with blood and pain before, but this was not just somebody's blood and pain, it was Hilda's, and he couldn't believe the volumes of gore that seemed to stream from her as the baby came struggling into the world. He didn't know what to do with the small, bloody human being he found himself holding, still attached to Hilda's womb by an odd-looking, ropelike thing that Ezra could hardly believe existed. His eyes raced to the window in one more helpless glance as he found his pocketknife, heated it over the oil lamp to sterilize it, and cut the cord. Then he waited for what he felt certain would be a piercing wail from the baby. But nothing came.

He thumped it once, then again, harder, then again. Finally a weak protest emerged from the tiny lungs, but it was not a wail or even a cry, just a whimper. Ezra looked pleadingly at Hilda, who lay with her eyes closed, her legs still spread in the attitude of birthing, her head soaked with sweat, blood still coming from her womb in incredible volumes—it seemed to him. He couldn't tell if she was asleep or unconscious. He pressed an ear against the baby's chest and listened. He barely heard a heartbeat, weak and irregular, and he felt a new kind of fear growing inside him, settling in his stomach like a tightening knot. He had never felt it before, but it overwhelmed him. For a moment he thought it would kill him.

The young Ezra stood paralyzed, holding his infant in his arms, watching to see it trying to breathe, gasping from time to time, flailing tiny fists weakly, unable to find the strength to open its eyes. He judged the weight to be too light, too sparse to live, but living it was, and the young father didn't know how to keep it that way, how to help it at all. Hilda, also, worried him beyond reason. What, he repeated to himself a hundred times, do I do now?

Suddenly he made a decision and, without considering further, he wrapped the tiny creature in sheets and an oilskin, thrust it as tightly as he dared beneath his own slicker, and charged out into the storm. The wind and rain blinded him, but between flashes of lightning he kept on the road and avoided the deepest puddles as he set out on the fifteen-mile trek to town and help.

The walk became a hypnotic nightmare. He didn't remember putting one foot in front of the other, only that he somehow managed to keep going. From time to time he would kneel down and shield the baby as best he could from the driving storm and check its breathing; then he would replace it in his coat and move on, holding his free arm in front of his eyes and hoping against reason that Dr. Cooper's car would somehow appear and make everything all right. Every step he took reminded him that he was moving away from Hilda, who might well be dead by now, and guilt and frustration almost drove him to wish the baby would die so he could turn around and rush back to her, although he had no idea what he might do for her when he got there.

At length he reached the crossing of Blind Man's Creek, a wooden bridge that had threatened to fall down a hundred times since Ezra and Hilda had moved out onto the farm right after they married. He rested against one of the stakes that marked the bridge's entrance, and he peered into the blackness before him, unable to comprehend what he saw and heard.

Beneath him Blind Man's Creek was raging out of control. The water was five or six feet higher than the usual banks, and the normally sleepy stream had become a river of torrential proportions in the wake of the spring storm. And the bridge, the old bridge he had cursed so often, was gone, washed clean away by the flood. He stood helplessly on the bank, the tiny infant tucked in his slicker, and fought to control his mind.

It was thirty miles around to the steel bridge over the creek where the main highway crossed it, and there was no guarantee that even that crossing was still up, so violently was the creek flowing. He knew it didn't matter; he could never make it. His legs were already buckling with the stress of walking through the muddy ruts of the road and the emotional wracking of the whole night's business.

The roar of the creek was deafening, and thunder and lightning crashed all around him. He used his free hand to wipe water from his eyes and stare across to the bank that would take him to town, to the senile old fool of a doctor who hadn't come in time—or at all—to help, when the flash of a bolt revealed a figure moving on the roadbed across the flooded creek.

He strained into the storm and spotted it. It was Cooper! In the driving rain he was pacing up and down the bank, a weak flashlight illuminating the space where the bridge had been. He was trapped on the other side, not more than a hundred yards from Ezra and his failing infant, not more than five miles from Hilda. Ezra's mind began to bend.

Kneeling down, he checked the baby's breathing one more time. He had it in his mind to try to swim the creek, brave the deluge that forbade him the help he so desperately wanted. But it was too late. The baby wasn't breathing at all. Ezra's fingers found no pulse on the tiny wrist or neck. The baby was dead.

Holding the diminutive corpse aloft in the rain over the black waters of the flooded creek below, Ezra screamed so loudly that Dr. Cooper, who had not yet seen the dark figure across the water, looked up, surprised and terrified. What he saw was the young deputy sheriff, thrusting a small bundle aloft, as if offering it to the raging storm as some sort of macabre sacrifice, and bellowing in pain and agony. The old doctor realized what must have happened, not in detail, but the implication was clear, and he felt a creeping pity and horror come over him.

He dropped his flashlight into the creek, then raced back to his car and found his bag. Without hesitating, he plunged into the icy waters of the creek. Struggling to fight the current, he found himself washed down nearly a quarter of a mile before he snagged a limb and managed to pull himself ashore on the opposite bank. He had kept his bag, but his shoes were gone and he was soaked through.

He slogged back to the road and found that the specter he had seen was gone. At first he thought he must have imagined it, but as he groped around in the continuing downpour, he suddenly noticed a small, muddy bundle resting on the edge of the road near where the bridge used to be. It was the baby, or the body of the baby, he soon ascertained. And he wondered if Ezra had plunged into the creek and drowned himself.

By the time he waded up to the Holmes farmhouse, the small corpse tucked under his arm like a bindle stiff, the rain had subsided and only occasional drops fell to keep his bare head wet. The sky was light with morning, and the ravages of the terrible storm were visible in the fields on both sides of the road.

Ezra opened the door for him when he knocked, smiled curiously at him, and led him into the bedroom where Hilda was now sleeping peacefully. Dr. Cooper worked on her a bit, taking care of obstetrical details Ezra had been ignorant of, and pronounced her fit but tired and weak. He prescribed some broth and waited in the parlor while Ezra dried his clothes by the stove in the kitchen.

In the meantime Ezra went outside and worked on the pickup. He worked quickly to finish the work the storm had interrupted the previous afternoon, reassembled the axle and jacked the vehicle down, then drove it around to the front of the house to pick up the doctor and drive him back to town.

Barefoot but dry once again, the doctor moved across the yard and started to get into the pickup. Ezra stopped him with a cold look, then gestured to the still wrapped, muddy bundle Dr. Cooper had left on a chair on the porch. "Best take that with you," the young deputy said. "It don't belong here." And the aging doctor had hobbled back, picked up the dead infant, and installed it in the back of the pickup. Ezra took him back to town. Nothing more was ever said about it in Ezra's earshot.

The images began to fade as the storm came up over the top of the courthouse behind Ezra and Imogene.

"No," he said softly, surprised that only seconds had passed since she had asked her question. He was almost

111

shaking with the violence of the memories she had evoked. "We never did."

"I see," Imogene said flatly, noting something far away in his eyes that called a halt to further prying. Then she said something else.

Ezra didn't hear her comment, for he was mentally adding, "But I know what it's like to lose a child!", words he could never bring himself to say, but words he had thought he would never want to say, either. Out in the cemetery, next to Hilda's grave, was a flat space. No mound, no marker. Beneath it, Ezra knew but had never consciously acknowledged, lay the body of his child, son or daughter he had never known. Had he asked, and he never had, he would have learned that it was a boy, born with a defective heart, premature, and doomed to die before it ever saw life. But that was information he had not sought, and neither Hilda nor anyone else had ever asked him if he wanted to know.

They had stayed on the farm for another month; then he had sold it and they moved to town, never discussing what had happened except to refer to her "sickness" during the Great Flood of Sandhill County. There had been no other attempts to have children, and Ezra never questioned Hilda's reasons any more than she asked what happened on the rainy, muddy road to Agatite that cold April morning. It was just something they came to understand and accept, allowing their love for each other to overcome any doubts they may have had about what might have been.

"What?" he said, realizing that Imogene was saying something.

"I said," she continued, "if you had, you might understand better how I feel." There was no malice in her voice, only a kind of sadness that touched Ezra's heart.

He thought of old Dr. Cooper, who had died a week later of pneumonia brought on, it was said, by his dous-

112

ing in the flooded creek. And he thought of how much he hated it when it rained.

"Yes, ma'am," he said. Then he looked up. "I think we better get inside." As he spoke great drops of water came pelting down on the lawn, and they both rose hurriedly and began jogging toward the courthouse. Ezra suddenly turned away from Imogene's retreating figure, however, and made for his car. He got in, slammed the door, and started up the Dodge, backing out and steering west into the face of the storm toward Blind Man's Creek.

A few minutes later he arrived at the old crossing. A sturdy steel bridge was visible through the summer thundershower, and the sheriff stepped out into the rain, oblivious to the force of the rain on his face and hands. He moved over to the edge of the bridge and looked down into the gurgling creek below him.

This will be no flood, he thought idly, just another rainstorm. The creek bubbled happily below and almost drowned out the sound of rain hitting the steel girders of the bridge. He looked across to the other bank and tried to conjure the images again, but they wouldn't come. And he was glad. These wouldn't return to him in dreams, he felt sure, and that was a comfort. That memory would be stored again, and it wouldn't emerge so easily next time.

He got back into the car and shivered as he watched the water course down his windshield. Maybe talking to her every day isn't such a good idea, he said to himself. Maybe it was a habit he needed to break if such daytime nightmares were to be the result. But he knew it was a habit, and he knew he would continue to talk to her at least until he found out what had happened to Cora McBride, or until she gave up and left. "And that ain't likely," he said aloud.

He looked through the rain-streaked car windows into the fields on either side of the road. Did some maniac grab her, kill her, bring her out to some field like one of these and bury her? Maybe down along the creek bed, maybe in somebody's pasture, or behind a barn someplace. He had thought often of starting a search, bringing up some dogs or something and combing the county for the buried body of the girl. But he didn't know where to start. It wasn't a small county. He had lived here his whole life, and there were miles of it he had never done more than drive through. If a killer was of a mind, he could bury a body so it would never be found. Without a clue, something pointing to a place, there was no hope for that sort of search, and the only result would be to call attention to what he strongly suspected was already being noticed by a good number of people—his obsession with the crazy woman on the courthouse bench.

It was futile to search, he knew; it would only give Imogene false hope—and tempt her to stay where she was. It could also make his dreams worse, and that he didn't need.

He smiled at the thought of what people were thinking when they saw the two of them sitting on the bench, chatting and laughing together. It was a danger for a sheriff, and it would be devastating to a younger man, but it didn't matter to Ezra, for the thoughts would never become gossip or suggestions. Ezra Stone Holmes was not a man people wagged their tongues about.

S E V E N

On one hot late August day Imogene's sister, Mildred, arrived on the *Noon Flyer*. She sat in the heat beside Imogene and argued with her for more than two hours. Sheriff Holmes watched them from his office window, and he prayed hard that Imogene would listen to reason,

114

pack up her few remaining things, and go back to Oregon with her sister. But after a long while Mildred appeared at his office door.

"Imogene said you might give me a cup of coffee, Sheriff," she panted as she fanned herself with a white handkerchief. She was older than Imogene by a margin and much, much heavier. Perspiration ringed her underarms, and sweat beaded on her upper lip under the faint hint of a mustache.

"Yes, ma'am, come on in," Ezra boomed, wishing he didn't fall into this country-boy accent every time somebody from out of town came near him. "You'd be Mildred, from Oregon, I suppose." He poured her a cup of coffee from Dooley's pot and handed the cracked cup over to her as she heavily seated herself in one of the wooden office chairs.

"That's right. Lordy, Lordy, what a trip!" She squirmed around in the chair, trying to find a comfortable position for her enormous hips. "It took me three days and nights, you know, and I had to sleep sitting up. I couldn't afford no sleeping car." She paused and looked around the office. "And it looks like it was all for nothing."

"She won't budge." Ezra made it more of a statement than a question.

"Not for love nor money," Mildred agreed, sipping, and then pulling away in horror from Dooley's awful brew. "What in the Lord's name *is* this?"

"Coffee." He grinned. "Sort of. You got to acquire a taste for it. My deputy, or—well, assistant makes it. Awful stuff until you get used to it, ain't it?" *Isn't* it, he irritably corrected himself.

"That's the Lord's truth," she said, setting the cup down on his desk. "You know, Sheriff, Imogene seems to think a lot of you. I'd say she's sweet on you if I thought it was proper."

Ezra turned red. This was totally shocking. After sitting with her every day for so long, he had come to regard her as a good friend, a good, good friend, but nothing more. She was with his thoughts, however, all the time, and while he was aware of how important to him she had become, he was unable to admit to the feelings that Mildred's statement stirred up. The old feelings of guilt came back. "Hell . . . uh, I mean, shoot, ma'am," he stammered, "I ain't done nothing to encourage that." He began to see himself as the greatest old fool any country town had ever produced. There was an awkward silence. "She seems to think *you're* about the nearest thing to heaven there is," he offered, scrambling mentally for a way to change the subject. "She was on her way to see you when . . ." He faltered.

"When Cora run off," Mildred finished for him. "That's what she did. There's no point denying it. She just flat run off."

Ezra sat straight up in his chair. The country boy accent disappeared. "Do you know where she is?"

"Me? Of course not," Mildred said. "But it's plain as day. My lands, a blind man could see it. She just run off. She never was any good. Too much money, too pretty. Too much like her daddy. I shouldn't be surprised to find out that she's been holed up in Atlanta all this time, probably living high on the hog while her poor old mama sits out there and soaks up the heat and Lord knows what."

"I don't think she's in Atlanta," Ezra said, pulling his pipe out of an ashtray. He began to work the tobacco in the bowl. In point of fact, he knew she wasn't in Atlanta. He had worried the police of that city to death trying to track her down. He'd gotten them to send a police report to him every week and distribute Cora's picture to all officers in Georgia and other major cities from Miami to Houston. If she was in Atlanta or anywhere in between, she was well hidden, and if McBride knew it, he was the biggest liar since Simon Peter denied Christ. He had talked to Imogene's husband five times since the first call, and each time he became more convinced that McBride not only did not know where Cora was, but also didn't very much care.

That didn't go with what Imogene had told him about how close Cora and her father had been. But Ezra had had one of the officers in Atlanta check that out too, and from Cora's friends they had learned that she was slightly fearful of Harvey McBride, and she knew he had other women and drank too much.

"I assume you've checked out her friends and such— Cora's, I mean," Mildred said.

"Oh, yes," Ezra answered dully, noticing the white ring of skin on Mildred's hand where a wedding band should have been. "None of them have heard from her. There was one boyfriend, a special one, Joe Don something, but he's married now to someone else. Got married last month, in fact. Apparently a shotgun affair." He wondered why he was telling her all this.

"Oh, Lordy!" Mildred breathed out heavily and began to pull her bulk out of the wooden office chair. "What are these young people coming to?"

"Are you, uh, married, Mrs.—"

"Fletcher, Mrs. George Alan Fletcher," she finished for him, then noticed her empty ring finger. "Oh! I see. Mr. Fletcher went to his reward three years ago. He was killed in an industrial accident. The ring just wore off. Just plumb wore down to nothing and fell off. I keep it in my medicine chest at home, what's left of it."

"I'm sorry." Ezra rose.

"Oh, no bother," she said, laughing. "Silly thing never fit anyway. Oh, I see! You mean about Mr. Fletcher. That's no bother either. I put my faith in God, Sheriff. He is the Truth and the Way!" She started toward the door.

"I suppose I'll go down and have one more try at moving Imogene." She sighed. "Lordy, I do wish she'd get on that six o'clock train with me. You know, I had to find out about what happened to her and Cora from the newspapers. She never wrote or called me. What do you think about that?"

Ezra shook his head and applied a match to his pipe bowl, frowning when he realized there was no live tobacco left inside. "I guess I knew she didn't." He frowned. "She hasn't used a telephone, to my knowledge, since she came here. I guess I should have called you, but to tell you the truth, I didn't know your name."

She raised her hand as if to say "never mind," and started out the door. Suddenly she turned and put a hand on a massive hip. "Sheriff, what do you think happened to Cora? Really?"

"I honestly don't know," Ezra replied.

"Lordy, children can be such a burden," she said, and she turned and moved down the hall.

"So can their mothers," Ezra said in a whisper as she disappeared. "So can their mothers."

E I G H T

Sheriff Ezra Stone Holmes had come to a point where he dreaded going to bed at night. After preparing his evening meal or late snack, undressing, and getting into bed, he would try to lie awake, stare at the ceiling of his bedroom, and will himself not to fall asleep. He knew that once he did drift off, the dreams would begin.

At times, of course, he was too tired to resist. And when he did sleep, his dreams would float around him like great birds of prey, waiting for his weaknesses to show so they could swoop down and make his rest unbearable. Imogene, Cora, Hilda, and now even Mildred paid him nocturnal visits, often standing around his bed and talking to each other about the misery of poor Mrs. McBride, or the shameless behavior of the Sandhill County sheriff. They talked about other things, of course, but he couldn't always remember what, and usually, upon awakening and finding himself bathed with sweat and his heart racing, he didn't try.

In almost every dream, however, he remembered the clarity with which he saw Imogene's face or Mildred's, or even Hilda's, but oddly, he never could catch a glimpse of Cora's countenance. Always a spill of blond hair covered her eyes and features, always she turned from his dream's eyesight just as he was about to fix on her face, and always she appeared in black and white, even when the rest of the figures were in bright colors.

One source of relief, however, was that no more "clues" appeared in the dreams, no more half-seen recollections to come bursting out at him the way the keys had in some sort of accusatory way, blaming him for not noticing things that pertained to his job.

Another source of comfort was that he had done no more sleepwalking, at least none he was aware of, and that one horrible dream of kitchen coffee and bright lights had not come back at all. But it wasn't entirely gone, entirely stored, either. While he could keep it away from his conscious mind, his subconscious retrieved it freely when he was sleeping, and while he never actually experienced it again, in his dream state he often recalled it, took it out and turned it over, examined it for unnoticed details and uncatalogued emotions.

Once or twice he actually dreamed he was dreaming it, if—he qualified to himself—that made sense. He would wake up after such a dream and almost rush to the kitchen to see if the coffee was poured, if the door was open, but it never was. Still, it was a disturbing experience, this dream within a dream, for he found that he often would go farther than he had when it was merely a sleepwalking nightmare. Sometimes he would go all the way to the end of the sidewalk, and then he would awaken himself with a cry of terror at what he saw lying there, but he never could recall what it was when he awoke, and something told him to be glad he couldn't.

But that sort of dream, the dream within a dream, was more rare than the simpler visions he had almost every night. In some of them he played an active role, and the women would talk to him; in others he was merely an observer. Some, he recalled, were vividly bright; others were shadowed. Men sometimes came into his mind's eye as well. Harvey McBride made more than one appearance, although Ezra had no idea what the man looked like. Even so, the sheriff preferred to believe his dream phantom was fairly close to the genuine article. The burly, pushy, intolerant man of his dreams always seemed to appear in a casually angry way, and Ezra soon came subconsciously to accept the fact that Imogene's leaving him had been her only alternative for survival.

The other man who often came into his dreams was Pete. And this had a far more disturbing effect on the sheriff's mind. This particular dream ghost was usually in his drugstore, behind his soda fountain or his prescription counter, dressed in his usual stained smock and sporting his usual three-day-beard—*had* Pete shaved on the day Cora disappeared? The question rattled around in Ezra's dreams, but he couldn't remember well enough to answer it for sure—still, there had been a razor in the sink, and the soap—grinning and nattering on as Pete usually did about fishing or the weather or somebody's particular brand of illness for which the only hope was the medicine that Pete himself would brew up. But flitting around behind him would be a swash of blond hair, not quite visible, but always blocked by the stained smock or the Chesterfield smoke that was almost always coming out of Pete's nostrils as if a fire smoldered inside him.

After such dreams Ezra would awaken, sweating in spite of the droning fan in his bedroom, with dawn still hours away and the night hovering over him like a knowledgeable part of the horror that refused to emerge into the open and be seen. His habit, then, was to rise quickly, dress in the clothes he had taken off a few hours before, and drive around, although he carefully avoided the downtown streets for fear of spying Imogene's ghostly figure perched as it always was, he knew, on the courthouse lawn's bench, staring, if she wasn't sleeping, at Pete's Sundries and Drugs' darkened front, waiting for her errant daughter to emerge like Lazarus coming forth from the grave.

He would check the gas stations and restaurants out on the highway, drive through the trailer park on the edge of town, and usually he would wind up on top of Mary and Buddy's carport, smoking and waiting for the sky to lighten so he could go home and eat and change to go to work. Never, he often thought, had Agatite had such efficient police protection. But in all his wanderings he never found a prowler or a crime being committed or cause to talk to anyone.

On the last day of August he found himself seated in the canvas chair in the predawn hours once again. The dreams had become more vivid than ever after the horrible recollection during the thunderstorm, and he found that he was speculating through them now, wondering what had indeed become of Cora McBride, and conjuring up images of young girls—not Cora, not usually—murdered and destroyed by monstrous killers.

He knew why he was dreaming about such things all of a sudden, and it wasn't the conversation about his having children. A truck's headlights broke the horizon in the west and began to grow as they were joined by a whine from the engine bringing its load through the small town. During the past several weeks since Mildred's visit he had immersed himself in case study after case study of missing persons, especially girls, especially teenage girls. Ranging back to the Lindbergh kidnapping, he had ordered official documents and case reports, written off for police journals and criminal records to try to find out if there was something else he might yet do. He should have tried to obtain a set of Cora's fingerprints, he admonished himself. He should have gotten right down to it, lifted them off something that had belonged exclusively to her, that only she had touched. But he hadn't thought of it in time. Now the luggage, the trunks, almost everything Imogene owned was gone, sold to finance this continuing absurdity of waiting for Cora to come back. Besides, he thought, he hadn't had—and didn't have—the equipment or the knowhow to take what he had read were called "latent prints" for comparison to police records elsewhere. He wasn't that kind of lawman, and his pride wouldn't let him ask for help from the Highway Patrol or Texas Rangers or especially from that prissy, disbelieving FBI man who had snubbed him so. But fingerprints or no fingerprints, he felt compelled to continue investigating as best he could. He was pretty much convinced that the girl was either dead or hiding—on-purpose hiding—but figuring that the former was yet a possibility, he did what research he knew how to do.

Sitting in his office under a dark gray cloud of tobacco smoke, he had carefully read each document, scanning them for similarities in particulars, but there was little help there.

The more celebrated cases were all special in some way. Killers whose motives were obscure marched across the pages of the reports and journals like a parade of

122

monstrous perversions. Most of the cases that were not out-and-out kidnappings for ransom—these he put aside as there was no indication that Cora had been kidnapped—involved sex crimes of some sort. The journals and reports were jam-packed with details that were too delicate to make the press coverage, not even the *Police Gazette*, which seemed to thrive on gore and mayhem. And the photographs were fairly standard police fare, revealing of the violence that accompanied death, but not explaining the central question of why it had happened in the first place.

For the most part the killers had been caught and tried and either put to death or jailed for life, and when they weren't, the reports indicated that some unfortunate individual who was killed in an apprehension attempt was likely the perpetrator they sought. But occasionally, and distressingly, the killer or abductor was not caught, and the missing girls were sometimes never found, and these intrigued and worried Ezra the most.

In the distance the whistle of the 5:15 westbound freight caught his ear just as the truck he had been watching roared by on the highway beneath him. Other lights broke the horizon now, and soon the gray light that was beginning in the east would cover the sky. It was a familiar ritual, and a comforting one, he thought as he relit his pipe, noting that it tasted like cow chips rather than tobacco.

He let it go out and allowed his thoughts to wander a bit more.

Usually the other cases, when they were solved, revealed something wrong with the killer or kidnapper, not with the victim, but Ezra's mind clung to the idea that Cora had had some sort of sinister hand in her own disappearance. It was too neat, and it was too fast. She had to cooperate in order to get away, he reasoned, and so

123

. . . and so . . . and so did Pete. It was hard to figure that, and he put the thought away.

Oddly none of the cases was exactly similar to this one at all. The children were either younger or involved with some sort of shady business if they were older; or it was an out-and-out abduction and part of a series of such crimes perpetrated by the same person. And after days of studying the grisly accounts of hacked-up bodies, sexually abused children, and death cults that seemed to crop up in California for some reason, Ezra found himself unable to continue to delve into the macabre details of human perversion.

But it was not in the police reports and journals that he found something to stimulate his thoughts in another direction, away from the idea that there was a monstrous killer stalking his town ready to snatch away pretty young girls from ice cream counters, but in the Fort Worth *Star Telegram*'s Sunday edition instead.

It was a small item, really, just two columns and a picture, but the reporter told a story that was so like Imogene's that it moved Ezra in a new way.

The story was set in Guthrie, Oklahoma, a water stop for passing trains, where twenty years before a woman and her daughter on their way to visit relatives in Sacramento had disembarked onto the station platform to stretch their legs while the locomotive took on water. With a nickel in her hand, the ten-year-old girl had left her mother and gone inside the depot seeking some treat or other, but she never came out. The woman frantically sought her and finally browbeat the local sheriff into starting a manhunt, but he found nothing. After six months and apparently when all her money had gone, the woman, whose name was Tillman, reboarded a passing train and returned home.

Twenty years later she returned to the town, and the local newspaper reporter wrote the story which the *Star*

Telegram picked up from the wire. She came back on a sentimental journey, of sorts, she said, with no real hope of finding a trace of her long-lost daughter but with a desire to see one more time where she had disappeared. She had never heard from her, and the girl had never turned up dead or alive. She simply vanished. The people of Guthrie turned out and gave her a welcome that was, Ezra thought, more like a homecoming celebration than a memorial, and the picture the paper ran with the story showed an elderly woman standing and looking a bit forelorn on the old railroad platform, pointing to the depot's door where she last saw her little girl. Inset into the photograph was a circle containing a portrait of the frowzy-haired ten-year-old looking happy and bright for the camera.

The story included an account of the efforts the woman and her family had made to find the little girl, the private detectives she had hired, the money she had fruitlessly spent. She attributed her failing health and her husband's early death to the girl's sudden disappearance as well. But the girl never turned up, and she apparently never would, and the story ended with Mrs. Tillman boarding yet another train to return to her empty house in South Carolina.

There were remarkable similarities in the two cases, Ezra noted, grinningly squinting into the brightening east. She just disappeared with a nickel in her hand, and no amount of searching turned her up. The mother had spent a good deal of time and money trying to find her, but had failed. And the girl was still missing, gone for good. But there were differences too. Other people had seen the girl, the train conductor, for one; and the woman had a ticket in the child's name, a sleeping berth, and that photograph, which, the story said, had been taken at a studio in Memphis during the trip.

But the main difference, of course, was that the mother

had finally seen the reality of the situation and packed up and left for home. Her money ran out, her patience, her hope, and she went home. Imogene isn't going to leave, he continued to himself.

He stood and stretched, feeling his bad knee protest from the unnecessary exertion. It needed heat, he thought, and he should stay home in bed with a hot-water bottle or heating pad on it, but he couldn't, not anymore. Home was where the dreams were, and he hated being there even when he was awake. He'd rather hurt.

Imogene wouldn't leave because she had no place to go. Oregon had been a foolish plan in the first place. Imogene was sophisticated, worldly, a lady. Mildred was crude, ignorant, superstitious, and the two of them would be like oil and vinegar together. She couldn't go back to Harvey—she had effectively and efficiently burned that bridge—and there was no place else for her. Her parents, she had told him, were dead, and aside from Mildred, there were no other relatives. He shook his head. She had no money, no future, nothing but the hope that Cora would somehow miraculously appear and things will return to the way they were. But, he knew, they wouldn't, they couldn't, not even if Cora did turn up and was ready to go on. There was no place to go, only the goddamn bench and the hope the nightmare would end.

Ezra went over and leaned against the steel rail that ran around the carport's rooftop. He needed to sleep, he needed to sleep without dreaming. He was nearly exhausted. He thought of asking Pete or even Doc Pritchard to give him something to help him, but he didn't dare. Dooley wasn't capable of handling stuff that might come up, when it came up, which might not be often. But if something did happen—fire, disaster of some kind, bona fide crime of any kind—he needed to be alert and available. Sleeping pills wouldn't do for a sheriff.

He realized with an uncomfortable grunt that his feelings for Imogene were growing stronger every day, and the realization disturbed him more than the dreams did. There was a feeling buried down deep that he couldn't really identify. It came to the surface when he was near her, and it came when he dreamed about her. It bothered him, nagged at his mind, and made him wish he could do something to help her.

In one dream he suddenly and shockingly recalled as if for the first time, although he knew he had remembered it before, he had taken her in his arms. She was crying hysterically the way she had done after he had questioned her about Cora's morality, but this time she was admitting that her daughter was a tramp, and he held her tightly to comfort her. He was patting her back and smelling her hair and telling her it was all right. He remembered the phantom looking up at him, replacing the piercing hatred in her gray eyes with a tenderness that melted his heart and made him vulnerable and weak.

In the dream he had wanted to kiss her, he remembered, and he was about to when he woke up. And he had an erection. It was a rare thing for him, and he acknowledged the sinful nature of his subconscious thoughts, the betrayal of Hilda, and the shame he felt. It made him shake all over, and for the first time since Hilda died, he wanted to cry. But he didn't. He stored the dream next to the others in the back of his mind, and he wondered how long it would be before the storage compartment there would be as crowded and disordered as Pete's back room. And, he thought with a reluctant speculation, how long would it be before the cluttered seeds of memory would cover suspicious and secret evidence of something terribly, terribly wrong?

He moved over to the trapdoor and metal stairs and stopped before descending. The highway was now alive with early morning traffic, carrying farmers and workers to their various assignments in the county. A truckload of Negro field hands creaked by, and several of the field hands grinned and waved as they recognized the sheriff high atop the carport looking down on the open bed of the ancient half-ton truck.

His mental hand went back to the storage area of his mind as his physical hand raised to return the Negroes' greetings. The mental fingers poked and prodded the stored contents of his mind to make sure none was stirring. Then he went down the stairs.

"Mornin', Ezra," Mary said, sweeping as she always was when Ezra made his descent. "Gonna be another scorcher."

"I reckon so," Ezra agreed, stopping for a moment to silently remark on the girl's gentle beauty that was complemented by the fresh air of early morning. The straps of a bathing suit were clearly visible beneath her blouse, and he figured she would spend at least a part of today up on the carport roof taking sun. "Where's Buddy?"

"Still asleep," she replied. "We didn't fill up till after midnight, an' he was pretty beat." She stopped sweeping and looked at him. "You want some coffee? You look tired."

He started to shake his head but realized that every morning for the past several months that he had found his way to the carport roof she had offered him coffee and he had turned it down. It wasn't polite. "Sure," he said, "I could use a cup." He limped into the office behind her, and she leaned her broom against the counter and poured two mugs full of the black liquid. It was good coffee, Ezra noted as he sipped it.

"Truckers like it hot and strong." Mary smiled over her own mug. "I guess I've gotten to like it that way too."

Ezra nodded to indicate that it pleased him and glanced out onto the highway, where traffic seemed awfully heavy for a small town. "Dooley's coffee is about like crude oil," he finally said.

They stood silently for a while, but it wasn't an awkward silence. Although they weren't close, they had the common knowledge of each other that small-town people acquire over time. There is the need for privacy, for solitude, for minding one's own business. So when Mary broke the silence after a few minutes, it was a difficult thing for her to do.

"Ezra?" she said. "What's wrong with you?"

"What?" He was startled and put off balance by the intensity of her voice.

"I don't want to pry into your business, but I think a friend ought to ask. What's wrong with you? You've been comin' out here every night for the whole summer, and that's not like you."

"I don't mean to bother you." He felt himself redden under the gaze of this pretty young girl who was talking to him as if they had known each other for decades.

"You don't *bother* me," she snapped, almost angrily, "You know you're welcome here, day or night, rain or shine." She softened a bit. "Tell you the truth, we sleep better knowin' you're up there." Her eyes shot up toward the carport roof. "But that don't mean you should be, and it don't explain why you're up there at all. What's wrong?"

"I've been having trouble sleeping," Ezra admitted, hoping the confession would put an end to her questions.

"It's that crazy woman, ain't it?" Mary flashed her eyes at him to see if her question struck home. "She's got you all torn up, hasn't she?"

129

"She's not crazy," Ezra said, too quickly, he thought. "She's upset and frustrated, and maybe she's gone a little bit off because of what happened, but she's not crazy."

"You ask me, she's crazy," Mary declared with certainty, but Ezra didn't respond, and they fell into silence once again.

"Ezra," she said slowly and softly, "you ever think about gettin' married again?" She studied him with her deep blue eyes over her coffee mug.

Ezra was positively shocked by the question, but he fought with himself to control any reaction. "Me? Naw. Hilda's—"

"Been gone a long time," Mary said quickly and folded her arms under her breasts, waiting defiantly for his next argument.

"That's right," he agreed. "And I'm an old man. I'll be retiring soon, and I have no intention . . ." He trailed off.

"You're a good-lookin' man, Ezra Stone Holmes," Mary said suddenly, "and if I was ten years older and Buddy wasn't around, I'd make a play for you myself." Ezra blushed deeply and set his coffee mug down. "It's none of my business," she continued. "I know that. And I don't want to stir up any grief. . . ." Ezra's mind conjured the mound over Hilda's grave, and it began to stir, just a bit. "But I think you need to put that crazy wo—" She caught herself. "—that woman on the courthouse bench out of your mind. There's nothin' you or anybody else can do to change what happened. And that girl, if there was a girl, is gone. That's that."

"I suspect you're right," Ezra said, as if he were turning over what she had said, as if he were hearing it for the first time, as if the idea had never occurred to him before. He wanted to get out of the motor court's office and go home, and he wanted this conversation to end.

"So why don't you come over to the church this Sunday night? We're havin' a covered-dish supper, an' you can socialize a bit. It'll do you good, and maybe you'll meet somebody. . . ." She trailed off, teasingly twirling a strand of her dark hair in one long pretty finger. But behind her sparkling eyes he could see her plotting and planning.

"Look, Mary," he said, "I might marry again. Who knows? But I'm too old to go on the prowl, especially among the grass widows and old maids over to the First Baptist Church." He saw the light dim in her scheming eyes. "I'll do what I got to do in my own time."

"In other words, mind my own business?" she said, smiling at him.

"In a manner of speaking, yes." He returned her smile to show there were no hard feelings as a result of her prying.

At that moment a trucker came through the door.

"Goddamn it!" he said. "I left a wake-up call for six, an' here it is damn near six-thirty, an' you standin' here jawing with this old foo—" He stopped, and his jaw dropped open when he saw the sheriff's badge on Ezra's chest. "Oh," he said sheepishly. "Mornin', Sheriff."

"Mornin'," Ezra returned the greeting. He was more amused than he showed in his gruff manner. "Think you could watch your language around here?"

"Yessir," the burly man replied, "Guess I'm not awake yet. Ain't had my coffee."

"It's over there." Ezra nodded toward the coffeepot on a small table, and Mary moved around behind the counter to the register to start preparing the trucker's bill.

"Thanks for the coffee." Ezra replaced the mug and started out the office door.

"No problem." Mary smiled from behind the counter. "Come back any time." Ezra started through the door. "I mean *any* time," she said, and her eyes looked upward toward the carport roof.

"Sure thing," he said, and he promised himself to

make sure he was gone on future mornings before she came out to sweep. He went out to his car and got inside.

That morning, instead of going home and changing clothes and making his breakfast, Ezra did something he had almost never done except on preplanned occasions. He drove out to the Sandhill County Memorial Cemetery and sat for more than an hour by Hilda Holmes' grave. He sat and stared and allowed the memory seeds to burst open and their stored recollections to swarm around him like a crowd of angry gnats. But however much he wanted to, he would not let himself cry.

N I N E

In late September Imogene's money was all but gone. She had cut back to one meal a day, and that was often nothing more than a bowl of soup or maybe a leftover dinner salad from the Town and Country Restaurant. Her clothes were wearing out, and her shoes were running down at the heels from her quick walks up and down Main Street every afternoon. She had quit buying cigarettes, and her one remaining coat had become threadbare, missing large patches of fur from having been wadded up and used as a pillow all summer.

Her hair was no longer curled and soft, but now she pulled it back in a severe ponytail, stretching taut the dry, tanned skin of her forehead. Her gray eyes wore a haunted look much of the time, and they flicked up and down the street between long glaring stares at Pete's Sundries and Drugs. People were so used to seeing her on the bench—*her* bench, everyone now called it without thinking about it—that they spoke or waved as they passed by, and she usually waved back, smiled briefly, and then returned to her vigil.

A couple of private detectives from Dallas and Atlanta came to town and bothered her for a couple of days, trying to get her to guarantee a large fee if they could find and return Cora. They hinted that they knew where she was, but Imogene wasn't fooled by them, and they left, one after Ezra had given him a talking-to. None came to take their places. Most had read the newspaper and magazine stories and knew that she had little or no money, and Ezra figured that McBride was getting more of this sort of thing than Imogene was; at least he hoped so.

She was also spared many visits by spiritualists, seers, mystics, and other quacks and loonies who usually were drawn to such a phenomenon as Imogene had become. A few had arrived, however; some claimed they only came to pray or offer to share a vision they had had of Cora from "the other side," but Imogene patiently exasperated them by asking them to identify the ring Cora had worn on the day she disappeared. They would guess diamond, sapphire, ruby, even plain gold or silver, but Imogene would just shake her head and dismiss them with a flick of her hand and a kind of braying noise she made with her lips.

One morning Ezra looked out his window and noticed a group of people setting up a tent and waving some large snakes as they chanted and danced around Imogene's seated figure. He ran out shouting and brandishing a nightstick. Finally they left, but he had been forced to help a couple of them up into the back of their war surplus truck with the toe of his boot. He limped back to where Imogene sat, feeling the ache in his knee and huffing and wheezing from the exertion.

"Lord!" he said, catching his breath and flopping down on her bench beside her. "Why don't you just give me a shout when these nuts show up? Why put yourself through this?"

She caught at her bosom and tried to regain her breath, and he realized that she had been genuinely frightened by the snakes and the wild-eyed holy rollers, but then she surprised him by laughing out loud. "Oh, Sheriff," she gasped between chuckles, "I really don't mind all this nonsense. *This* group was particularly bad, but normally I kind of enjoy seeing them. They entertain me. There isn't much for me to do, you know."

He almost asked her why she didn't see how foolish and insane the whole thing was, why she didn't just get on the westbound train and go on out to Mildred's. He would loan her the money, he knew. Hell, he thought, he'd give it to her if she would just give up and go. But he knew what she would answer, and he really didn't want to spoil her good mood. "Tell me something," he asked. "What kind of ring *was* it Cora was wearing?" He couldn't recall seeing a ring in any of his dreams, and the question intrigued him.

"Why, Sheriff," she said, feigning shock, "don't tell me *you've* had a vision!"

"No." He wanted desperately to reveal what he had been having almost every night since she came to town, but he didn't have the courage. "I just wondered, that's all."

Her eyes narrowed into sly slits, and she glanced quickly around to see if anyone was in earshot, then whispered as she leaned close to Ezra's ear, "She didn't have on any ring. She was allergic to gold and silver. They made her break out. She didn't own any jewelry."

They had a good laugh over that.

T E N

During the first week of October Imogene put an ad in the paper to sell her rosary. At first there were only lookers, curiosity seekers who were more interested in seeing her close up than in buying something from her. Since there were few Catholics in Agatite, and even fewer with the cash to buy a jeweled rosary, she didn't have much luck at any price. Finally a jeweler from Wichita Falls got wind of it, and he came over and paid her well for it. She wouldn't tell Ezra how much she had gotten, but she said it was a good price and would keep her going a while longer.

Ezra didn't know much about Catholics, but he didn't think he'd ever seen her pray using the beaded rosary or any other. She'd bowed her head when the preachers came by, but he noticed, once when the First Christian minister came over, that she kept her eyes open. He finally worked up the nerve to ask her about it.

"I prayed for the first forty days," she replied. "One of the men who came here was the Catholic vicar. You know, they only have mass here twice a month? Anyway, he heard my confession, blessed me, and came back a week later and gave me communion. Then I stopped praying. I won't pray again until I see Cora."

Sadness filled Ezra and almost overcame him before he turned it, without realizing it, into a genuine affection for her. He took a chance and asked her to call him Ezra, and he was pleased when she not only agreed but asked him to call her Imma, a name, she told him, Harvey hated. They spent more and more time together on her bench, Ezra recounting adventures of his life, reluctantly displaying his partial ear where a holdup man's bullet had wounded him over a decade before, and telling her more and more about himself and his feelings.

She looked over fifty now, although she had been in Agatite only six months. Her hair had lines of gray in it, and her skin had become tough and hard from the harsh southwestern elements that crossed the courthouse square in an endless parade of climatic changes. Her nails, once lacquered and long and beautiful, were now cut short and had cracks in them, and he could see the bones of her shoulders where they stretched against the dry, wrinkled skin. She wore no perfume, but she took care to bathe regularly, and the fresh smell of soap was always about her. Ezra thought of Hilda more and more, and his dreams became more and more bearable as he grew closer to Imogene. Whatever there was sinister and dangerous about her seemed to melt away as summer reluctantly changed to fall and her vigil continued.

The big problem, he knew as he sat beside her and luxuriated in the warmth of her charm and attention, was not that he truly liked her. He unconsciously slipped an arm along the back of the bench and pulled his ankle over his good knee and felt more relaxed than he had in years. She seemed not to notice, and at first he didn't either. He felt at home here, on the bench, peaceful and content. Suddenly he realized what he was doing and sat upright, pulling his arm back and folding it in his lap, sheepishly glancing out of the corner of his eye to see if she noticed his awkward recovery. But she paid it no mind and continued to watch the traffic moving past Pete's Sundries and Drugs across the street.

What if anyone saw? Ezra wondered almost aloud, and he let his eyes roam around the courthouse square to see if anyone was staring. Probably, but what did it matter? Tongues were bound to carry tales even when things didn't happen. He could always deny it, but why? What difference did it really make? He liked her, he knew, and on this one morning, anyhow, that wasn't the real problem.

He studied her, and again she seemed to pay him no notice. She seemed to be as comfortable as he was to share the bench. It was more than that he truly liked her, he realized; it was that he was growing more than a little fond of her. But the big problem, he said to her with his thoughts, wishing she could hear them and that she would turn to him and show that she understood, the big problem, Imogene McBride, is how to tell you, to utterly convince you that Cora is never coming back.

PART

3

For the terrible one is brought to
nought, and the scorner is consumed,
and all that watch for iniquity are cut off.

—Isaiah 29:20

O N E

In the middle of the month Mayor Samuel F. Perkins summoned Ezra to a special meeting of the city council. Ezra was, at first, delighted, hoping that the mayor was finally going to respond to his long-standing request for a new sheriff's car, but his anticipation evaporated when Perkins opened the meeting by insisting that Ezra arrest Imogene McBride.

"On what charge?" Ezra asked.

"Charge?" Perkins yelled at him, his cheeks flaming bright red as they always did when he was agitated. "Creating a public nuisance. Vagrancy. I don't care." He looked around the table at the other city fathers, who were vaguely embarrassed to hear someone talk to Ezra in such a tone. "It's a goddamn disgrace! That woman sits out there day after day, week after week. Jesus H. Christ, Ezra! It's your job to keep those benches clear for public use!"

"Oh, hell," Ezra grumbled back at the fuming mayor, not showing the consternation he was feeling. "She's not half the nuisance your damn kid is, running around in that hot rod you bought him with a belly full of Oklahoma beer and tearing up people's lawns and scaring folks half to death." Perkins winced. He knew that more than once Ezra had called him to come pick up Tommy rather than jail him. "She's not vagrant," Ezra continued, "since she's paying her own freight, and she's a sight better-looking than that silly Civil War statue with one arm missing and bird shit all over him on the other side. You want to get rid of a disgrace, there you are."

Perkins opened his mouth, but Ezra pointed his pipe at him and cut him off. "And those benches are there for folks to sit on, and as far as I can see, that's all she's doing. She ain't costing nobody nothing. She ain't hurting nobody. If you want her arrested, you can by God go arrest her yourself and quit telling me how to do my goddamn job!" He stood and started to walk out of the meeting. He felt himself flush.

"Ezra," Perkins called to him in a mock teasing tone, stopping the sheriff at the office door, "this *is* an election year."

"Yeah," Ezra said, turning and lighting his pipe slowly, "and I hear that kid over to the Ford dealership's going to give you a run for your money. But I'm too old to worry about that." And he left. That was all he heard from the city council about Imogene McBride.

T W O

That same day, or, really, the next morning, after the city council meeting, events took a turn that temporarily removed everyone's mind from the crazy woman on the bench in front of the courthouse. The news came to Ezra while he was sitting again on top of the carport at the Holiday Motor Courts.

The early morning October wind was out of the north, and while it was by no means cold or even cool, it hinted at things to come in the harsh winter that Ezra and everyone else in the region expected after such a hot, dry summer. There was a ragged, cutting edge to it, like an old razor blade that has been used once too often. He shuddered to think of the first norther blowing in off the cap rock, and his thoughts shifted to Imogene and how she would make out when the really bad weather arrived.

His mind was with her and lost in that night's dreams when he heard the radio in his car crackle and Dooley's voice calling him. Quickly he rose from the canvas chair and pocketed his pipe with a quirk of regret. It had been the first enjoyable smoke he had had for months, it seemed, and it had almost convinced him not to give up the habit, something he had been contemplating.

He half stumbled down the metal stairs, and finally he reached the car's window and snatched the mike from the radio mount.

"Yeah," he barked. "What is it?"

"Cattle thieves! Buster Swinson called an' said they was at it, *right now!*" Dooley's voice was excited in spite of the lateness of the hour. Ezra checked his watch and noted it was 4:28. Early in the morning for cattle thieves, he thought, but almost perfect for a small town where there was only one sheriff. Of course, he mused, who would suspect a sheriff would spend half his night wide-awake?

"Where are they?" Ezra asked.

"Buster said he was calling from the phone booth at Neeley's Gas Station," Dooley went on. "Said he'd meet us at the old barn near his yards."

"Which yards?" Ezra patiently inquired. Sometimes he wondered if keeping Dooley wasn't more trouble than he was worth. He was only about half there, the sheriff thought, and loyalty can't count for much in a situation like this.

"North End Yards," Dooley replied. "Said you'd know the barn. It's the one where Barney Hitchcock hung hisself." Ezra nodded over the mike. He remembered the barn. The stockyards and slaughterhouse were adjacent, but the barn was well behind them in a grove of elm trees. "You want me to meet you there, or you gonna come by here an' pick me up?"

"You wait at the office," Ezra ordered. "I got Buster

141

out there, and I can deputize him if I have to. You stay by the radio in case this turns into something we can't handle and you have to call for help." Ezra clicked off the mike and tossed it into the front seat before Dooley could argue with him. Dooley would give his eyeteeth to be there, Ezra knew, but he would only get in the way. He meant well, but having a man who was more than a brick or two shy of a full load was too dangerous, especially if this turned into a shooting problem.

The sheriff moved around to the trunk of the old Dodge and opened it. He took out a 20-gauge shotgun and broke it open, checked it, then reached into a box in the corner of the trunk and took out two slugs and filed them into the twin chambers. A scatter-gun load at night, he reminded himself, was too uncertain. And—he smiled grimly—if I wind up hurting one of Buster's animals, there'll be hell to pay. He had no intention of firing the weapon at all, but if he did, he wanted to be sure to stop what he hit, and a slug was the best load for that.

He slammed down the trunk, returned to the side of the car, and carefully placed the shotgun on the front seat. He got in and steered the car toward the North End Yards to meet Buster.

Buster was a self-made man who had fought his way up from ranch hand to owner and developer of one of the biggest cattle businesses in six counties and beyond. He not only raised his own beef; he also slaughtered it, shipped it on his own trucks, and made a fortune every month, if one could believe him. He ran three separate stockyards in the county, a rendering plant, and he was putting in a large poultry plant as well. A good many businesses in Agatite found his name on a percentage of their net worth, and he sat on the bank's board of directors and the school board as well.

Ezra had never liked him. He suspected that Buster had pulled off more than one shady deal, and he found it difficult to trust the giant, gruff, irritating man who perpetually wore faded work shirts and jeans even though he could well afford custom-made suits. He also owned and drove a variety of worn-out vehicles, never buying new cars or trucks except for his business, and he continued to live in a broken-down old farmhouse on the edge of town next to his South End Yards, a place that was continually bathed in the dusty, stinking refuse of his primary source of income.

Buster was unmarried, abrasive, impulsive. He had few real friends, but he had the respect of most of the community since he had long ago proved himself to be a good businessman and a shrewd haggler. Ezra had never found anything in the man to admire, but he had no reason to suspect him of being anything other than what he was, either, so they regarded each other with a mutual understanding based on respect and wariness.

About a month before, Buster had come into Ezra's office to complain that somebody was rustling cattle right out of his yards. He claimed that more than twenty head were missing, and it seemed that they were taken all at once.

Ezra went out and looked things over, and he studied the paperwork Buster thrust under the sheriff's nose to show that the counts were off. But there was no hard evidence at all. The books clearly showed that cattle were missing, but there was no sign of how it might have happened.

Since roads or a highway bordered all three of Buster's stockyards, he had had great ditches dug all the way around them. Ten feet deep and twelve to fifteen feet wide in some places, they made access to the yards possible only by way of heavy steel gates, which, of course, were locked up tight at night. No cow could cross one of those gorges, and few men were willing to lug cattle through the briers, tumbleweeds, and other debris collected in the bottoms of the great trenches.

Ezra suspected that Buster was up to something, and he didn't look real hard at the paperwork. He figured the old rancher was probably stealing his own cattle, butchering them, then claiming the loss on his insurance. It was an easy way to make a buck, and since one butchered cow looks like any other, it was almost impossible to trace. Only Buster and one or two chosen employees need ever know.

But when Ezra had suggested that it might be an inside job, Buster had flown into a rage. So the sheriff went out and had another look around, but he didn't find anything.

He finally told Buster that without more to go on, he couldn't do very much. He toured the yards on his nocturnal drives after dreams drove him from his bed, and he inspected them during the day whenever the chance came up, but nothing seemed amiss. Still, by the time Ezra steered his Dodge into the driveway leading up to the old barn, Buster was out almost two hundred head, and he had become a regular feature of Ezra's afternoons, fuming and storming about the loss of assets and the value of beef on the hoof.

Overall, the sheriff felt a little guilty about the whole thing. If Buster had really caught somebody making off with livestock, it was a clear sign that Ezra hadn't been doing his job. He should have been spending sleepless nights sitting out here and waiting for potential thieves to show up, not woolgathering on top of a carport. He swore silently. It's Imogene, he realized. She's in my head and she's interfering with my life—and my job! Goddamn it, he swore at himself. More than forty years a lawman, and suddenly you can't even cope with a little cattle rustling. Forty years shot because of some crazy old woman and her little lost lamb.

His headlights picked out Buster in the old barn's door, and Ezra immediately killed the lights and parked the Dodge off to one side. Across the road behind him the North Side Yards stood black against the sky, and Ezra could hear the low noises made by livestock moving around in the pens and smell the sweet manure fragrance wafting in the night air.

"About time you got here," Buster growled in a low whisper. "Why didn't you just go ahead an' use your siren to let them know you was comin'?"

"Evening, Buster," Ezra replied, getting out of the car and pulling the shotgun out behind him. "Where are they?"

"It's damn near mornin'," Buster corrected. Then he gestured with a rifle he carried in his hand. "They're well over to the west side," he said.

"How many?" Ezra noted that Buster also had a giant pistol strapped on low, tied down like some absurd parody of a Wild West gunfighter.

"I counted four for sure, but there may be another one in the truck," Buster replied.

"Truck? What sort of deal they got?"

"Well, it's smoother than a moose's root," Buster said with reluctant admiration. "They got them a semitrailer on the road, an' they pull a kind of runway out of it an' lay it across the ditch. Then they saw down some of the fence and just lead the heifers, one at a time, across the runway an' right up a ramp into the back of the truck. It's blacker than hell out here, an' them cows don't know what's goin' on, an' in a bit they're loaded an' gone. They just patch up the fence with some wood glue or somethin', I guess, hit it with a dab of paint or stain, an' that's that." Buster's face was invisible in the early morning gloom, but Ezra could imagine the expression on it.

"Any other cars?" Ezra asked.

"Nope," Buster replied. "Just the one truck." He

145

paused a moment, then went on. "I would have taken them myself, but they got guns. Every man jack of them is wearin' some business of some kind. This is some kind of professional setup."

Ezra was pleased. Buster might be irascible and hard to get along with, but he had a good head on his shoulders. He had better sense than to start a shoot-out with four armed men without the law on his side.

"Which way's the truck pointed?" Ezra asked, reckoning that the road on the west side of the yards was too narrow for it to pull around or make a U-turn.

"North," Buster said.

"Like to block that road," Ezra said, scratching the stubble on his chin.

"Get to it!" Buster ordered, and Ezra noticed for the first time two more shadows standing in the barn's doorway. They moved closer, and in the dim starlight he recognized two of Buster's men. "You heard the sheriff. Take my pickup an' block off the road. And do it right, goddamn it."

"Hang on," Ezra said, still startled to learn that he and Buster hadn't been alone. "Who's that?"

"Fernando an' his brother, Miguel," Buster answered.

"You men got guns?" Ezra asked the shadowed figures.

"'Course they got guns!" Buster exclaimed. "You think we're damn fools?"

"Well, leave them here," Ezra ordered, then he continued before Buster could argue, "I can't deputize the whole damn county over this. You keep your rifle, but you leave that hog leg here, too. You men take his truck over as quiet as you can, block off the road, then get down in one of the ditches and keep your heads down."

The men muttered and stacked their rifles against the barn. They faded off toward Buster's pickup, started it, and drove off at a low speed with the lights out.

146

"Well," Ezra said as they disappeared into the night, "Buster Swinson, you're a deputy sheriff of the County of Sandhill, State of Texas. You're sworn in and you're bound to follow my orders. Now, get that pistol off, and let's go."

Buster reluctantly unstrapped the pistol belt he was wearing and laid it across the sheriff's car, then he checked the load in his .30-30. The two of them crossed the road and walked down to a gate which they scaled and began to make their way across the feed lot among heifers and steers bound for auction or slaughter. The smell of manure was heavy in the night air, and its cloying sweetness overwhelmed Ezra's pipe. The sheriff winced as he felt his boots strike puddle after puddle of wet, soggy dung on the floor of the pens.

This sort of thing—the prospect of violence—was too rare for Ezra to grasp all at once. He would be called over to the colored section of town every now and then to settle something or other, and there had even been a murder or two over there, but mostly his experience had been in chasing down bootleggers trying to bring booze over from Oklahoma or in picking up the odd prowler. What rustling took place was mostly a matter of some minor investigating, asking some questions, and finally turning over what he found to the Highway Patrol to make the arrest, unless it was some local boy who was down on his luck. And that didn't happen often enough to merit mention. There were suicides, beatings, or some drunk hell-raisings after a high school dance or football game, but nothing, in recent years anyway, rivaled this stealthy walk across a feed lot to catch armed cattle thieves. Ezra wondered if he was really up to it.

He had been in one or two real shoot-outs in his career. One about ten years ago had actually made the national papers. A bank robber with a place on the FBI's most-wanted list had held up the First Security Bank in

147

the small town, then strolled as pretty as you please into Central Drugs across the street and ordered a sandwich. While he waited for the sandwich, Ezra showed up and tried to arrest him. The man pulled a gun out and fired, taking off a piece of the sheriff's ear, but by the time the pain and realization of his wound reached his senses, Ezra had pulled out his .44 Colt and fired back, splattering most of the back wall of Central Drugs, including the counter girl, with blood and brains.

He had little recollection of the entire incident, but he did get a five-thousand-dollar reward from the Texas State Bankers' Association, and he made the one and only trip he had ever taken out of Texas and southern Oklahoma when he went to the National Conference of Sheriffs to speak of the business. They paid his way, he recalled. As he moved from pen to pen, reaching out his hand to calm the beasts who crowded together in the stockyard, he found that the old robbery had begun to stir in its memory seed, and it was threatening to burst.

He could feel the fear and apprehension of that sticky August afternoon trying to erupt, and for a brief moment he wanted to just give in to it, go back to his car, and retreat to his carport roof. He remembered suddenly that one reason the robber had gotten the drop on him so easily was Hilda. He could visualize the man's hand reaching into his coat for the butt of a large pistol, and he remembered telling his hand to drop to his own weapon, then hesitating. He was thinking of Hilda, and what she would do without him if he got killed, of how she would react to the news. Then he saw the smoke and the flame leap from the black barrel of the man's gun, and the rest was a blur. He moved his hand instinctively to the half ear and felt it to make sure that it hadn't all been a dream.

He had hesitated because of Hilda, and he had damn near gotten his head blown off because of it, he thought.

The shotgun was heavy in his hands as he and Buster moved close enough to make out the outline of the large trailer. He could see the men moving about in the far pen, and he realized with shock that it was already growing light in the east. It wasn't near dawn yet, but everything had the kind of pale outline to it that preceeds daylight, and he had no trouble seeing them moving cattle through the narrow opening in the fence and across the wooden runway Buster had described.

"There they are," Buster whispered in his ear as they crouched down.

Ezra's heart was racing, and his knee was yelling at him for bending it so forcefully. He felt sweat breaking out on his forehead, and he wondered if he was actually going to be able to go through with this. He had never had a failure of nerve before, he realized—only that one hesitation. He cocked the shotgun's twin hammers and got ready to rise, but something held him back. Something in him wouldn't let him move.

It was her! Imogene! he realized. He found himself worrying about what she would say if he got hurt or killed. How would she go on? What would become of her? Would a new sheriff be as kind to her as he had? Would a new sheriff be as tolerant? Would he defend her to goddamn Mayor Perkins? Would he—would he dream about her?

Ezra bit off the questions as hard as he could. This was ass-hole stupid, he told himself. How could he even consider the possibility that she would give a good goddamn what happened to him? But even as the question intended to quiet his anxiety flowed out, he knew it didn't matter what she thought. He had become dependent on her, and somehow, he believed, she was dependent on him, too, whether she knew it or not. He felt something for her he had not felt for anyone in a long, long time. He was so unused to the feeling that at first he was perplexed and confused. What was it? Then he knew, and the recognition made all his memory seeds stir uncomfortably.

"Ezra, goddamn it!" Buster's voice hissed in his ear again. "You takin' a shit or what?" Buster half raised to get a better look, then crouched again. "We just goin' to *sit* here?"

"No," Ezra said with determination. He swallowed hard. "Let's go. Stay behind me." He wished he had made Buster leave his rifle behind along with the pistol.

He stood up and struck for the opening in the fence, then thought better of it and veered off a bit to the left. He climbed through and walked along the fence side of the ditch, cradling the shotgun in his arms. He was aware of Buster's footfalls directly behind him.

"All right, boys," he said in a loud voice. "That's it. Let's just stand quiet."

The men were fussing over a heifer that refused to budge from the center of the wooden runway across the ditch, and they froze when they heard Ezra's voice.

"Who's that?"

"This is the sher—" Ezra started to say, but as the first words left his mouth he saw the men moving. One was raising a pistol, and another reached for a rifle leaning against the fence. At the same time, the struggling heifer was shoved violently off the runway into the ditch, bawling, and the men scrambled past her on the wooden planks.

Ezra's brain screamed at his hands to level the shotgun and fire before the man with the pistol had a chance to get off a shot, but before he could act he saw the face of Imogene McBride swim briefly before his eyes, and he hesitated a second too long.

From his right a blinding flash knocked him off balance, and the thunderous explosion that followed it milliseconds later made his ears ring. He found himself incomprehensibly falling, with great pain searing through his skull from right to left, and he flailed out his arms into the air to try to find purchase on anything he could.

A stickery but thick bed of tumbleweeds broke his fall in the bottom of the ditch, but try as he might, he couldn't find his balance. His head was bursting with pain, and his right eye was smarting from what he finally realized was the muzzle flash of Buster's .30-30 exploding in his ear. As he wrestled around in the thorns and brambles in the ditch's bottom, he tried to locate the shotgun, but it had fallen out of reach, and overhead he finally came to hear the crackle and pop of a first-class shoot-out going on. Because of his semideafness caused by the big rifle's blast, he seemed to hear the gunfire at a great distance, and he imagined that he had fallen a long way from the battle.

Drawing out his .44, he tried again to scramble to an upright position. The brambles that had cushioned his fall were two and three feet deep, however, and all he could do for a few minutes was thrash around and swear. He felt rather than heard something heavy thrashing around as he was, and he dimly remembered the cow that had fallen into the ditch just before him and hoped that it was far enough away not to come stampeding over him.

Finally he reached out, found the ditch's wall, and began scrambling up. The loose soil made climbing difficult, especially since he kept his pistol in his hand, but somehow he found a reserve of strength and made it to the top.

"All right!" he screamed into the sounds of gunfire that met him loudly when he reached the top of the trench. "That's e-goddamn-nough!" He fired once into the air. "*Stop it!*" The gunfire ceased abruptly. "I'm the

151

goddamn sheriff of this county, and you're all under arrest!"

Ezra fought to catch his breath and lay his face down into the loamy soil at the top of the ditch. Wearily he hoisted himself up and stood facing the rustlers. "You boys lay down your guns and keep your hands where I can see them," he ordered in a steady voice, fighting not to let them know how old and out of breath he was. "Buster, you okay?"

Buster wasn't entirely okay. He had taken two hits, one in the shoulder and one in the leg, and he was losing blood fast. But he had done his share of damage, Ezra learned in the next few minutes. Two of the rustlers were hurt worse than the rancher, another had not been shot but had been almost trampled to death by the terrified heifer in the bottom of the ditch where he fell after the shooting started. But the other two were unharmed, one because he had stayed in the truck.

The rest of the business went fairly smoothly. Fernando came helling down the road, brandishing a recovered rifle, and Ezra sent him to get Doc Pritchard and an ambulance for the wounded. He found Miguel to guard the others while he sent for Dooley to come pick them up.

Doc Pritchard beat the ambulance to the scene and pronounced Buster hurt but not about to die. "He'll limp like hell, though, Ezra," the doctor assured him, and Ezra nodded with more satisfaction than he liked to admit he felt. All three of the injured thieves were shipped to the security hospital wing of the Wichita Falls Police Department.

It turned out that they were part of a large rustling ring that had been stealing cattle from all over north Texas and southern Oklahoma for more than a year. Normally they just took one or two head at a time, but they had sized up Buster's yards as easier pickings and had gotten greedy—and caught. The two healthy captives were installed in the holding cell in the sheriff's department until they could be moved to more secure and permanent accommodations the following week.

By the time Ezra sat down to do his paperwork, noon had already passed. He had found his pipe and shotgun in the ditch, and after working on his report for an hour, he rose and poured himself a badly needed cup of coffee. He stood at his window, puffing on the pipe and choking down Dooley's coffee and watching Imogene out on her bench.

She looked like hell, he thought. But then so do I. Recollections of the flood of confusing and appalling emotions of the morning came to him in a quiet, disconcerting way. "I wish you'd never come to this town," Ezra said quietly to the figure across the lawn from his office. "I wish to God you'd just passed right on through and gone to visit Mildred and taken your ghostly bitch of a daughter with you and never come here." His eyes lifted to Pete's Sundries and Drugs across from her gawky figure, and he shook his head. "And I wish—"

"You say somethin', Sheriff?" a voice interrupted him, and he turned to see the snaggly-toothed grin of one of the rustlers as he leaned against the cell bars.

"Nothing to you," Ezra said. "Shut up or I'll gag you." The man moved lethargically back to the cell's cot and spat a glob of tobacco juice at Dooley's can. He missed.

Ezra moved back to his desk, trying once again to shove all his memories back into their proper slots. There would be a lot to explain on this one, he thought. A citizen, temporarily deputized and not properly sworn, starting a shoot-out while the sheriff rested out of harm's way in a ditch. Jesus. Thank God no one was killed. He shook his head. It won't look like my fault, he thought wryly, but it was. I hesitated, and I damn near got myself killed. It was my fault, he said firmly to himself. And hers. He lifted his eyes to the window where the October sky taunted the community with memories of summer. "Yes," he said under his breath, too low for the prisoner to hear, "it was very much her fault."

T H R E E

Imogene had heard the gunfire from what the local citizens would come to call the shoot-out at the North End Yards, and it had frightened her. She was spending the night out on the bench again, something she had taken to doing in the realization that the weather would soon turn foul and she wouldn't be able to anymore.

She didn't question too much the logic of it all, of waiting all night every night for Cora to come back—she just did it—and each nocturnal period was, for her imagination, a wholesale terror. She had never gotten used to spending the night outdoors.

Cat fights and other night sounds had ceased to frighten her, and she no longer gave in to foolish fantasies when she heard the trains coming into the station. But the eerie deadness of the darkened town never failed to fill her with dread, and she waited with growing impatience until the sky began to lighten and dawn would come to relieve her watch.

The gunfire had erupted suddenly, and she had jumped, catching at her throat with one hand, her eyes wide with fear, and then she realized what she was hearing and tried to find some logical explanation for it. It was far in the distance, not threatening to her, and she glanced quickly up to the sheriff's office window and noted with satisfaction that the light was on and Dooley's form could be seen peering out in the direction of the noise. She almost got up and went inside to ask him what was going on, but then she thought better of it. She was enough of a bother to Dooley, she thought, and she didn't need to get in the way of official business.

After a few minutes the gunshots ceased, and on the north wind she thought she could hear shouting, but it was soon gone, and she began to relax. Her thoughts went to Ezra for the first time since the noises began, and with a small start she realized that he could be involved in something unpleasant, possibly even in danger.

Rising and pacing a bit, she wondered if there was something she should do for him. In spite of his exasperation at her stubborn decision to stay right where she was, his patience with her had been wonderful, she acknowledged. He and she had talked about so many things in the past month that she felt that they had become quite close, almost like brother and sister. It was a nice feeling.

Suddenly she heard the wail of a siren, and an ambulance screamed past her. She walked out to the curb and looked down the street after it, wondering if it was Ezra who had been hurt, and feeling a tremendous pity for the aging sheriff who had—after some prompting, admittedly—been so kind to her. He was a good man, she thought, who asked so little from her and seemed so willing to do whatever she asked him to do. Why couldn't Harvey have been like that? she angrily asked herself. That would have made things so much simpler, and Cora would never have pulled this silly prank.

The thought of Cora moved her back to her bench, and she sat again and stared at the drugstore. She had had no more monster visions of it since the first night, but she had no trouble associating it with the cause of all her misery. Suddenly she stamped her foot on the ground in frustration. "Cora!" she called across the empty downtown district. "Cora! Come out here this minute!"

It was a call she often made, and while the futility of it was apparent to her, it seemed to make her feel better.

The ambulance returned after a while, and the sky lightened. Imogene remained on the bench. She still had not seen Sheriff Holmes, and no one had come near enough for her to call to them and find out what had gone on. That something unusual had happened was apparent; the citizenry seemed to be positively abuzz with news of some great occurrence, and Imogene had a mixed feeling of pleasure, in that she had known about it as it was actually going on, and frustration in being ignorant of what it was.

By midmorning she spotted the sheriff's car pulling into the courthouse parking area, however, and she breathed a sigh of relief as she watched Ezra hobble up the steps to his office. He was limping much worse than usual, she noted, but besides an awfully dirty uniform and a missing hat, he did not appear to be hurt or damaged in any way. She found herself able to relax then, and she promised herself a nap before she took up her watch for the night, but in the back of her mind she found it more than slightly disturbing that he hadn't come by to speak to her as he usually did, and she made a mental note to chastise him for ignoring her on this fine autumn day.

"It's a great pity," she said softly to herself, "that people can't be a little more considerate of others as they go about their day-by-day routines."

F O U R

A week later Ezra got the phone call. As usual it came late at night, well after midnight, and as usual, he was dreaming about Imogene. His heart was pounding in his

156

ears when he came awake to the phone's ringing, and for a few seconds he tried to recall the details of the dream, but they vanished. He fumbled for the jangling instrument as it rang a second time.

"Yeah?" he growled into the receiver. He didn't feel like being clear and calm tonight. He fully expected Dooley's voice to be telling him of another "ot-tow" accident.

"Sheriff Holmes?" It was a woman's voice. No. A girl's, but it sounded funny, muffled, and Ezra's breath caught. Cora? his mind asked.

"Who is this?" he asked, trying to concentrate hard on the voice, detect any background noises, listen for clues.

"I won't tell you," she said. Ezra thought she must be talking through a handkerchief or a towel or something— like in the movies. "I wanted you to know, though . . . uh, that some of the kids . . . on Halloween night . . . well, they . . ." She finally trailed off, and Ezra's breathing started a regular pattern again. He recognized the voice.

"What?" he asked. "What?" It sounded like Sylvia Conners, who went around with that damn Perkins kid. This was a break! Usually he didn't find out about that crowd's Halloween pranks until the next morning when there wasn't anything to do but clean up the mess.

"Well . . ." She hesitated, then plunged in. "Well, you know that crazy old lady at the courthouse? You know, the one who's looking for her daughter?"

Ezra felt himself go cold all over. "Yeah," he said. "What about her?" It was Sylvia all right. She was a good kid, member of his church. All she ever did wrong was hang around with Tommy Perkins and his gang. But then, he *was* the mayor's son. Probably old Perkins had taken his argument with Ezra home from the city council meeting, and Tommy had gotten some ideas. Bunch of damn thugs, Ezra thought.

"Well . . . some of the kids are going to do something to her. On Halloween night," she gasped out. Ezra realized she was whispering, and he got a mental image of her under her bedclothes secretly snitching on her best friends.

"What kind of something?"

"I don't know. Really I don't. They won't tell me because I said I felt sorry for her. Anyway, they're up to something. And it's bad." She spoke rapidly, warming to the gossipy flavor of her report.

"But you're not going to be there, are you, Sylvia?" He chanced a guess at her name.

"No, sir!" she said quickly, dropping the whisper and whatever she had over the phone's mouthpiece. "Not me! Uh . . . I'm not . . . oh, *damn!*" The line went dead.

That's good, Ezra thought, chuckling as he rolled his legs out of bed and onto the floor. I'll keep this little secret for her, and she'll be good for another tip in the future. She'll know she can trust me not to tell who snitched.

He dressed, pulling his boots on and noticing that his knee had gotten much, much worse since his fall in the ditch. There would be no more sleep this night, he wearily acknowledged, and then decided to take a drive out to the lake and check some of the cabins. Someone, he was sure, had been prowling around out there.

Ezra's car's headlights fingered their way hesitantly along the overgrown road that led down to Medicine Lake. It was paved, or it had been at one time, but aside from a handful of West Texas Utilities employees who still worked in the hydroelectric plant on the dam, and the odd fisherman, almost no one still used this road for access, and weeds and grass grew up in the cracks in the blacktop like a mini-forest. The primary recreation area was on the south side of the lake, where Blind Man's Creek still flowed into it and brought catfish and perch in

158

numbers and sizes to entice Sunday crowds, and where the water was deep enough for swimming and boating.

It never had been much of a lake. It was more a deep hole in the ground that the Army Corps of Engineers had dredged out and filled up with creek water in an attempt to provide electricity for the rural cooperatives in the area. During the war, however, it had run full tilt, and the company had built a group of cottages, about thirty in all, along a circular drive parallel to the lake and near the plant. They were small buildings, really, none with more than two bedrooms, designed mainly for the men who worked at the plant and their families.

They had always been a source of irritation to Ezra. The men who moved into them were never local folks, but they were usually railroad riders and bums who needed work and who were practically drafted by the company when the army had taken most of the able-bodied men away. Although the circular drive enclosed a park and there was a community house with a dance floor and kitchen, Ezra figured that he had spent more time breaking up fights and arresting drunks than enjoying picnics and Fourth of July dances in the diminutive community.

In front of the creepingly slow tires of the sheriff's vehicle, cottontails and jackrabbits raced madly from one overgrown ditch to the other. Ezra didn't recall ever seeing so many rabbits in one place.

"Good place for hunting. To hell with the fishing," he grumbled as he automatically stepped on the brake to keep from crushing a fleeing rabbit.

After the war the company had cut back operations by more than fifty percent, and postwar prosperity made it possible for workers to own their own cars and live in town. The cottages were then sold to people for lake houses, but they were too near the city to be of much use for weekend stays, so the houses mostly went to ruin, except for the one or two that a few folks tried to keep up in hopes that the property might someday rise enough in value to make them worth selling. No one at all still lived out there, and it had been years since the sheriff had ever known anyone to spend the night there legally.

Of course, the high school kids were fond of the spot. It was a favorite place to go for parking under a full moon and a bit of necking. Ezra figured that more than one family had been accidentally started on the circular drive. It was just large enough that if a parked couple spotted a car coming in the gate they could start their own vehicle and sneak out the other way before the sheriff could get around to them.

But aside from sex and an occasional drinking party, it was also a favorite place for teenage mischief. Once, two years before, Ezra had made a routine summer night's sweep along the drive and was horrified to see a man hanging from one of the overgrown trees in the park area. He had raced over, tripping over a rusty seesaw, only to discover Paulie Hazelwood dangling from ropes that threatened to do no more damage than burn his wrists a bit.

Paulie was to be a freshman in high school the following year, and some of the outgoing seniors thought that he deserved a little taste of hazing in advance. Aside from being scared and sore, Paulie wasn't hurt, and he refused steadfastly to name his tormentors.

Since then Ezra had tried to swing through the cottage area a couple of times a week. He figured that his appearance on a regular basis would discourage more of the same sort of foolishness that could have, if Ezra had not happened along, turned out badly for poor Paulie.

Ezra squinted through the bug-encrusted windshield and located the two hand-lettered boards that indicated the terminals of two trails that forked off the main road. One board read FISHING DOCK, and an arrow pointed down to the left. It was a dead end, Ezra knew. No one had fished the old dock since two men drowned there years before. The cause of their drowning was never discovered, and many tales of horror had been told around campfires in Sandhill County since their bodies were pulled out. But as far as Ezra was concerned, there was no indication of foul play or anything more mysterious than what might come out of a whiskey bottle.

Even so, late at night when he usually came to the fork in the road, he always felt a small shudder as he glanced down the completely overgrown trail that curved down and out of sight toward the old dock. He knew there was nothing down there, of course, and he knew that no one was about to go down there, especially after dark. But as he guided the car past the sign and its announcement, CABIN AREA, he gave the other trail only a bare glance and breathed a silent prayer of thanks that his eyes hadn't seen anything that might entice him farther into the ghostly darkness.

The rabbits thinned out as he approached the gate to the cabin area. To his left the giant hydroelectric plant hovered over the dam. A steady hum drowned out all other night sounds close to the building, and the bizarre array of giant electrical gadgetry surrounded the building, hissing and buzzing like a hideous monster, illuminated by the yellow light from the few windows that hadn't been painted over. A skeleton crew worked the plant at night, and Ezra counted the usual number of vehicles in the parking lot beneath a single streetlamp as he turned the car through the gate and onto the circular drive.

The cottages were arranged on the north side of the drive and stood one after another in a row all the way down to the lake, where the community house dominated the drive's curve. The south side of the road bordered the lake all the way back to the gate, and between them were about seventy-five yards of grass, weeds, and trees hiding rusted and broken playground equipment, demolished picnic tables, and discarded liquor bottles, beer cans, and junk that had collected over the years since the last families had moved out.

From the driver's side of the car, Ezra couldn't see the cottages very well, but he trained the spotlight from its mount next to him as best he could on each building, trying to see if anyone moved behind one of the windows.

He had had a complaint from Doc Pritchard and another one from one or two other people that someone had broken into their cottages and moved things around. Nothing, aside from the locks, had been broken or stolen, but they wanted him to keep a closer eye on their worthless property, and he felt a bit guilty that he hadn't done so.

About halfway down the drive he thought he saw something move inside one of the houses, and a tingle of excitement crept up his neck. He had been barely moving the car, but he suddenly stopped it and trained the light directly on the window where he was sure he had seen movement. Nothing came back to him but the spot's reflection.

Reaching beside him in the seat, he grabbed his flashlight and got out, leaving the light brightly holding the window prisoner. He warily circled around behind the car and moved up to the cottage's porch. Peering through a side window, he splashed light around the living room of the small house, but nothing appeared to be out of order.

"Hello!" he called, noting that it was very late at night, and if the owner, whoever he might be, was there, he was likely asleep and wouldn't be expecting the sheriff to be shining a light through his window. "This is the sheriff!" he called again, marveling at how loud his voice sounded in the dead silence of the cottage area. It echoed across the playground and disturbed a colony of bullfrogs which set up a massive croaking in response.

He shrugged and moved around behind the cottage, not completely relaxing, but almost entirely convinced that his imagination and fatigue were getting the best of him. This place was eerie, he thought as he surveyed the row of cottages from the rear. Overgrown with weeds and mesquite thickets, surrounded on two sides by a dying lake, the empty cottages boasted happier times, and all of a sudden Ezra realized that what bothered him most about coming out here was the terrible sadness the place called forth. The buried playground, now void of children, the snug little cottages, now empty of light or life, the enormous plant, now cut back to nearly a dead stop owing to the cheapness of gas-fired electricity. This had been a regular town once, with people, laughter, hopes, and all the other emotions a community had a right to. Now it was nothing. It wasn't even a ghost town. It hadn't existed long enough for that. It was just empty.

He had turned and started back for his car when he noticed that the one-car garage behind the cottage was open. The door had been pried away from its hinges and then leaned back in place. Ezra stared at it for a minute, trying to comprehend what he was seeing. He looked around at the empty cottages to his left and right. Each one had a garage, and each garage, like each cottage, was identical to the one next to it. But each door that he could see in the beam of his flashlight was fastened shut. This one wasn't.

He swallowed hard and laid his right hand on the butt of his holstered .44. He walked deliberately over to the garage door, gave it a kick, and jumped back as it fell forward.

Inside was nothing that shouldn't have been there.

The garage was barely large enough to hold a car and allow the driver to get out after it was parked. A few shelves lined the far wall, but they were empty, and spider webs told him that it had been a long time since anything had been stored there. He walked inside and looked around briefly, shining his light up and around, and then he shrugged. Someone just took the door down, he decided. Nothing suspicious about it at all. He felt foolish.

The garage did have an odor, though. A familiar, gasoline and oil smell. It was too fresh to have been left by a former owner, Ezra noted, but who would want to use an old garage like this? He didn't have an answer, but he could tell that a vehicle had been there recently.

He tried unsuccessfully to replace the door without putting down his light, but the door would only lean awkwardly, and he finally gave up and moved back to his car. He turned off the spotlight and pulled his pipe out of his shirt and lit it, surprised to feel the cool night air on his wet shirt. He had been really afraid, he told himself with surprise. But of what? An empty cottage? An empty garage? It was foolish.

He stood smoking and listening to the night lake sounds compete with the buzzing from the hydroelectric plant's electronic gadgets, and finally he concluded that he would find nothing at the lake tonight. But as he got into his car, his eye picked up movement again.

This time it came from down the drive, toward the community house, and there was no chance it was his imagination. He started the car and hit the spotlight at the same time, catching the bright red glow of a vehicle reflector in the spot's beam. He raced the engine and spun gravel behind him as he drove toward the end of the drive. It was a pickup, an old one, and it was parked so that the tailgate just protruded from the corner of the community house facing the drive's curve.

Pulling up right behind the truck, Ezra snapped on his red light and stepped out of the car, shining his flashlight toward the cab's rear window. He called out, "You there, in the truck. C'mon out. This is the sheriff."

No one moved from the truck, and Ezra slowly made his way to the door and looked inside. It was empty. He backed off and looked around, across the road, and then behind him into the windows of the empty community house.

"Another stupid thing to do," he spoke his thought. He had pulled a classic blunder. He had come helling up, red light flashing, shouting and carrying on when there might have been someone really dangerous in the truck. But there wasn't. No one was around. He was lucky.

He studied the truck. It looked familiar, and suddenly it dawned on him that he knew it. He checked the plates and then double-checked his hunch by looking at the registration spring-chained to the steering column. It belonged to Dub Hankins, Pete's son.

"Hey, Ezra!" The voice came from the blackness of a mesquite thicket between the road and the lake, and the sheriff almost jumped out of his boots. His hand automatically fell to his pistol, and he almost crouched with the pain he felt knife down through his bowels as they tightened in fear. "What're you doin' here?"

It was Pete. He came sauntering out of the mesquite thicket and moved easily up alongside the pickup opposite where Ezra stood.

"I might ask you the same question."

"Well, don't go all God-almighty on me," Pete snorted, and Ezra felt the resentment swelling in his old friend's voice. "It's a free country, ain't it?"

"This is private property, and you know it." Ezra sounded colder than he meant to, but he was still shaking a bit from fright.

"Hell, don't I know it." Pete slapped the pickup's side.

"Rich folks got the best goddamn fishin' holes in the county all to themselves. They don't use them, though. So I figured somebody ought to."

Ezra said nothing. He looked down into the pickup's bed. An ancient cane pole rested against one side and protruded over the tailgate, but there was no sign of any other tackle.

"Been runnin' trot lines out here for more 'n a year," Pete offered to Ezra's silence. "Got me a nine-pound cat last week. Sure enough, an' I had one bigger than that this time, but watermoskins got to him an' ruined him."

Ezra shook his head. "Trot line?" he asked stupidly. He knew no one had ever pulled a nine-pound cat out of Medicine Lake. Never.

"How come you never invited me out here to fish with you." Ezra tried to sound friendly, cajoling, attempting to capture something of the friendship they had enjoyed before Imogene and Cora McBride had come to Agatite.

Pete spat into the dirt. "Shit, Ezra. You're the sheriff. I mean, I didn't think you'd say much to me, us bein' friends an' all, but I didn't figure you'd want to come out here an' actually break the law. This *is* private, like you say."

The sheriff nodded. "Well, I don't suppose it hurts anything. Just don't mess around with these cabins. Somebody's been breaking into some of them."

In the lowered flashlight beam Ezra caught Pete's eyes widening. "No shit?" He sounded incredulous. "Which ones?"

Ezra gestured with his light. "Oh, number twenty-four, I guess, and Doc Pritchard's, too."

Pete whistled and took a couple of steps around the back of the truck. Ezra noted that he was wearing nice slacks and a sports shirt. He was clean-shaven, too, and his hair, sparse as it was, was neatly combed back. "Man, I been comin' out here for a long time, an' I never seen nobody." He looked intensely at Ezra. "What'd they do?"

"Nothing much." Ezra lowered his eyes. He realized he had been staring at Pete. How did a man run a trot line and not get wet or muddy? he wondered. Where was his stringer? Where was his gear?

"Well, that's a goddamn shame," Pete said, shaking his head and moving past Ezra toward the driver's side of the pickup. "Damn kids'll do anything to get in trouble, I guess."

"I never said it was kids."

"Well," Pete offered as he opened the door and climbed into the truck, "who the hell else would it be? Not everybody's as lucky as me to have a boy like Dub."

"Say!" Ezra had a quick thought. "Where's that fancy fishing rod he got you?"

"Fishin' rod?" Pete pulled a cigarette from his shirt pocket and searched around for a lighter. "What fishin' rod?"

"The one he got you for your birthday." Ezra pulled a book of matches out of his pocket and tossed them into Pete's lap through the open door.

Pete took his time lighting his cigarette. "Oh, yeah, that," he said at last. "Cost damn near a arm an' a leg, it did." He drew in on the smoke. "Made him take it back. I don't need no fishin' rod." He gestured into the truck bed. "Got me a damn good cane pole an' a trot line. What I need a fancy-dan rod for?"

"Yeah," Ezra said, noting that suddenly he could see everything a bit better without the light. Dawn was coming slowly, but clouds kept the light dim and delayed.

"Hey!" Pete exclaimed suddenly. "It's damn near mornin'. I got to open in a couple of hours."

Ezra nodded and waved silently as he moved back to his car and switched off the red light and the spot. It was still dark, he noted, and the false light of the dawn gave only a bare outline to things.

"I'll keep an eye peeled for them kids," Pete called as he fired up the old pickup. Ezra waved again and sat down wearily in the car.

Pete wheeled around and drove back up the north side of the drive, and Ezra watched him in his rearview mirror as he refilled his pipe and tried to think. Something in him made him want to scramble down to the lake through the mesquite thicket and search for Pete's trot line. But what would it prove if he didn't find it? he wondered. What would it prove if he did? Trot lines popped up all over the lake. Boaters constantly complained about unmarked lines that fouled their engine props, and even if Pete had been lying—and Ezra was certain that he was—what was he trying to cover up? Why was he out here in the first place?

A thought, dark and sinister, shot across his mind, and he brushed his forehead with his hand as if to wipe it away. No, he thought, not that. He didn't know what had happened in the drugstore, in the back room, but he knew that Cora wasn't out here. Not with Pete. That was too much.

He glanced up through the pipe smoke into the mirror once again. Pete had stopped. Ezra figured he forgot to say something and would come back. In the back of his mind he found himself imagining that Pete had remembered his tackle, his stringer, and was suddenly coming back to get them, and he stepped out of the car to greet him, help him if he could. But Pete wasn't turning around.

He had stopped the old truck directly in front of the same cottage Ezra had investigated, number twenty-four, and he was waiting. The gray light now flooded the entire cottage area with morning, and Ezra could see the truck clearly, Pete's shadow outlined in the small rear

168

window of the cab. Suddenly he saw his old friend's hand come out the window and gesture toward the cottage, and, to his horror, a woman raced across the weed-choked lawn toward the pickup.

Ezra called out, but his voice wouldn't work, and his pipe fell from his teeth and spilled bright red ashes all over his shirt front as he caught it awkwardly. "Cora!" he finally managed to yell, but it wasn't clear. Still, it was loud enough to make her stop just as she reached the passenger side of the pickup's cab, and she looked up.

Her head was covered with a scarf, and she wore a bright print dress. She stood for a moment staring toward the sheriff's car parked only a short distance away. Ezra strained his eyes, then he was sure. It wasn't Cora.

It was Glenda Powell, a woman from town. Twice divorced, once from a Negro, she had a reputation that sent the hands of Christian women all over Agatite fluttering around their throats. Ezra had never known her to be any trouble to anyone. She made her living cleaning houses, even, he recalled with a grimace, old Pete's. She wasn't young by a long shot, but she was far from Pete's age, and she wasn't bad-looking for a woman who had had nothing but trouble in her life.

She stood for another breath, then ducked her head and jumped into the truck, which had already started to drive away before she could close the door. Ezra sighed. That seemed to solve the mystery of the cottages, he thought, and he confirmed it when he noted to his surprise that the lights of Pete's truck were clearly visible as they passed the fork in the road and the signs where Ezra had paused.

"I wonder how long he's been coming out here with her?" Ezra thought aloud. He started the car and continued his circle around the drive. Then he wondered silently if they were in love. Pete never could marry her, not here, not in Agatite. It would ruin his business forever. No decent folks would even speak to him. And they couldn't use Pete's house or a motor court. Dub lived at home, and there were no secrets in Agatite, not about motor court romances, anyway.

Of course, it might not matter. Ezra's car clattered through the gate and back out onto the road leading back to the fork. If Imogene kept up much longer, Pete was probably ruined anyway.

It was full daylight when the car reached the fork and the sign. Ezra pulled up, stopped, and looked out across the mesquite and weeds toward the cottages. It had been so long since he had been out here in the daytime that he had forgotten that the road curved around and came up almost directly behind the cottages. It would take him maybe two minutes to get to the gate at the speed he had been going when he came in, maybe another two to get around far enough to see that particular cottage and its driveway. That was plenty of time for Pete and Glenda to see him, get his truck out of the garage and put the door back up, and drive down the drive far enough to throw him off the track.

"It's a damn good thing it was Pete and not some mean son-of-a-bitch," Ezra lectured himself as he put the car into gear and started toward the highway.

He decided to punish himself by not letting on to Pete that he had seen anything, by not interfering with an old man's happiness. He owed him that much, and buying a small lie seemed a small price to pay an old friend.

Even so, it disturbed him to find out that there was a darker side to Pete's nature than he had ever known, that his childhood buddy could lie to him so easily, so casually, so believably. And it bothered him even more when he realized that such a dark side, such an ability to lie, could indeed have had something important to do with the disappearance of Cora McBride.

170

FIVE

Ezra approached her on that cold, clear Halloween morning. She looked bad, he noticed. She had lost so much weight that her skin was sagging on her neck, and there were dark hollows around her gray eyes that now looked almost bleached out with staring. In fact, he silently remarked, they were almost empty, lighting up only when he came to speak to her, and the realization warmed his heart. He saw none of the old indefinable something behind them that he had noticed the first day he met her, but he took the absence of that subliminal force to be a good sign. She was wearing out, sure, he thought, but she was also softening.

"Morning," he said as he approached with a thermos of coffee under his arm and two mugs in his hand.

"Good morning, Ezra," she said brightly, smiling. "Don't tell me you brought coffee? Dooley's?"

"Nope. But not much better," he said, sitting beside her. "Mine." He set the cups down and began pouring coffee into them, enjoying the pleasant sensation of watching the steam rise off them on this first really cold day of the year. It was just above freezing, the courthouse thermometer said.

"Say, Imma," he said as he sipped from his mug and watched her hold the warmth of her cup in both her hands. "I was wondering . . . tonight's a busy one for me and Dooley, and I usually don't try to go home to eat. But later on—I was wondering if you'd care to join me over to the Town and Country for a bite of something."

"Why, Ezra Holmes!" she exclaimed, and smiled grandly. "Are you asking me for a date?" She became coy, and he could detect her former prettiness coming out in the flush of her cheeks.

"Well . . . uh, not exactly," he said, fighting off the

171

temptation to dig a toe into the yellowing grass. He was unable to meet her laughing eyes. "I just thought wȧ might eat a little supper inside where it's warm and sort of talk about things . . . other things, something—"

"Other than Cora," she quickly added.

"Yeah," he mumbled.

"Well, I really shouldn't." She looked around and then shot a hard glance across the street where Pete was sweeping the sidewalk in front of his store. "I mean, my place is right here until Cora decides to quit this business and come on back. But since you asked so nicely and you've been so kind to me, I accept."

His heart leaped. "Fine," he said, realizing that he was more elated than he should be, since his purpose was merely, he kept telling himself, to get her off the street when he figured the kids would come by. "It'll have to be late. Tonight being Halloween and all. Dooley and me got to make the rounds of the schools and churches, and there's always a lot of local calls. How about nine-thirty?"

"That sounds fine, Ezra," she said, cupping a fresh cup of coffee he poured from the thermos in both her hands and holding it close to her face so its steam could bathe her in its warmth. She needs gloves, he thought. Winter's coming soon, and it'll make this morning's chill feel like mid-July. "I'll be right here, waiting for you," she concluded.

He knew she would.

After he made the early rounds and came into the courthouse by the back way, he sent Dooley over to the high school to watch for pranksters. A few calls had come in, but he radioed his assistant to check them out and get back to the school as soon as he could. Agatite had good kids, mostly, and Ezra didn't worry too much. But last year somebody had painted the green front of the school building with white paint and had written all sorts of ugly, obscene sayings about various teachers on

172

it. It was a harmless enough prank, but he had caught hell from the principal, Francis Holstein, and he didn't want to see a repeat performance.

He had loaded a 20-gauge shotgun with rocksalt and laid it across his knees as he watched from his office window. He could see Imogene down on her bench. He didn't know what the kids would try to do or exactly when they would try it, but he wanted to be ready.

There was a Halloween party over at one of the kids' houses, and he figured they would come out of there around ten or so, full of spiked punch and ready for mischief. If they came by and found her gone, maybe they would just give up and go on home, Ezra reasoned.

He watched her sitting primly and ramrod straight on the bench. What did he feel for her? He had trouble analyzing his emotions. She made him feel tongue-tied and foolish when he talked to her, and at the same time, when he was away from her, he often felt angry toward her, frustrated about her. Still, he found that he spent more and more time at the courthouse than on patrol. And even though he blamed it on advancing age, he knew that there was more to it than that. She was too much and too often on his mind. He couldn't really come to grips with how he felt, but he knew that it was a strong emotion, and he also knew he needed to be careful with it.

At nine-forty-five he went to the bench to pick her up. He offered her a small paper-wrapped box. She opened it and discovered that it contained a pair of fur-lined leather gloves.

"They were Hilda's," he muttered as she squealed with delight and poured out her thanks. "We got them for a winter fishing trip we never took, and I don't think she ever wore them." He wanted to tell Imogene of the agony it took for him to go up to the attic and haul down the one or two boxes of Hilda's things he hadn't had the

173

heart to give away, of the stirrings of his memory seeds as he pawed over the scarves and handkerchiefs and other personal things he remembered were stored with the unused gloves. But he said nothing as she briefly and insincerely protested the gift, pulling the gloves on and off several times, luxuriating in the rabbit fur lining.

Imogene had really done herself up for their "date," Ezra noticed, feeling a bit ashamed of his reasons for asking her out on this particular evening. Although her hair was still done up in the pony tail, it was freshly washed and held back with a colorful ribbon rather than the rubber band she usually used. She had put on a touch of makeup, also, and her red lips and eye shadow restored the prettiness he had noticed in her the day after they first met. Her nails were covered with polish, too, and even though she still wore a faded, worn dress and raggy coat, she looked almost radiant in the streetlamps' glow as they walked across the square to the Town and Country Restaurant.

S I X

The meal had been over for an hour and they were drinking coffee and smoking the cigarettes he had bought for her. She insisted he share one with her in lieu of the pipe which, she confessed, bothered her stomach sometimes. He grinned inwardly as she told him this, for Hilda had made the same complaint, forcing him outdoors with it periodically. Still, he rarely smoked it in the house. Whatever discomfort he had felt around Imogene before evaporated, and she sat playing with the lit cigarette and chatting with animation about her life in Atlanta, although she carefully avoided mentioning Cora or, of course, Harvey.

"You know," she said at last, "tonight has been so very good for me, Ezra." She sipped the last of her coffee. "I cannot tell you how wonderful this whole evening has been!" Her gray eyes danced in the dim light of the restaurant's lamps. "Why, I think I might just call it a day and turn in early. It's Halloween, you know!" Her nose wrinkled in a playful display of fright, "All sorts of things happen on All Hallow E'en!"

This was better than he could have hoped for. "Yeah," he answered slowly, crushing out the cigarette and wishing he could now light up his pipe. "Agatite's kids are good kids, but a few are rotten and try to spoil it for the rest."

He began to feel a strange, warm feeling creep all over him. It was a familiar pleasant sensation, and at the same time, he sensed, it was dangerous. But it suddenly gave him a recklessness, and he heard himself speaking, incredulous at his own words.

"Say, Imma, I'm getting old enough to retire." He held up a palm to ward off her protests. "I am. I'm sixty now, and I been sheriff of this county for a long, long time, deputy before that, and Texas Ranger for a while. I even did two years as a marshal. I'm up for reelection next month, and I been thinking seriously about not going through with it." He paused and sipped his coffee, gathering courage for the next leg of what something inside him told him was a dangerous journey. "I don't have much money saved up, but I still got most of Hilda's insurance, and I got the reward money from that fellow I shot back in forty-two socked away, and, of course, I'll have my pension and social security." He studied her face, but it was simply curious as to where he was leading her. "I always wanted to go up to Canada and fish some of the streams in the high Rockies."

"Well, I think you should." She picked up her water glass and sipped a bit. "I'll miss you, though."

He should have taken the hint, he thought later, but the strange sensation had completely overcome him, and with a quick check to make sure none of the memory seeds associated with Hilda were angrily stirring—and they weren't—he plunged ahead. "Well, actually, Imma, what I mean is . . . well . . . what I was thinking was that maybe you, uh . . . might, uh . . . want to give all this up and go along with me." He breathed out heavily. There, he thought, it's done.

"What?" she asked as if she hadn't heard him properly. The water glass froze halfway back down to the table. He spotted the old, indefinable something flitting around her gray eyes that had gotten large and ominous.

"Oh," he said, "now, I know I'm a lot older than you, and I don't mean . . ." The feeling was disappearing. "I don't mean nothing like *that*. That is, uh . . . not unless you, uh . . . wanted it that way. . . . I mean, you—well, hell, I don't know what I mean. . . ." The feeling was completely gone, and he was asking himself what in the world he had been trying to say in the first place.

The water from Imogene's glass hit him full in the face, bringing with it a sharp coldness and slight hurting where an ice cube struck him over the eye. "You son-of-a-bitch!" She glared at him, all warmth and affection in her gray eyes replaced with a cold fury Ezra had seen before and found dreadful. He opened his mouth to say, "No!" but it wouldn't come out.

"You *lured* me over here as a *friend*, a *friend*!" she rushed on. "Goddamn it! I'm not one of your slutty tarts! Your damned whores! Is that what you think I am?"

He reached out for her hand, trying to calm her down. People were turning to look around. Thank God, he thought quickly, the place was almost empty at this hour. "*Don't touch me!*" she shrieked at him, rising and upsetting the table so the dishes and ashtray fell to the floor with a clatter. "I'm a *married* woman! Not some fly-by-

176

night trash who sells her life *and* her body for a cheap dinner and some damned, damned gloves!" She pulled her cracked and weather-beaten bag from the floor beside her chair and wrenched a tear in it ripping it open. She jerked out Hilda's gloves and threw them in Ezra's face. "I'm going outside now," she said, stretching herself to her full height. "To wait for *my daughter!*" And she ran out of the Town and Country, leaving him still seated at the overturned table, empty and weak.

Suddenly he came to himself and got up, leaving the gloves on the floor where they had fallen. He pushed past Dinah, the waitress, and caught Frank out of the corner of his eye waving him past the cash register the way someone might wave an emergency vehicle past an intersection. He reached the sidewalk just as Imogene reached her bench, sat down, straight as a flagpole, and took up her vigil of Pete's Sundries and Drugs across Main Street.

Ezra took a deep gasping breath and began to form the words of the apology he knew he had to make, more for himself than for her, he realized, but he had to do it. He took a step off the curb, then stopped cold. A shiver of horror shot from his feet up his body to his head and made his hair stand on end. Across Main Street, coming out of the shadowed doorway of Pete's Sundries and Drugs, was a tall, blond girl wearing a long, white dress. She was smiling, he could see in the streetlamp light, almost laughing as she skipped down toward the street corner.

Ezra was frozen to the spot. He felt the night air cooling his face and chest where Imogene had wet him with her water. He opened his mouth to yell, but the words caught in his throat, and he recognized the familiar, dreamlike feeling of helplessness. But this was no dream, he insisted to himself. This was real!

Imogene saw the apparition at the same time Ezra did and rose quickly from her bench. She started toward the

177

street corner on her side as if to meet the figure that looked so much like Cora. But as she reached the corner, the dancing, laughing figure ducked around her own corner by the side of the picture show and was gone. Imogene cried out something Ezra couldn't understand, and then he realized what else she saw. Another one! The second "Cora" came from farther down Main Street, away from where Imogene stood with her arms stretched out. This one was yelling, "Mama!" in a loud voice filled with terror. Imogene ran down the sidewalk away from the corner toward the second blond figure, dressed exactly like the first. Imogene was shouting, "Cora! Cora! Come here this minute!"

Ezra suddenly remembered himself and took a few steps forward, but before he could reach the courthouse lawn, a third figure came out from another doorway, parallel to Imogene, and started yelling "Mama!" and running in the opposite direction.

Imogene ran back and forth along the sidewalk, not knowing which figure to cross the street toward and unsure of all three. She was waving her arms and screaming, "Cora!" at the top of her lungs while the ghostly dancers stayed just far enough away to taunt her with their nearness.

So this is what they were up to, Ezra thought as he finally reached the courthouse lawn. Imogene's bench was between them, about fifty yards away, but she had run down to the other corner now, chasing the third figure as fast as she could, her voice cracking with emotion and bouncing back to her from off the empty buildings across the street. When she reached the corner, the figure there seemed to disappear, and another took up the teasing call, "Mama!" and Imogene ran to the opposite end of the block, then when that figure vanished, she spotted another and chased it. She looked, Ezra thought with a grimace, like a duck in a shooting gallery.

He took a few more steps, trying to figure out how to catch the three girls who were playing this horrible trick and force them to confront the woman they were torturing. Then he heard the roar of a car's engine and saw headlights pierce the darkness of the side of the courthouse.

A blue Chevrolet hot rod bounced over the curb onto the courthouse lawn and pulled between Imogene and her bench. She didn't hear it at first, concentrating as she was on the last of the dancing figures disappearing into the darkness of a side street. The Chevy was loaded with kids who jumped out and began throwing things at Imogene, running to cut off her escape in any direction except across the street toward the phantom figures of her daughter.

Ezra began to run toward the car, but before he reached the sidewalk that bisected that side of the square, his knee, abused and neglected as it had been for so many months, collapsed, and he fell painfully headlong onto the yellow grass of the courthouse lawn. Pain, hot and agonizing, swept over him like a fever; he could feel the beads of sweat on his forehead being cooled by the night air even as more came out to replace them. He cried out between gritted teeth, and he reached for his pistol that he ordinarily carried everywhere but had left behind this evening when he went to pick up Imogene.

The sheriff tried to pull himself up on his good leg, but the pain came over him again and he became sick to his stomach. He leaned over and vomited up the veal cutlet he had eaten, noting the vegetables swimming in his stomach fluid, and then he heaved and retched again. Finally he managed to rise on his good leg, fighting off a new wave of pain, and he yelled at the kids. His throat was burning from the vomit, and he couldn't hear himself over their yells and Imogene's screams. She had ceased trying to run away from the attacking mob of youngsters and was now just holding her palms up, trying to stop the kids from pelting her with whatever they were throwing. There must be twenty of them, Ezra thought, and he suddenly started hopping and hobbling toward the steps of the courthouse.

He stopped twice to allow the pain to subside, but he finally made it into his office and grabbed the shotgun. He almost fell, trying to raise the window, then pulled off the first barrel with the gun pointed high in the air. The effect was stunning.

The kids froze like statues where they stood, some with arms cocked and their loads ready to fire, some with their arms under Imogene's bench, apparently trying to pry it up from the steel anchors that kept it secure on the courthouse lawn. Imogene also froze, one hand covering her face and head, the other thrust out in front of her for protection. Then, as if on signal, the kids scattered in twenty directions at once. Ezra sighted on two or three of them, intending to fill their pants with a painful but basically harmless reminder of this Halloween prank, but he saved his reserve barrel. He knew the one he was looking for, Tommy Perkins.

All of a sudden the hot rod roared to life and gouged out great tracks in the lawn before the tires caught. The Chevy raced around the side of a building, followed closely by the load from Ezra's second barrel.

"Missed the little coward," he growled. "Didn't even have the courage to get out of the car. Stayed out of sight. The little bastard!"

"What the hell's goin' on?" Dooley's voice came from behind the sheriff. He had apparently been asleep in the holding cell, and he was hitching up his suspenders as he came out into the office.

"Why the hell aren't you over to the school?" Ezra yelled at him, taking his anger and pain and frustration out on the sleepy man in front of him.

"Francis come by and said he'd watch for a while so I could get some shut-eye," Dooley said, wounded and defensive. The sheriff almost never yelled at him. "You wasn't around to check it with."

"Oh, shit!" Ezra said, and he turned and started hobbling down the hall, leaning heavily on the shotgun as if it were a crutch, and ignoring Dooley's asking him what the hell was all the shooting about and why was he limping so badly. He reached the outside door and stepped outside onto the steps. Imogene was crawling on her hands and knees and was halfway up to meet him.

"*You!*" she said when she spotted him and began to struggle to her feet. "You vile, *vile bastard!*"

Ezra was suddenly reminded of drunks he had seen trying to stand. It had always struck him as funny before, but not now. He limped down a step or two and put his hand out to help her.

She struck his hand when he reached her, knocking him backward and off balance, and he sat down hard on the steps. Pain screamed from his knee when it bent, but he clamped his jaw tightly shut and fought back nausea.

"You are a loathsome beast!" she brayed at him, pulling herself totally upright and swaying a bit. She was covered, he saw to his horror, with egg yolks and shells. Her hair was slimy and the egg ran down the sides of her face, mixing with her makeup and making it sticky and gooey. Egg shells hung from the patches of fur in her coat, and one of her eyes was red and swollen shut from what Ezra deduced was a direct hit by an extra-hard shell. The stench came to him, also. Rotten eggs! The little bastards had thrown rotten eggs at her! God!

"You don't understand," he said, trying to rise but stopped by the flooding pain from his knee.

"Oh, I *understand*! I understand *plenty*, Mr. God-almighty High Sheriff! I *understand* more than you'll ever know!" Her voice was totally out of control, hysterical, and the shrillness of it bounced off the closed businesses on Main Street. In the distance, between her gasps for breath, he could hear the eleven o'clock eastbound blowing its whistle.

"You're all alike, you goddamn men!" Her good eye flashed in the light reflected from inside the courthouse behind Ezra. "You think every woman wants the same thing. A quick toss in the sack, and you're done! Oh, you son-of-a-bitch! You *old, old* son-of-a-bitch! You'd do anything to get me off that bench and into your bed! Wouldn't you? *Wouldn't you?* Get away from me! Get away from me and never come near me again! Never! NEVER!" On the last word her voice reached a pitch she couldn't sustain, and it cracked, and she broke into sobs and retching, vomiting up her dinner as Ezra had his only minutes before.

He watched silently until she finished, then he said as softly as possible, "Imma . . ."

He couldn't go on, but it didn't matter, for she put her hand out, thrusting it stiff-armed in front of her the way she had fended off the eggs thrown by the pranksters. Then she drew herself up as tall as she could and half walked, half staggered over to her bench and sat down. With the hem of her skirt she tried to clean the rotten eggs from her face and hair, bending over almost comically to reach it. Then she sat up straight and stared at Pete's Sundries and Drugs. She would, he knew, remain there all night.

Ezra suddenly felt more tired than hurt, more weary than angry. He slowly hauled himself to his feet and climbed painfully up the steps and entered the courthouse. He still limped along on the shotgun.

When he got to the office, he saw Dooley sitting in a chair, looking down at the woman on the bench and the deep tire marks in the courthouse lawn. He held a cup of coffee.

"Get over to the school and tell that goddamn Francis that you're the goddamn deputy, and it's your goddamn job to guard the goddamn school!" Ezra barked.

Dooley rose silently and started out, taking the shotgun from Ezra's hand as the sheriff transferred his support to the corner of his desk. Ezra looked dumbly at Dooley's retreating back and called him. "What're you going to do with my shotgun?" he asked.

"That's *my* shotgun," Dooley said, startled, then he corrected himself. "Least, that's the one we keep in the car. I brung it in, it bein' Halloween and all . . . you know, kids."

Ezra gestured, and Dooley handed the weapon over. The sheriff broke it open. Slugs. He had fired 20-gauge slugs at those kids. My God, he thought, I could have killed one of them. I could have blown Tommy's gas tank up. My God in heaven. He looked over and saw the butt of the other gun, the one loaded with light rocksalt, where it had fallen between the wall and his desk. He must have knocked it over when he came in, he thought. The two guns were identical. Remingtons. Double-barrels. He had loaded the car gun with slugs the night of the cattle rustling shoot-out, and he had never unloaded it, just left it in the trunk of the car like some damn fool without a lick of sense. "Jesus God!" He whistled through his teeth. "Slugs."

Dooley still said nothing. In all his years with Sheriff Holmes he had never heard him swear as he had this night, and he knew better than to ask a lot of questions.

Ezra motioned him out, and the deputy took the shotgun and left. Ezra thought how much he'd wanted to put a load of rocksalt into that little punk Tommy's car or the seat of his britches. But he would have killed him for sure if he had hit him with a slug. How could he make a mistake like that? Slugs felt different from a regular load when they went off. Hell, he thought, rubbing his chin,

183

they felt a lot different. His hand was shaking as he stumbled over to the window and looked out, then groped his way back to his desk chair and fell into it. And his pistol! He'd been out of the office without it only a couple of times in his career, a funeral—Hilda's, he thought with a shock—and a wedding. Hell, he even wore it fishing. Why had he taken it off tonight?

But he knew the answer to the question before it formed. It was her. He put his head in his hands and smelled the vomit on his shirt and hands. She had done this to him. She had turned him inside out and thrown him into spins and loops. She had been nervous about the pistol—oh, she never said anything, but he could tell the way her eyes kept flicking to the big Colt whenever they talked, and so he'd taken it off. But this was business tonight, not pleasure! Why had he taken it off when he knew mischief was afoot? What was it the kids had been calling her out there as they pelted her with rotten eggs? Witch? She *was* a witch, he declared to himself. They also called her crazy—hell, the whole damn town called her crazy—and she *was* crazy, he thought, not in the way most people meant, however, but in a far more dangerous way. That much he was sure of.

But the bitch of it, he thought as he cradled his head in his hands and faced the admission for the first time, the *bitch* of it was that he loved her.

On a small table next to his desk was a bulging manila folder with heavy black letters: FILE—MISSING PERSON: CORA LEE MCBRIDE. He pulled it to him and opened it. Inside were all the reports and letters pertaining to the case—that is, if it could be called a case. His notes on phone calls and interviews. Carbon copies of police reports and the FBI's three reports were all there. Everything, in fact, that he had on the case was there. Also included in the folder were clippings from magazines and newspapers, articles he had been able to get his hands on, hoping that one of them might have a shred of information he didn't that would solve the mystery of Cora Lee McBride's disappearance. Some of the clipped articles were kind: "Mother Waits for Lost Child." Others were less so: "Insane Imma of Agatite." He shoved the folder under his arm and rose with great pain and stumbled over to the file cabinet. One of the drawers was labeled CLOSED CASES/DEAD ISSUES. He pulled it out and pushed the thick folder into the back of the drawer.

As far as Ezra Stone Holmes was concerned, he told himself, it *was* a closed case, a dead issue. Imogene and her crazy obsession! He had gotten caught up in it and then trapped by it. Because of her! Her. He had wasted all the time he could on her. He had a town to run, and he was going to by God run it! Run it until he retired.

He slammed the drawer shut and stood for a moment with his hand resting on the metal handle. His mental hand forcefully took all associations he could gather that had anything to do with Imogene McBride and compressed them into a seed, and then it shoved the seed back into the deepest recesses of his memory, beyond Hilda, beyond the young deputy who had carried his dying infant through a driving rainstorm, back as far as he could. And as it was placed, he prayed harder than he ever had in his life that it would rest.

The pain in his knee was reduced to a low, pulsing throb now. This is more than arthritis, he thought. Maybe I should go over to see Doc Pritchard. He slowly moved across his office, buckling on his gunbelt as he went, almost falling with every step. He snapped off the lights, ignoring the telephone, which suddenly started to ring. As it rang, he stood in the doorway of the office and looked across at the open window through which he could see the lights from the street dimly filtering in. The darkness of the office struck him as the telephone rang its tenth ring and stopped. Suddenly, he started to cry.

S E V E N

Winter came early to Agatite, and there was hope of a white Christmas. Imogene sat through all the coldest days, bundling herself into a blanket she had purchased at the newly opened Army and Navy Surplus Store, pulling it up over her head like a tent when the weather started to rain or sleet on her. She retreated indoors at night, but she was up before dawn every morning to greet the milkmen and farmers. People barely noticed her at all anymore, or, if they did, they merely clucked their tongues in pity for her and hurried on against the icy north wind.

When the snow finally did come in late December, she sipped hot chocolate or coffee from a leaky thermos, and she grew more and more witchlike in appearance. People stopped speaking to her when they passed, for she no longer spoke back. From time to time a reporter from New York or Chicago would come down for an interview, but she always asked them for money now, and they usually left without much of a story.

As the winter grew more severe, the churches took a renewed interest in her, and one of them, the Bible Baptists, actually got her to come to a service on one cold Sunday night. She converted to their faith right then, but she warned them that she would only attend evening services, and then only occasionally. They got her a new blanket and often stopped by with hot food and some prayer every day, but she didn't seem to care much for them and refused to bow her head when the skinny preacher would lift his hands toward heaven and announce in ponderous tones, "Let us pray!"

In February she got a job as the night dishwasher at the Town and Country Restaurant. So the woman who had once given orders to servants found herself up to her elbows in dirty, lukewarm water, listening to the obscene

Spanish chatter of the busboys, and slicing open her hands on the cutlery of the café.

About the only pleasant event in Imogene's life was a new friendship—of sorts—she had struck up with the head waitress at the Town and Country, Dinah Mae Cross. They hardly talked at all, but unlike the other waitresses or busboys at the small restaurant, Dinah always seemed to take an interest in what Imogene's opinion was about almost anything. And while Imogene never said very much about most of the things Dinah brought up, she had a feeling of guarded affection for her fellow worker. She tended to see Dinah as a person who was always hoping that there would be a change for the better in her life, maybe tomorrow, maybe the next day, or just someday. She talked a lot about wanting to run her own place, and she never tired of criticizing the way the Town and Country was managed. But Imogene knew that it was all a lot of idle dreaming, and she indulged her because her understanding of what it meant to hope against hope went deeper than most people could fathom.

Sometimes, when things slowed to a standstill in the restaurant, she and Dinah would simply sit silently and share cups of coffee, each lost in her own thoughts and content for quiet company in which to gather them without silly gossip interfering.

Imogene had never said anything to Dinah to indicate that she liked her, appreciated her company, or even thought of her at all, though. She knew of too many people in the small town who simply wanted to pry into other people's lives, and though Dinah never asked any personal questions or tried to draw Imogene out in any way, she still didn't quite trust her, and they kept their distance from each other.

In the daytime, as the north wind howled around her, sweeping dusty snow in great swirls across the courthouse square, Imogene would sit for hours, rising only to stamp her feet a bit and keep her circulation going, blowing on her hands and beating her arms against her thinning body like some great emaciated bird trying to take off in the snowstorms.

That winter cattle died by the hundreds in north central Texas, and the frigid wind from the cap rock froze three people to death. But Imogene remained on her bench, her stare at Pete's Sundries and Drugs never varying, her determination to wait for her lost daughter never faltering. If anyone in Agatite had had any doubts about her sanity before, he was now convinced, and more than one citizen had intoned that Imogene McBride had become a kind of living curse on the small city, a constant visitation from God that the community was harboring something deep and wrong. But no one really believed such sayings, and they all stood amazed at the strength and determination of the woman on the bench in the courthouse square.

E I G H T

In early March the whole town found cause to pass by the courthouse and gawk, for Harvey McBride came to see his wife. He arrived on the eleven o'clock westbound and came directly to the square, trailing smoke from a large cigar and sporting an expensive-looking suit and gold watch chain. He stood directly in front of her for almost two hours, smoking and flailing his arms in the air and yelling. But it was a windy, dusty day, and the roar of the March gales drowned out any specific words he had for eavesdroppers' ears.

Finally he took to pacing up and down in front of her, smoking the third in a series of cigars, and going red in the face. At one point he got down on his knees and seemed to be begging her for something, but she only shook her head and stared past him as if he weren't there, and he got up, checked his gold watch, and stormed out of her sight back to the depot. There he gave the stationmaster, Henry Fisher, hell because the east-bound was fifteen minutes late.

Two months later Dooley brought out an official, blue-backed paper that informed Imogene that Harvey had divorced her on the grounds of mental incompetency and desertion. She simply glanced at it and let the breeze carry it away. Harvey didn't matter anymore.

She sat there for the rest of the spring and summer, and into the fall of the following year. There were no more Halloween pranks, no more teasing and baiting by kids of any kind. Imogene was as much a part of the town as any fixture or building was. Everyone just came to accept her as a fact of life in Agatite.

Pain finally brought her down in early November. An operation removed a kidney and took her away from the park bench for three weeks. It also ruined her financially, plunging her into debt, a condition she refused to tolerate and met by taking her total earnings from the Town and Country over to Doc Pritchard's office and dumping the money on his receptionist's desk every payday. By the time she was able to resume her place on her bench—which Haskell Johnson had thoughtfully repainted in her absence—she was truly destitute. Mrs. Sweeney had to turn her out of her room, and Imogene spent three days and nights on her bench, leaving only to go over and wash dishes at the Town and Country, and braving the early northers under her threadbare blankets as best she could until she earned enough to move back into the boardinghouse two weeks later.

The weather turned really nasty that December, and although there had been no snow yet, the wind had a knife's edge to it as it came screaming down Main Street and sliced across the courthouse square. Her blankets developed holes, and the Bible Baptists had more or less lost interest in her, so no one brought her anything anymore, except Dooley, who would sneak out a cup of coffee to her from time to time when Sheriff Holmes was out of the office.

She spied the sheriff on occasion as he limped up the sidewalk from his car, his pipe steaming in the frosty air, and she wondered how he had hurt his leg. She didn't ask him, though, and she didn't ask Dooley. If he wants me to know, she reasoned to herself, he'll tell me.

She had no recollection of the awful Halloween night when she had banished him from her life, and she thought of him—when she thought of him, which was mostly when she saw him—as a sort of old acquaintance with whom she had temporarily lost contact. She felt no hatred toward him, only a kind of dull resentment that he, too, had abandoned her and probably, like everyone else, thought she was crazy. That was all right, she said when she contemplated the problem, for he didn't matter anymore either. But she didn't think of Ezra often, and when she noticed that he seemed to take the back stairs more than the main entrance to the courthouse, she simply assumed that it was because the back steps were fewer, and that would be easier for a man with a cane.

NINE

In truth, Ezra did take the back stairs more, but the cane had nothing to do with it. He regarded the slender pine crutch as a constant reminder of his unprofessional foolishness and a fit reward to boot. His leg would never completely mend, Doc Pritchard had told him. Ligaments were ripped apart in there, and after winning the election and wearing a cast for six weeks, Ezra found himself in the undignified position of being the only lawman in the whole state who had to use a cane.

His main regret about the whole thing, however, was that it forced him to retire when this term expired, something he had really been thinking about, of course, but something he had hoped to put off. He had wanted to run one more time, just to prove he could. But now the practicality of that overruled his pride, and he found it too painful to move. His people deserved a better sheriff than a crippled-up old man.

His stupidity on that Halloween night had almost completely undone everything he had ever built up in the way of self-respect in his life, and he had decided, before he acknowledged the truth about his bum leg, to stand one more time for election after his present term was over to show himself and anyone else who might be interested that Ezra Stone Holmes still had what it took to sheriff a county. But that was ego talking, he knew, and he acknowledged that he thought too much of the people of this town, that he owed them too much to give them a gimpy sheriff for protection.

Even so, he still had his pride. A new man, a war hero, local-boy-made-good, Abel Newsome, was being touted by the city council as a likely replacement for Ezra when—and there's *no* hurry, the grinning idiot Mayor Perkins had assured him—he did decide to retire, and Ezra bowed to the inevitable by taking the young giant out with him on patrol from time to time to show him the ropes. The sheriff stubbornly refused to deputize him permanently, however, in spite of Mayor Perkins' encouragement and unsolicited okay. "If we can't afford no new sheriff's car," Ezra had growled at the mayor, "we can't afford no deputy. I reckon me and Dooley can handle things just like we always done." And that had been that.

But it was his pride, also, that made him take the back stairs. He just wanted to avoid Imogene. He didn't want to be reminded of his own foolishness, and, he thought with a frequent grimace of pain, he wanted to avoid her pity, her goddamn understanding, and he wanted to avoid the possibility of having to tell her what he knew. For the previous summer Sheriff Holmes had discovered what happened to Cora Lee McBride.

The envelope arrived on a scorching Friday morning. It was a thick, brown, official-looking mailer, and the return address read: "New Orleans Police Department." Under his name on the address label was printed in official-looking letters, "FOR OFFICIAL INSPECTION ONLY— Official Police Business." He knew what was in it.

The details of its contents were unimportant. What mattered most to him was that it was so late in coming to him. If he had gotten a sealed, official report a year before, he would have almost gleefully ripped it open, anxious to discover what relationship such a message might have to Cora and Imogene. But now, after so much had happened, it was too late. If it was good news, if it would restore the normalcy of the past, patch up things between him and Imma—or even between him and Pete—or even between him and his dreams he would have welcomed it as a child welcomes a Christmas package. But in the world of official police communications, good news came by phone, sometimes a telegram. Official Police Business envelopes were for tragedy, or, worse, for speculation, and he was afraid to open it and left it on his desk, glaring at him every time he entered his office until the following Wednesday.

Finally he forced himself to sit down at his desk and pick up the envelope. The hot, sticky afternoon filled the office with an oppressiveness that seemed to underscore how he felt. His dreams had continued even after the fateful Halloween night. No amount of compression or

192

storage of memories could stop them, it seemed, and Cora kept coming to him in them. He wondered what effect the contents of the envelope would have on his nocturnal visions, if they would make his nightmares worse or make them disappear completely. With a deep sigh that expelled a massive volume of smoke from his lungs, he ripped open the oversized envelope.

Four eight-by-ten black-and-white photographs fell out, clipped to an official police report of an apparent suicide. "Victim's name: Unknown," Ezra read at the top of the report. A friend he had made in Atlanta during his original search for Cora had suggested that this might be the long-missing Cora Lee McBride, and the NOPD had sent him the information with a request for assistance in identification according to a handwritten note stapled to the report. "H. McBride uncooperative," it said. "Show to I. McBride and ID positive? Could be missing dau." It was signed "Dt. Stuart, Hom. NOPD."

Ezra pulled the note off the report and noted the particulars. The victim was female, about nineteen or twenty, blond, blue-eyed, and the same height and weight as the missing girl. She had been working as a prostitute in the New Orleans area for more than a year under a variety of aliases, none of which, apparently, she kept for more than a day or two. She had been arrested three times, each time under a different name, once for assault, once for soliciting, and once for carrying a concealed weapon. For reasons known only to her and God, she put a pistol to her head and pulled the trigger on May 30, but she had botched the job. The bullet tore away half her face and head, but it didn't kill her, according to the coroner's report. She was either too badly wounded or too dazed and blinded to finish the job or call the police or a hospital, and she apparently had bled to death.

Ezra's heart almost stopped as he read the condensed

police jargon that officially rehearsed the end of a human being's life. It was so cold, so final, and he sat stock-still, turning over the details in his mind.

Eventually he found the strength to turn the page and was shocked to find a second report—an abandoned child report—attached to the first. It seemed that in the apartment with the corpse a small child, a boy, about a year or so old—no birth certificate was located—was found in a crib. He was nearly dead from dehydration and starvation, but the doctors expected him to recover. Pinned to his dirty pajamas was a piece of newspaper where someone, likely his dead mother, had simply scrawled in eyebrow pencil, "Joe Don McBride."

No other identification was available. Ezra gazed stupidly at the copied fingerprint reports that identified Trudy LeBlanc, Jane Crawford—Ezra thought of Imma's disgust at Cora's fascination for those "trashy movie fan magazines"—and, he bit his lip, Imogene Jacobs as the same person. He scolded himself again for failing to obtain some prints of Cora's and send them along with his many inquiries. It was the modern way to investigate a disappearance, the modern way to fight crime, and, he ruefully thought, the modern way to prevent tragedies such as this one.

But he hadn't thought of it in time, he rationalized, and there was the equipment problem. But something underneath his arguments told him that he could have done something about it—called the Atlanta police, gotten them to go to Harvey's house and find some prints, something—if he had really believed she was missing. Or, the thought emerged icily, if he really wanted to find her at all. To find her meant to lose Imma forever. He had known that all along. So maybe it wasn't just his silly pride that wouldn't allow him to call in more professional help. Maybe something more serious kept him from doing what he should have.

His eyes went back to the report. There wasn't much more. The tenants living around the scene had only known that a prostitute and her baby had lived in the ratty apartment. From their scanty comments made to the New Orleans police, Ezra deduced that the girl's neighbors led lives that weren't much better than hers had been.

Ezra slipped the photographs from the paper clip and gagged. The top photo was a police record shot of the body as it had been found. Sprawled across a wooden floor, legs still hanging from a sheetless mattress, was the completely naked body of a young girl. Black pools and stains were everywhere, on the walls behind the bed and spreading from the long strands of blond hair that were strung out behind her head. What he could see of the apartment around the bed was a collage of dirty clothes, cracked walls, and movie star pictures, some of which were splattered with the dark substance. "Blood," Ezra whispered.

The second photo was a closeup of the girl's face, showing her wound. Half the head was indeed gone, leaving one eye open and staring silently and blindly into the camera's flashbulb. It was almost more indecent than the death pose in the first photograph. How could anybody live through that? Ezra wondered, noting the raw fingers of flesh, covered with bone fragments and brain matter streaming out to mix with the blond tresses beneath it.

From those two shots, Ezra knew, it was impossible to tell whether she—*that*, he corrected—had ever been anybody, let alone Cora McBride. But suddenly a mental picture swam before his eyes, and he thanked all that was holy that the phantom Cora of his dreams had never swept back her long, blond hair and exposed her face to his sleeping eyes. That, he grimly admitted, would have been too much for him to handle, and he knew now that

195

something somewhere protected him from what her blond tresses concealed, and he was incredibly relieved and grateful.

The third picture was a mug shot. Ezra stared at it and noted the bare defiance in the eyes of the arrested prostitute. A scowl glared into the police camera, and the hair was matted and dirty. She had a large bruise on her jaw, and her eyes seemed glazed and distant. This looked more like the picture of Cora he had seen, but it was a far cry from the beautiful high school junior who had smiled at him from the pages of her yearbook.

Yet there was something else as well, something behind the eyes that the scowl and distant, distracted stare couldn't entirely conceal. He knew what it was, for he had seen it in Imma's eyes too many times before, and he knew it well enough to fear it even in the eyes of a dead girl's photograph.

The final shot was of the baby. He was a filthy little boy with a nasty looking mark on his cheek, possibly a bruise, or—Ezra didn't like to think it might be—a burn. He lay on an ambulance stretcher and was simply staring vacantly up into the camera. A nun was kneeling beside him. Another handwritten note was clipped to this shot also, and Ezra lifted it up to read, "If this is g-son of I. McBride, please make arrangements. H. McBride not interested."

Ezra walked over to the window, wincing from the pain in his knee and reminding himself to get the cane every time he rose and tried to walk. He could see Imogene sitting on her bench, staring over at Pete's Sundries and Drugs. Poor old Pete, he thought. Was it worth it? Something had struck him in the first photo, and he limped over to his desk and picked it up. There, on the nightstand, by a stack of magazines and empty Coke bottles lay a pack of Lucky Strikes. It didn't prove anything, of course, but something in him made him wish Pete was there to see it.

Pete. His old friend's face swam briefly in front of Ezra's eyes and took on many shapes before the sheriff ran his hands over them to erase it. He was, on some mornings, entirely convinced that Pete had been directly responsible for Cora's disappearance. All the circumstances pointed in that direction, and Ezra's dreams and speculations inevitably led him back to the storeroom in the drugstore, the cot, the razor, the back door.

After the episode out at the lake, Ezra had decided that he was completely sold on Pete's guilt. But why? Why should an illicit tryst in an abandoned lake cabin make him more guilty than he otherwise appeared? In fact, with Glenda on his string, why should he take a chance with a little tramp like Cora? There was no evidence, none at all. A pack of cigarettes—common brand—Pete's anger, a fresh shave—maybe he had been meeting Glenda back there and was afraid Ezra would find out if he poked around too much—Pete's casual ability to lie to his oldest friend. Now that might be something, but it was nothing to make a case out of, nothing that really meant anything except that Ezra was not as good a judge of men as he'd always thought he was.

Other times, therefore, Ezra was just as completely convinced that old Pete knew nothing of Cora McBride's disappearance. Maybe she never went into the drugstore at all, just as the druggist contended. Maybe she slipped into a doorway, was briefly hidden by a passing van or car, and took advantage of the opportunity. Maybe she just told her mother that she was sick of the whole business of running away and was leaving her right then and there. Maybe—Ezra rubbed his forehead and felt a headache coming on—maybe she just vanished into thin air.

He didn't know. He never would know. And no matter what he found out now or ever, he could never take it to Pete and confront him with it. And he also knew he could never apologize to his old friend and mend the terrible rent that had formed in the fabric of their relationship.

But he still wanted to know what Pete knew or at least to know that, truly, Pete didn't know anything. He never would ask him, however. And he realized that now, especially now, it didn't make any difference.

He sat down again at his desk and ran his hand through his thinning gray hair as he stared at the pictures. "Was this Cora McBride?" he asked aloud, making it more a statement than a question. Visions of the little boy came before him, and he raised his eyes to the window. He couldn't see Imma from his desk, but he knew she was there. She had no place else to be. She had nothing else to live for but to stay on that bench and wait for a daughter who, now for sure, would never return.

He took a piece of stationery from his desk and smoothed it out in front of him. Finally he wrote: "ID positive. This is Cora McBride. G-mother I. McBride is now indigent." His hand paused. Holding the pen over the paper, he noticed that it was shaking just a bit. He bit his lower lip hard, then wrote, "Hold action on g-son until"—he stopped again and looked at his desk calendar—"further notice—one week max." He felt a responsibility, but he also had an idea. He signed the page, folded and sealed it in an envelope, addressed it, and carefully placed it in the "Out" box on his desk. Then with a single motion he swept all the pictures, reports, and official envelopes into the wastebasket on the floor. He took a match from his pocket and lit the edge of the brown mailer. After it had become ashes in the bottom of the can, he poured a half cup of Dooley's coffee on it.

He got up, grabbed his cane, and limped to the office door. He was planning to drive over to Kirkland and talk to a family that had been wanting to adopt a child for the past two years. They were poor as dirt farmers could be, and they already had more than they could handle. But they had been asking him to help them locate a child; they weren't even particular about age or race, because as the woman put it, "God just gave us too much love to waste." They were good people, hardworking people, and they were Catholic, rare for white people in Sandhill County, and maybe they could make up for something Ezra sensed had gone terribly wrong in his county. It was a piece of unfinished business he wanted to put right, and once it was over, he could then take all the loose ends of the case of Imogene McBride and stuff them forever into a seed of memory and store it away for good. He was confident it would never stir again, and he knew that he could now retire in peace.

He moved out of his office, limping heavily with the cane, and made his way down the courthouse steps. For a moment he stood and stared at Imogene's gaunt back. Her head was stiffly erect, her eyes still trained on Pete's place, her hands still primly folded in the threadbare skirt that covered her lap.

Ezra took a step or two down the sidewalk, then stopped. He drew in a deep breath and then hobbled over to the bench and sat down. Imogene never turned her head or took any notice of him at all.

The sun beat down on them and sweat crept out from under his Stetson and rolled down his forehead. He looked at her face, noting that no perspiration showed on the leathery skin that still fought to retain its lucidity and youthfulness in spite of the abuse Imogene had exposed it to for so long.

There were a thousand things he wanted to say, to apologize for, and something vindictive down inside him wanted to blurt out the truth about her slatternly daughter, about her neglected and abused grandchild, about her unconscionable foolishness in torturing herself, Ezra himself, and a whole town because of a myth of Cora's virtue that she wouldn't give up.

199

"Hot, ain't it?" was all he could muster, and once again his country-boy accent betrayed the nervousness he felt. He chewed his lip and waited.

After a long moment she replied, "Yes, I think it's warmer than yesterday. I don't know how people stand it." She never looked at him or moved at all.

Ezra wondered how she stood it, but he had learned long ago not to ask how she took the climate. That was a secret she kept from everyone, probably because she didn't know herself. "I hear they're going to put a fifty-pound block of ice over by the bank, and then they're going to sell chances to guess at exactly what time it will all melt." He tried to animate his voice to lighten the mood that had settled around the bench.

"What foolishness," she snorted. "How people hunt for things to waste their time."

"Oh, I don't know." He tried one more time. "I thought you might be interested. There's a fifty-dollar prize for the correct guess, down to the half minute they say." He stared at her, trying to get her to look around at him. "And nobody I know is a better expert on heat—or cold—than you are. . . ." He trailed off, ready to surrender.

Suddenly, however, her head snapped around and her fierce gray eyes glared at him, full of hatred and almost, he thought, red-rimmed with acidic resentment. Although it was only a second or two, it seemed like several minutes that her stare penetrated his face, her eyes unswerving, unrelenting, attacking his inmost thoughts and, he thought as he physically leaned back away from the incessant gaze, his soul.

Then, just as suddenly, they softened, and her familiar laugh emerged from her cracked, dry lips, and Ezra found himself warming inside as he reacted to her white teeth and the fleeting revelation of a younger woman trapped in the disguise of a hag. "You know," she laughed, "you may be right! Who spends more time outdoors than I? Not even farmers, I'll say, spend as many hours a day measuring the hourly changes in temperature."

He nodded, relieved and afraid to speak further for fear of arousing that beast inside her, the one that he had always seen lurking behind her eyes, and glad that she was laughing.

"Maybe I shall enter the contest," she said, and she reached down for the ragged purse beneath the bench and opened it to find her coin purse. "How much are the entries selling for?"

"Ten cents," he lied, for he knew they were asking a full dollar, and she probably didn't have a dollar to waste. "Alex Bateman over at the bank is taking the guesses. The proceeds are supposed to buy some swings for the city park."

"He's a nice boy, but he'll be a fat man," she concluded as she fingered a dime out of her coin purse and handed it to Ezra. "Now, let me see. When are they putting the block out?"

"Around five this afternoon."

"So it'll sit all night." She placed a cracked fingernail under her chin, closing her eyes and thinking hard. "I would say it won't last much past noon tomorrow." She clapped her hands and smiled, and Ezra felt his heart jump in spite of himself. "One o'clock. No! One-thirty. I'll say one-thirty. Is that a fair guess, do you think?"

"I'd say it's a good one." He pocketed the dime, and she turned again to stare across the street. "I'll put it in for you right away so no one else can claim to have guessed first. First guess of each time has priority if it's right."

"Where's your pipe?" she asked without looking at him.

He felt his shirt pocket and remembered it was still up

in his office. "Trying to quit," he said without conviction. He rested his hand on his ruined knee. "I think I got enough health problems."

"I dare say," she said sympathetically, and looked at him again. "In fact, Sheriff—uh, Ezra . . ." She hesitated and actually reached out and put her weathered fingers on his gnarled, bony knuckles. "I've been wondering if you've ever thought about retiring?"

He was shocked. At first he didn't know what to say. The last conversation they had had was about his retirement. Could it be she didn't remember it? Could she have simply wiped out the memory of that horrible night, forced herself to expunge it from her thoughts? No, he thought, that wasn't possible. It was too grotesque, too terrorizing. But then he remembered that this was Imogene McBride, a woman who could force her mind to accept exactly what she wanted it to accept, to exclude exactly what she wanted it to exclude. She had proved that; her capacity for seeing what she wanted to see and nothing more had become a legend in Agatite, and it was only a short step from seeing what she wanted to see. Cora's mutilated face briefly flashed across his mind.

"Well, yes, as a matter of fact"—his hands reached again for his missing pipe—"I reckon this is my last term."

"You've done a good job, Ezra." She nodded and withdrew her hand. "You're a good sheriff and a good man."

He didn't know what to say. For a few minutes they continued to sit in silence, and finally he arose and began to walk to the car. He wanted to take care of the final business in Kirkland and be done with it.

He took a few halting steps and stopped, turning around on the burned August grass, and looked at her once more. "Imma," he said to her severe profile, "I'm . . . I'm sorry."

202

He wondered if she heard him, and he was about to turn and leave when she suddenly looked at him. He thought he had seen her gray eyes in all their moods—fiercely defiant, angry, soft and laughing—but what he saw in her face now was something different, new and surprising. Around the bottom of each eye a pool of tears was forming, spilling over to run down her cheeks in silent testimony to the sadness that now possessed her.

"Why, Ezra Stone Holmes!" She tried to laugh, her voice cracking with emotion. "Whatever in the world is there to be sorry for?"

He raised his hand in a half-gesture of acquiescence, but she snapped her head back around to her constant vigil, and she said nothing more. He turned again and limped out to his car, looking back over his shoulder once more to see her staring incessantly at Pete's Sundries and Drugs.

That night he had the best sleep that he had had in more than a year. He awoke two hours late for work when Dooley called him to check and see if he was all right, and for once the telephone didn't jangle him into a state of nervous excitement. That night he didn't dream at all.

T E N

Sometime toward the beginning of her third winter on the bench, Imogene forgot why she sat out there every day. She was no longer consciously waiting for Cora to return, not really. A voice inside her had convinced her long ago that Cora would never come back. She tried to tell herself that she sat there for vengeance, vengeance on a town that had let her daughter—no, *helped* her daughter—get away from her. She didn't know how, and she didn't know why. She really didn't care about it either. She just sat there and tried to hate all of them, and she knew that by being out there all day every day and most nights, she could make them hate her, make them regret that they had done such a horrible thing to Imogene McBride.

She knew that she bothered them more than they would ever admit, even to themselves, so she continued to sit. Besides, she had no place else to go. She could never stand living with Mildred and her crazy religious sayings. That she knew. Imogene wanted to believe that if they had simply told her the truth from the first, that Cora had wanted to get away, go back to Harvey—although Imogene couldn't quite accept *that*—then she could at least have gotten into the Hudson and put Agatite and all the horror of the past months behind her forever. She did believe she actually would have done that.

She no longer thought much about Cora at all; only sometimes when a pretty blond girl would cross the sidewalk in front of Pete's Sundries and Drugs would she make an idle comparison. Cora had gotten younger in her memory, as well. She most often appeared as a laughing eight-year-old with long blond pigtails and a mustache of milk across her delicate mouth. She was, to Imogene, a young girl at play, not an eighteen-year-old swishy-hipped woman who had walked away from her so long ago.

Imogene had now spent three days and nights on the bench. She still owed more than two hundred dollars to Doc Pritchard, and some more than that to the hospital. Her few belongings were contained in a battered cloth bag dumped beside her, a parting gift from the teary-eyed Mrs. Sweeney, who was again forced to turn her out when her fourth rent payment came due and there still were no funds available.

She didn't think she could hold out much longer. Although she managed to sneak leftovers out of the restaurant to eat, she realized she was slowly starving to death, and if hunger and weakness didn't kill her soon, she reckoned she would freeze to death before the week was out. She looked forward to the evening, when she could go to work and get warm in the dirty suds of the Town and Country's kitchen.

The wind whipped and swirled around her, and she pulled the raggy coat around her shoulders and pressed her broken-down shoes close together. Her teeth chattered and her eyes watered from the cold front that had hit that afternoon, plunging already near-freezing temperatures even lower. A tap on her shoulder startled her and made her jump.

"Hi, honey!" It was Dinah, the head waitress from the Town and Country. She had a thin white sweater pulled tightly across her uniform and was visibly chattering in the icy wind. "It's kind of cold," she said. "Can I sit down?"

Imogene smiled faintly and scooched over as Dinah sat on the bench, pulling the ends of her sweater together and digging her hands into her lap.

"I should have brought out some coffee, but I forgot," she said. "God! It's *cold!*" She moved closer to Imogene, trying to share her body warmth. "How in the world do you stand it? I heard that two fellows froze to death up near Amarillo last night. They broke down on the highway and tried to walk in, but they wound up froze hard as a board. That's the norther that's hitting us now."

"My, that's terrible," Imogene said, shocked to realize how glad she was for the company. No one had been out to talk to her in a long, long time, she thought. "I guess you kind of get used to it." A silence fell between them, broken only by the wind's howling and Dinah's chattering teeth. "Listen," Imogene said at last, "you didn't come all the way out here just to discuss the weather."

"No, I didn't. . . ." Dinah hesitated, then she spoke quickly through gritted teeth as she tried to stop their clicking. "I wanted to get you alone, without Frank around."

Imogene sat up a bit straighter, interested.

"Listen, I had an Aunt Myrtle who died down in Dallas last year, and she left me all her insurance money. It ain't a fortune or nothing, but I think it's enough to buy old Frank out. I know he wants to sell, and I just might be able to get his place for what I got, plus maybe a loan from the bank."

Imogene's eyes narrowed, watching for a trap. "So?" she asked at last.

Dinah shivered. "Well, if Frank sells he's going to take Cynthia and Delores with him and open this Dairy Freeze out on the bypass. He thinks there's a lot more money in ice cream and hamburgers. Anyhow, I can hire a couple of girls to wait tables, but I need somebody to help me run the place—a manager, I guess."

"And that's me?" Imogene set her guard on full. Her gray eyes were flashing with suspicion.

"Look, honey." Dinah looked her squarely in the eye. "I don't care what you do or where you come from. I read in one of them magazines about you that you used to run a big house back in Atlanta, and—well, running a restaurant ain't that much different, except you got to do your own cooking sometimes because folks is particular about their food." She waited for a reaction and, seeing none, went ahead. "I never finished high school, but I think you got something on the ball. You sure know how to stretch a dollar, if half the gossip I hear about you is true." She blushed in spite of the cold, and Imogene nodded to let her know she wasn't offended.

Dinah took courage from the nod. "Now, I don't know

206

why you think you got to be out here day in and day out, but you think you do, and I ain't got no quarrel with that. All I know is that you been as regular in that kitchen as anybody I ever seen. Except for your operation, you never missed a day. That's enough for me. Anybody who can wash dishes day in and day out the way you do and never complain ain't got to take nothing off nobody. Now, if you take the job, I'll pay you one-third of everything we bring in, and you can come out here between shifts and sit to your heart's content. But I ain't kidding, it's going to be hard work, and we might not make it at all. But we don't got a chance unless you're there when I need you."

Imogene took a moment to contemplate what she was hearing. It *would* be hard work—she knew that—but she also knew Dinah was being honest with her and that the offer was a sincere one. It was all business, too, and Imogene liked that. There was no hint of a lie or trick of any kind, no note of conspiracy. It was cold-blooded, and she liked that too. And, most importantly, Dinah was a woman. There would be no men to back her into a corner and hurt her. "I'd like to think about it," she said at last.

"Honey, I'm going to make Frank the offer this afternoon," Dinah chattered. "That is, if you're in. If you're not, I'm going to quit and leave for Amarillo or Dallas or someplace and get a better job. I'm getting no place in this hick town." Dinah's eyes were pleading with Imogene. "Besides," she added, quickly lowering her glance and then bringing it up full to show she was speaking from the heart, "I'll advance you enough for a room. You ain't going to make it through the night out here."

"All right." Imogene was surprised to feel so relieved and warm inside from the decision.

Dinah threw her arms around Imogene's neck and squealed into her ear, "That's great! I know we can make it over there! I just know it! Frank's been doing it all wrong since he opened!"

"One thing," Imogene cautioned as Dinah pulled on her neck again. "You ever try to keep me away from this bench, and I'll quit you flat."

"Imogene, honey"—Dinah smiled—"you got yourself a deal!"

EPILOGUE

Imogene suddenly yawned and stretched her arms over her head. She looked at the small Timex on her wrist and noted that she needed to be back at the Town and Country in ten more minutes to start the potatoes for lunch. They were having a Luncheon Special today, thanks to a load of shrimp Dinah had talked her brother Harold into bringing back from a fishing trip down on the Gulf. Dinah would have been cleaning and peeling the little delicacies since the breakfast work was over. They were charging only $3.98 for the lunch, with iced tea. When she had first sat down on this bench over thirty years before, Imogene could have bought a whole steak dinner for less than that. My, she thought, things have changed.

A lot had indeed changed since she first came to the bench, and she had watched them all. For one thing, the bench itself had changed. The wooden ones had all rotted away by 1957, and the city decided to put in these concrete ones. They weren't nearly as comfortable as the old wood, she thought; they didn't slope at all but were flat on the seat, and they didn't have any backs on them. Sometimes, at first, she had experienced terrible back pain from them, but she kept at it, trying to keep her posture straight, and finally she had adjusted. "People can get used to anything," she was fond of saying.

The town had changed too. Pete's Sundries and Drugs had been gone longer than the benches, replaced first by a little glassware store that hadn't lasted out the year, then by a flower shop that had also failed, and finally by a real estate and insurance office that had replaced the old-fashioned storefront with rock work and glass doors.

Pete himself was dead. He had a stroke right in his store. Imogene had visited him in the hospital as he was dying, paralyzed on half his body, dripping drool down his grizzled face. She walked right up to the bed and looked down on him. He recognized her—she could tell by his eyes, even though they wouldn't work right. She took her time, just standing there, and finally he made a noise, and she leaned down. It sounded like "I'm sorry," but she couldn't be sure. He died later that night.

Ezra was also gone. He had had a heart attack somewhere up in Canada, and they hadn't found him for two days. That made her sad. She found that she missed his figure walking into the courthouse with his pipe steaming in the cold morning air. He was a comfort to her in a way she didn't really understand fully, and she hated it that he died so alone. On his last day as sheriff, the day Abel Newsome replaced him officially he came out and sat beside her for a bit. They didn't say a word to each other, and after a while he got up and left. That was the last time she ever saw him.

Luke Short's garage was gone, too. It was a used-car lot now, with shiny but older cars lined up where dirty old Luke had once pumped gas and worked on engines. His son-in-law ran it after Luke had been killed when a car he was working on slipped the jack and landed on him. Imogene had been sitting right on her bench, and she saw the whole thing. It was a terrible shame.

She had been sitting there through so many terrible disasters: the big fire of 1959 that almost burned the whole of downtown to the ground, and would have if pumper trucks from neighboring towns hadn't shown up in the nick of time; an oil well had also caught fire and lit up the night sky over town for two whole days before the men came from somewhere far away and stopped it. And there had been the tornado of 1962—that was one of the few times the weather had really frightened Imogene and driven her inside in stark fear, where she cringed with the other county employees in the courthouse basement, emerging only to find the Civil War statue had been the only apparent casualty. Its other arm was now gone.

The Timex told her it was time to go. The little watch had been a present from Dinah one Christmas. They didn't normally exchange gifts, but one wintry afternoon a week before the holiday, Imogene simply lost herself on her bench. She had come out at her usual time of morning and just blinked her eyes and it was late at night all of a sudden. Dinah had been afraid to come out and get her. It had been a strange experience, and Imogene recalled that it had worried her some. She didn't have the heart to tell Dinah that even if she had had a watch it wouldn't have made any difference. That had also been the day of Mrs. Sweeney's funeral, and she didn't even remember seeing the hearse go by, although it passed right in front of her.

So many people had died. Harvey, she heard, died in 1970, but she didn't know of what. Probably drank and whored himself to death, she often thought when she considered Harvey at all. And Dooley—dear Dooley— who continued to bring her coffee long after Ezra was gone, passed away on his cot in the holding cell in the sheriff's office. He once told her that he had spent more nights in a cell than any other free man alive. That made her sad, too.

Dooley, in fact, had died on the same day Mildred died, her going in her sleep too. But that same afternoon there had been a big downtown pep rally and parade in honor of the Agatite Eagles' playing in the district finals, and Lord, how she loved parades, she thought. She especially liked the one on Thanksgiving when Santa would climb down from his fire engine and make a special trip over to her to give her a candy cane. These were the things she waited for now, although she didn't really know it.

My, yes, lots has changed, she remarked to herself. Businesses on Main Street had come and gone, people had come and gone. Lately, she thought, more had gone than had come, but she didn't worry about it. Even the Town and Country had changed. Now it was a Dinette rather than a Restaurant, a change in name to indicate a more restricted menu. And they weren't doing so well as Dinah had hoped at the beginning. In fact, they had trouble affording uniforms and shoes, let alone the expenses of keeping it all going. "But it beats working for somebody else," Dinah was fond of saying as she counted out the few dollars a week they shared. At least they wouldn't starve. Working in a dinette meant food was always around.

But Imogene didn't worry too much about that either. She only cared about the twice a day and sometimes three that she would spend in the courthouse square on her bench. Let Dinah worry about the new chain steakhouse and pizza places out on the highway. Mornings, afternoons, and pleasant evenings, rain or shine for the first two, sleet or snow, almost any kind of weather, she would sit and stare at Pete's Sundries and Drugs, which was now Randolph's Insurance and Real Estate. And in the afternoon she would take a turn down the cracked concrete sidewalks of downtown, glancing in shop windows, and cruise the aisles of the Ben Franklin store, then return to her bench and knit or crochet until time to go back to work. It was a way she had of renewing her hope, she told herself, for, as she was also fond of saying, "If you have hope, you have everything," and Imogene believed she had written the book on hope.

She stood and stretched. People still thought she was

212

crazy, she supposed. They thought she was still waiting for Cora, but the memory of Cora had vanished years ago, faded into a vague recollection of unpleasantness that floated through her mind like gossamer. The bench and the block across from it had stopped being linked with a blond girl in a white-and-pink dress years and years ago. Imogene didn't realize it, but in spite of that link, her life was inexorably tied to the bench. It was like living in a time machine, watching people come and go, remembering them as they were, watching them change. It was like a book Cora had once brought home from the library. Only that had been silly: there had been monsters in the book. There were no monsters in time, only people, ordinary people. The only monsters that existed were in the mind.

Some days she forgot what year it was, and her vision failed to record the current events that passed before her eyes. She would see a time in her mind, with people who had long since died or moved away still walking or driving up and down Main Street, still conducting the daily business of a decade or two before. She was never frightened by these ghosts. In fact, she was amused. She particularly liked the evenings in the summer when the weather was nice. She never watched TV, read a newspaper or magazine, or really talked to people. She did go down to the Methodist Church once or twice a month, and she had taken to reading the Bible and misquoting a scripture or two whenever one came to her. But her faith was spasmodic and unreliable. She had not prayed since the forty-first day after Cora disappeared.

Imogene walked painfully across the lawn toward the Town and Country Dinette, its flyspecked windows shining in the August heat. Maybe this afternoon on her walk through downtown she would go into Jason's and put a pair of nursing oxfords on layaway. Her feet *had* been bothering her lately. She saw Abel Newsome come out of the courthouse and nodded to him as he passed. He raised his hand in greeting and moved on to the sheriff's cruiser. She liked Abel, although she never thought he was as good a man as Ezra had been. But he was young yet, not even sixty, she thought. He liked her. He always complimented her biscuits.

When she stepped up onto the curb of the sidewalk in front of the Town and Country, she turned and looked back across the street toward the square and the bench— *her* bench. It was a good life she had, she thought, not the one she might have chosen, but a good one even so. It was a good town, too. It was *her* town. She felt a claim on it that people who had been born and raised here, who had borne and raised children of their own here could never make.

"Thank you, Cora," she said, suddenly and quietly, and then she looked around quickly to see if anyone had heard, but the sidewalk shimmered in the noonday heat and was empty. She blushed and lowered her head, turned, and went into the Town and Country to start fixing the potatoes for lunch.

AFTERWORD

Causes are never as interesting to me as effects.

Once, at a reception given for me by a women's book club, I was literally backed into a corner with demands that I explain what actually happened to Cora. I tried to smile it off, so to speak, but my readers pressed the point. I would like to have answered them, but I really couldn't. *I don't know what happened to Cora.* I never worried about it. *The Vigil* isn't about Cora; it's about Imogene, and in a larger sense, it's about Ezra. It's about what happened to them because of Cora. Imogene's missing daughter was the cause; their strange, sad love story is the effect. That is what inspired the book, and that is all the story I know to tell. What happened to Cora—whether Pete seduced her or vice versa or something else happened—isn't important, and to tell the truth, it isn't really interesting. What's interesting to me is Imogene and Ezra's experience after Cora disappears; that's the story I wanted to tell. And I suppose that's at least a partial answer to another question I frequently hear about *The Vigil*: What is it about?

Not long ago a friend of mine wrote and asked if I had this or that in mind when I constructed the plot and developed and named the characters in *The Vigil*. I read his letter carefully, and I was more than mildly surprised at the number of literary allusions and analogues he had found. Most of them, I objectively agreed, were cogent, and he had a good case for what I recognized as a well-founded critical appraisal of the book. The sad thing, perhaps, was that none of it was intentional. I had no idea any of it was there until he pointed it out to me. I selected characters' names at random, because they "sounded right," and my only concern was not to choose a name that another author I had read had used in a similar way for a similar character. I often wish writers could use just "Character One," "Character Two," and so on for the people in their books, as the Greeks did when they thought up the words *protagonist* and *deuteragonist*. But my friend found significance in characters' names, incidents, and other minor connections I had barely given a thought to when I included them.

The Vigil is not a mystery, nor is it a "psychological thriller." It's just a novel. But that's not usually a good enough answer. (What is a novel? The late Paul Scott once defined a novel as "a large number of pages with even printing on both sides, cut in a rectangular fashion, bound together along one edge and covered with a stiff paper or cloth binding." That, he said, is the only definition of the genre that has any meaning. Therefore, saying that *The Vigil* is a novel doesn't say very much about it. If it had just some fewer pages, it might not even meet Scott's criteria.)

The Vigil is a love story. It's about the love a man can develop for a woman who has no love to return. It's about the love a mother has for her child as well. But it's also about the love people have for life. Imogene is not a very likable person. She is prudish, fundamental in her emotions and her judgment of others. She is overbearing and a little loutish. She really doesn't have the capacity to love when she arrives in Agatite, and she doesn't find it right away. She is the object of her own contempt, a person who has failed to live up to her own sense of her responsibilities, in short, the sort of individual she despises. It's a hard thing to find out that you despise yourself, but it's that discovery that makes Imogene strong, ultimately; and it's that strength that Ezra falls in love with. He's a strong

216

man, and he admires strength in others. It's his undoing, finally, but I think these sorts of contradictions are what make us human.

Aside from the questions—What happened to Cora? What is the novel about?—the most frequent comment I hear about *The Vigil* is that Imogene's sitting out there all those years is incredible. Most people can't imagine such a thing. I never doubted it was not only possible but probable. What a lot of people don't understand is that she's not sitting out there because of Cora; she's not really waiting for her to return. But she has nothing else to hold onto. Imogene's past life is over the moment Cora walks into that drugstore, and she has no choice but to do what she does. In a way, she's lucky. She has Ezra—and Dooley—to protect her, to see to her needs. She has a town to belong to in a way that she has never belonged to anything before. In fact, if there's a conscious symbol in the book, it's the bench—*her* bench—which comes to stand for a vantage point for the whole town. In the end, Imogene understands Agatite from a unique point of view that people who are born, grow up, and die there never achieve. That understanding, plus her vigil, gives her a sense of purpose that is stronger and more sustaining than anything else she has found in her life. And, given its effect on the town—and on Ezra—Imogene's vigil accomplishes considerably more than a quick, violent self-destruction might, for by it she is avenged as well as redeemed. Ironically, her presence on the bench punishes those around her. The town suffers, Pete suffers, and, of course, poor Ezra suffers. But their misery is their own doing as well, and in the long run, I think, they mostly profit from it. Imogene may well be crazy, but it is the rest of Agatite that pays the price for Cora's disappearance and learns from it.

Much has been made—too much—of an idle comment I made before the book was published that I had seen an article about a real-life woman whose child had wandered away from a train while it was stopped in a small town in Oklahoma during the thirties. The child completely disappeared after entering the depot for gum or candy. A search was mounted, but the girl was never found. After awhile—several months, as I recall—the woman continued her journey, and in the mid-seventies when I saw the article, she returned to the town for a kind of reunion with the folks who remembered her. I read the article in a Tulsa, Oklahoma, newspaper sometime in the mid-seventies, and it moved me sufficiently for me to fictionalize it and use it in Chapter 8 of the novel.

But there is nothing of that story in Imogene's tale. The real little girl was a mere child of six or seven, and the story's factual particulars were lost to my memory long before I wrote the first line of *The Vigil*. What did stay with me, though, was what the woman must have gone through, what must have passed through her mind while the deputies searched for her little girl. How, I remember asking myself, could she just leave, go on like that? There were several possible answers: she had other children to worry about, she had a supportive husband and family who helped her get over her loss, she had somewhere to go. Imogene had none of these things. By divesting her of a past and a future, I leave her only with the present, where her constant vigil tries to keep time stopped so that the unthinkable will be undone. In time, and ironically, Imogene becomes happier than she has ever been in her life. Cora's disappearance gives her life a meaning, her vigil gives her a purpose. Few people are so lucky.

Finally, *The Vigil* is about the town. It's about the kind of people who populate a small town and who live out their lives with very little remarkable occurring to disrupt them. Some readers may feel that today our society is primarily urban and there is little value in setting stories in small towns, in rural America. They might complain that such settings, while curious, aren't relevant anymore. I don't agree. The rustic setting, the pastoral and nostalgic past are a part of our heritage that have become archetypal. Such images call forth our warm reactions to major holidays, family values, and something in the American past that is more worthwhile than that which might be found in the American present. (Not incidentally, they also are very effective sales gimmicks for breakfast cereals, cigarettes, luxury automobiles, wine coolers, even deodorant soap.) At the center of this mythic, rural America is the small town, and regardless of how urban we like to think of ourselves as being, small towns continue to exist and to exert enormous influence on how things are done in this country. In some ways the American small town is much more powerful than all the Dallases and Chicagos put together. It is more than an aphorism to say in a complimentary way of some major city or other that it "has a small-town 'feel'" to it.

Small towns like Agatite are greater than the sum of their parts. Like the clods of Europe, to paraphrase Donne, they are diminished when one person falls away, and conversely, increased when one is added. I have trouble believing that the same is true of cities like Houston, Los Angeles, or New York, where such "falling away" might, in a way, better the fortunes of those who remain, and where additions are often received with the creaking groans of strained capacity. The fate of an individual, then, seems more important, stands out more, set in the context of rural life.

Small towns have personalities of their own, and they reflect the good and evil in their makeup as clearly as a person may. In *The Vigil*, the town is more than a backdrop for Imogene and Ezra's story; it is a living part of that story, another character if you will. *The Vigil* couldn't happen anywhere but in Agatite, although I think Agatite could be in Illinois, Vermont, or California. Imogene and Ezra, Pete and Cora are part of the town and part of the story as well. I like to think of the novel as an integral whole, a reflection of my ideas about towns and places and people. Above all, I hope it's a good story. When people ask me why I wrote the novel—my first—I often tell them, "Imogene caused me to write it." Once I thought her up, I couldn't get her out of my head, and when I finally sat down and started trying to tell her story, she came alive for me. I've said that I'm in love with her, and I guess I am. If I can cause a reader to care for her, and Ezra, too, and to feel that a good story has been told in *The Vigil*, then my purpose in telling it has been accomplished.

Clay Reynolds
Beaumont, Texas

Questions for Discussion

1. Imogene McBride, Sheriff Erza Holmes, and Pete the drug-gist have distinct ways of coping with painful realities. What are the differences and similarities in how these three individuals deal with their problems?

2. The town Agatite collectively becomes a significant character in the plot's development. What purposes do the named and unnamed residents of the town serve?

3. Sheriff Holmes and Imogene McBride are beset with physical as well as psychic pain. How do these problems move the plot forward and give it cohesion?

4. Ezra Holmes has disturbing dreams about the fate of Cora McBride. How does the author use these dreams to develop the novel's plot and themes?

5. To what extent are Sheriff Holmes, Pete the druggist, Dooley the deputy, and other characters products of their small-town environment?

6. What does Imogene McBride's long vigil reveal about parental love?

7. Is Sheriff Holmes's doomed love for Imogene believable? Why or why not?

8. In time, the town's attitude toward Imogene changes significantly. How do you account for these changes?

9. Why did Ezra Holmes withhold from Imogene the news about what happened to Cora in New Orleans?

10. Why is there ambiguity about how Cora disappeared?

11. What is the significance of Imogene's survival as Dinah's business partner?

12. The novel's epilogue recounts the deaths of most of the characters who participated in the unfolding of the narrative. What is the effect of these disclosures?